PRAISE FOR *THE*

"Part mystery, part history, all spook, oiled sword at hand."

—Christopher Buehlman, author of *Between Two Fires*

"An almost Dickensian level of detail transports readers to medieval England in poet Douglas Nicholas's gorgeously written novel."

—*Library Journal*

"Marvelously descriptive . . . like a more profound Harry Potter for adults."

—*Kirkus Reviews*

"*The Wicked* is the rare sequel that surpasses its predecessor."

—*GeekyLibrary*

"Superb storytelling."

—*SFGate.com*

PRAISE FOR *SOMETHING RED*

"A hauntingly affecting historical novel with a touch of magic."

—*Kirkus Reviews* (starred review)

"Rich in historical detail, this suspenseful coming-of-age fantasy grabs the reader with the facts of life in medieval England and the magic spells woven into its landscape."

—*Publishers Weekly* (starred review)

"This darkly atmospheric debut novel is well worth its measured plot-building for its horrific, unexpected ending."

—*Library Journal* (starred review)

"This first novel is a beauty."

—Cecelia Holland, *New York Times*
bestselling author of *The King's Witch*

"Not for the faint of heart, this pulse-pounding page-turner grabs you from the start and never lets you go. A wickedly clever and evocative combination of history, horror, mystery, and magic."

—*Booklist*

"Nicholas goes for the throat with *Something Red*. Rich in history, ankle deep in blood, and packed with brilliant writing and whip-smart plotting."

—Jonathan Maberry, *New York Times*
bestselling author of *Flesh & Bone*

"Ably conjuring the beauties and drawbacks of the past, and with an engaging and unusual cast list, *Something Red* is a thoroughbred novel of nightmare terror, ruled by a force of sheer evil that seems, and may well prove, unstoppable. A Book of Shadows with a genuinely beating heart."

—Tanith Lee, award-winning author
of *The Silver Metal Lover*

"Nicholas's beautiful prose, his detailed portrayal of life in medieval England, interesting characters, and underlying supernatural themes make this book a real gem."

—*BookBrowse*

ALSO BY DOUGLAS NICHOLAS

The Wicked

The Demon (A Novella)

Something Red

Iron Rose

The Old Language

The Rescue Artist

In the Long-Cold Forges of the Earth

THRONE
OF
DARKNESS

A Novel

Douglas Nicholas

EMILY BESTLER BOOKS
—
ATRIA

New York   London   Toronto   Sydney   New Delhi

ATRIA PAPERBACK
An Imprint of Simon & Schuster, Inc.
1230 Avenue of the Americas
New York, NY 10020

First Emily Bestler Books/Atria Paperback edition March 2015

EMILY BESTLER BOOKS / ATRIA PAPERBACK and colophon are trademarks of Simon & Schuster, Inc.

Lines from the poem "Hyena," from *Collected Poems* by Edwin Morgan, are reprinted courtesy of Carcanet Press Limited.

For information about special discounts for bulk purchases, please contact Simon & Schuster Special Sales at 1-866-506-1949 or business@simonandschuster.com.

The Simon & Schuster Speakers Bureau can bring authors to your live event. For more information or to book an event, contact the Simon & Schuster Speakers Bureau at 1-866-248-3049 or visit our website at www.simonspeakers.com.

Manufactured in the United States of America

10   9   8   7   6   5   4   3   2   1

Library of Congress Cataloging-in-Publication Data

Nicholas, Douglas.
  Throne of darkness : a novel / Douglas Nicholas.—First Emily Bestler Books/ Atria Paperback edition.
     pages cm
  1. Magic—Fiction. 2. Great Britain—History—John, 1199–1216—Fiction. I. Title.
  PS3614.I3375T48 2015
  813'.6—dc23

                          2014036008

ISBN 978-1-4767-5598-4
ISBN 978-1-4767-5600-4 (ebook)

for Theresa

Part I

THE APOSTATE KING

1

Part II

THE EYE OF THE HYENA

137

Part III

THE MUTTERER

259

Pronunciation of Irish names:

Maeve = MAYV

Nemain = NEV-an

A glossary of Irish terms is to be found on page 329.

A glossary of archaisms and dialect terms is to be found on page 331.

Part I

THE APOSTATE KING

The whisper wakes, the shudder plays,
Across the reeds at Runnymede.

—Kipling, "What Say the Reeds at Runnymede?"

CHAPTER 1

HOB OPENED THE SIDE DOOR OF the tavern, stepped out into the squalid alleyway, and threw himself violently to the right. A faint rushing sound as the shaft of the cudgel clove the air, a glimpse of movement at the lateral extreme of the eye's ability—something had warned him, and thus the blow struck his shoulder, and that already moving away, so that he suffered no real injury, just shock and dismay.

He had a chaotic blurred vision of the wall opposite—whitewashed daub peeling away from the wattle, urine stains—dim-lit in this tunnellike passageway, the two buildings so close together, sagging toward each other at the upper storeys, the eaves almost touching. Then he was down in the mire of the alley, rolling frantically away from his attackers, toward the rear of the inn. He planted a palm in the muck and used his momentum to roll up to his feet, as Sir Balthasar had taught him, a trick of the Norman knight to recover when unhorsed, or when the horse was killed beneath him. Even as he regained his feet he was running backward a few paces. He ripped his dagger from its leatherbound birchwood sheath and staggered to a halt.

The youth found himself facing a small band of grown men. The alley—just a walkway, really, between the two buildings—was so narrow that only two could come at him abreast, and he had an instant to take in an impression of several shadowy forms behind the two leaders. The one with the club was on Hob's left; beside him was a knifeman. Behind them were perhaps four others; perhaps five. The group, recovering from the failure of its ambush, was beginning to advance again, the ones in front gauging the danger the young man's dagger presented, the ones behind urging attack.

Jack was inside the inn, but Hob had not had time or breath to call out, and his attackers were rapidly closing with him. A vision of Nemain flitted before Hob's eye: she had shown him some of Molly's battle sleights, and one involved her leaping at a boulder in a field, planting a foot, and bouncing off the stone to achieve a rapid change of direction in an attack.

Now Hob looked hard at the knifeman, on his right, and with a loud wordless cry ran at him. Three paces short of closing with the bravo, Hob sprang at the right-hand wall; his right foot struck it two feet above the alley dirt and he pushed off mightily, propelling himself leftward across the alley, landing in a crouch before the club-wielder. Hob's left hand came up to catch the man's wrist and check the cudgel's downward progress; his right hand also came up, up, the dagger-point leading, sliding beneath the man's rib cage, piercing his heart. The club-man froze, struck dead by this internal thunderbolt, and fell back, his body tangling in the legs of the men behind.

The bravo in the lead with the knife now swung backhand at Hob, a weak blow, an awkward blow, and dealt the young man a shallow cut on the shoulder. But Hob was already moving back, resetting his feet, weaving his dagger this way and that, seeking an opening against the lead attacker, as Sir Balthasar had taught him. His youth, his strength, and his reach of arm, coupled with intense instruction from one of the most formidable knights of the North Country, had made Hob a match for even a grown man, even a hardened thug.

But there was no chance of his living through an encounter with a half-dozen men. "Jack!" he bellowed, as loud as he could. At that moment the rearmost of his enemies gave a truncated yelp; his head was snapped partway around, and he toppled over onto his back. The group halted its advance, and the bravos turned to see what threatened them from the alley front, all except the lead knifeman, who did not dare take his eyes from Hob's blade, swaying this way and that, an adder preparing its strike.

Another man went down toward the rear. Hob heard the thud but was himself unable to take his eyes from his immediate adversary. A moment later the inn door banged open and Jack, a horrid gargling roar erupting from his ruined larynx, crashed into the group, pounding the first man he met into unconsciousness with a giant fist to the back of the neck, scooping the dropped cudgel from the ground, laying about him with irresistible fury.

Hob's attacker, unnerved, allowed himself to be distracted, a fatal mistake. Hob lunged. His right leg went out before him, his knee bent; his right foot planted itself well ahead of his body; his right arm speared straight toward the man's throat, the outstretched dagger tearing into muscle, artery, windpipe: an irreparable injury, the door to death flung open. The bravo's eyes widened in horror; he dropped his own knife to grasp his neck; he sank down, dying.

Hob looked about him. Jack stood in the middle of several men, one unconscious, the rest dead or dying in the mud of the alley. Beyond him, holding a cord of gray silk on which hung a gold coin, stood the grim form of Sinibaldo, "the shadow of the shadow of Innocent III," whom Hob and Jack had met only that morning.

CHAPTER 2

EARLIER THAT DAY, HOB HAD been acutely aware of the other Italian, who sat well back in the dark corner. He could make out only the indistinct shape of a head and shoulders, and, catching the light from the hearth fire, the figure's lower legs, clad in the finest gray wool, shod in the supplest red-brown leather.

"Sir Odinell?" asked Molly.

"Yes, Sir Odinell; he has recommended you to me, and I have heard that you are to the market, here in Durham, and I have somewhat to discuss with you. I trust that you will find it as helpful to you, my lady, as I hope it will be to me."

An elegant, well-spoken man, Monsignor Bonacorso da Panzano, a sprinkling of white amid his dark hair like that of an aging dog, lean, swarthy, with intelligent dark eyes and an expression that managed to be amused and chilly at once. Despite a pronounced accent, which resulted in "I have heard" sounding to Hob like "I 'ave 'aired," the priest's English was nearly flawless; the young man found it an extremely pleasant voice, a dark tenor, musical, somewhat nasal, the accent giving the familiar words an unfamiliar spice.

Monsignor da Panzano had sent a page to Molly's wagon with a message that was an exquisite blend of courtesy, enticement, and threat. The summons had specified all four of the members of Molly's troupe: herself, her lover Jack Brown, her granddaughter Nemain, and Molly's former apprentice Hob, now Nemain's husband. Molly had swiftly weighed their choices, and accepted the invitation gracefully, although not without misgivings.

They had come to Durham Priory, a stronghold of the North England Benedictine monks, and been shown to a small windowless study, furnished with a quiet wealth that showed in the oak paneling, the richly carved table that served as a desk, the silver candelabrum on that table, its seven branches casting a warm but wavering light. Behind the table sat the monsignor, who identified himself only as "a humble agent of His Holiness," come to England as quietly as possible in these times of acrimony that lingered between King John and Pope Innocent III, despite their apparent reconciliation; da Panzano was not quite hiding here among the monks of Durham Priory, but he was certainly calling no attention to himself.

And the times called for discretion from everyone: no

one knew where the center of power would be from month to month. In that late spring of 1215, the seventeenth year of King John's reign, the king and the barons were circling one another like stiff-legged, ears-flattened fighting dogs. Rebellion was in the air, especially in the North Country.

There were negotiations: the banished and reinstated Archbishop of Canterbury, Stephen Langton, and the great knight William Marshal both tried to bring the parties together. There seemed to be progress, but here and there were clashes, skirmishes, small battles between partisans of the two factions. In particular the barons' men clashed with King John's foreign mercenaries—Flemings, Poitevins, and others—who were generally disliked. And now this agent of Pope Innocent III, one of the most dominant politicians of the age, had shown an unwelcome interest in Molly's troupe.

From the beginning of the interview, another Italian had sat in the shadows of the corner farthest from the candles, and made no sound except to answer curtly when addressed, nor indeed had he moved. Monsignor da Panzano had not introduced him, and only asked him a question or two, as one who seeks to confirm a memory, but the two had spoken in Italian.

Now da Panzano said something to the shadow, and that person stood and came into the light. The man went to the door, opened it, and spoke to one outside. He turned and put his back to the door, folding his hands in front of him. Hob looked at him with frank curiosity.

He saw a man of middle height, broad of torso and shoulder but flat-stomached, with long arms and hands that seemed to belong to a larger man. A thick neck, a cap of dark-brown hair, and features that were blunt-cut, almost to the point of brutality. A large nose, with a pronounced curve, presided over a wide, thin-lipped mouth. His eyes were darkest brown, perhaps even black, and looked back at Hob with the flat emotionless menace of a reptile.

Over a cotehardie of gray-brown wool was a coat of black linen, its laces left undone so that it hung open at the front. On the left breast of the coat had been embroidered two crossed keys, one in silver thread and one in golden.

"But what a beast I am!" said da Panzano. "I have not presented my associate: this is Sinibaldo, more precious to me than my own right hand. He is a man of many accomplishments, and is an invaluable agent to me, and to the Holy Father."

The Italian against the door gave a brief bow that managed to convey, if not arrogance, certainly a measure of stubborn pride.

A very short while later there was a diffident knock at the door. Sinibaldo turned, put a foot near the bottom of the door to guard against an attempt to burst in, and opened the door a little way. He looked out; Hob saw his head turn this way and that, a suspicious inspection up and down the hallway, then he stepped back and opened the door fully. A novice came in with a tray holding a glass bottle in the Venetian style, and a set of small silver cups. Sinibaldo, his eyes narrowed, his expression one of keenest vigilance, divided his attention between the novice and the partially open door. The young man placed the tray on the desk before Monsignor da Panzano and withdrew.

Sinibaldo closed and locked the door behind the novice, crossed to the desk, and plucked the glass stopper from the bottle. Hob saw with fascination that he did everything with his left hand—was his right hand enfeebled? But both hands were large, square, and heavily muscled, the veins prominent: hands that might belong to a professional strangler. Sinibaldo lifted the bottle, sniffed at it, stood a moment with an abstracted expression, as though thinking or remembering. Then he nodded and began, working left-handed, to fill and distribute cups to the company, first to Molly and then to the others, and then to Monsignor da Panzano. He moved with the surefooted economy of an athlete, or of a dancer, always on balance: a man who would be braced, as Marcus Aurelius advises, against assault from unexpected quarters. He did not pour a cup for himself, but turned and went back to the obscurity of his seat in the corner.

But when he turned toward the corner, the motion spun his coat open, just a little, and Hob could see, slung to a leather belt, on the right side, a long Italianate dagger, wasp-slim, wasp-malignant, with an ornately turned hilt made of what seemed to be a dull copper. Just before the coat swirled closed again, Hob caught a glimpse of a leather strap that fastened to his belt and ran up and over his left shoulder beneath the coat. There seemed to be loops in this strap, seven or so, that held—Hob could not tell what they held: small complicated items of some sort.

Hob took a sip from his cup. A deliciously sweet taste, in which he could detect cinnamon and clove, and an aftertaste as of nuts, but with the sting of alcohol, strong as the *uisce beatha* that Molly produced from the portable vessels slung from her wagons. A delightful warmth settled in his stomach and ease spread out along his limbs. He smiled with the pleasure of it.

"You enjoy it, I hope?" Monsignor da Panzano said to the company in general. "I am bringing several bottles with me, all the far way from Rome herself, and before that from Venice to Rome."

"'Tis a grand taste," said Molly, who enjoyed a drink as well as anyone, "but 'tis not for this you've brought us here, and it's unable to rest easy that I'm finding myself, and we not knowing if 'tis some danger we're slipping into."

The priest made a supple motion with outspread hands and lifted shoulders, not quite a shrug, that seemed to say *I understand your concerns completely.* "A thousand apologies, madam, you have the right of it. I am thinking to set you first at your ease with my poor refreshments, but perhaps we should be—what is the word?—*blunt*, yes, blunt. Or is it *direct*? Well. We—myself, and through me the Holy Father, and through him Holy Mother Church—we are needing your help against the king."

He sat back and watched for the reaction to this startling and mortally dangerous set of words.

Molly sighed and made as if to rise. "If it's treason you want to speak, I've no wish to be hearing of it. He's not my king, but I am to understand that it's a dim view that's taken of such loose talk, and I've no wish to be drawn and quartered, and you with a man in the shadows there, and he a possible witness against us."

"Hear me, hear me, dear lady, but a moment. You are in a frail ship in tempestuous seas: on one side are the rocks of King John's enmity, on the other the great cliff that is the Church, and already you have sailed far too close to the cliff. I am offering to bring you to safe harbor, if you can render us the type of service you rendered to Sir Odinell. You have my guarantee of safety in perpetuity from prosecution by the Church against your . . . *unusual* practices and abilities. And later, when you come to set foot again on your native shore, you will have the Holy Father as your patron against your enemies, and against the Church in Ireland itself."

Molly sat back at this, but with a deepening scowl. Hob cast a sideways glance at her, wondering what she would decide. Molly often called the troupe to a council of war, but only Nemain would think to disagree with her at all, and even Nemain obeyed her in most things, recognizing that the authority was Molly's and also that she was the wisest of them by far.

Molly was Queen Maeve back in Erin, as Nemain was Queen Nemain, hereditary chieftains of their clan. Their kinfolk had been betrayed and murdered, their clan scattered, and their land usurped by rivals, and she and her granddaughter had fled to England, where they traveled under the guise of musicians, and healers. Maeve began to use the Christian nickname *Molly* rather than the pagan *Maeve,* and now only Jack called her *Maeve,* on those rare occasions—usually moved by passion—when he chose to ignore the pain and difficulty that speech cost him.

Slowly she had begun to accumulate wealth and allies,

always with the hope of returning to Erin to regain her position, and to exact revenge. But these plans were known only to a few confidants, and it plainly disturbed her to learn the extent to which da Panzano was aware of her activities. Sir Odinell knew of them, but Hob thought that the knight never would have told the papal agent Molly's secrets; rather, he would have recommended her for her abilities in hope of securing her another patron, or to blunt any animus the Church might feel toward her. Hob stole another glance at Molly, but her stony visage told him nothing. For this moment, thought the young man, it remained only to determine how much of a threat da Panzano represented, and what path led out of the thicket into which they had stumbled.

"Sit, enjoy my hospitality," said the priest, "and listen for a short hour. Learn to trust me. I will tell you things of the king that not a handful of people know, and you will understand why you are here, with your people."

Molly gave a sign of assent, and the papal agent sipped from his cup, and began.

CHAPTER 3

UT FIRST—LET ME EXPLAIN Sinibaldo," said da Panzano. "I am a special sort of *legatus missus,* a 'sent legate.' You may think of me as the shadow of His Holiness: I do his bidding, sometimes in the dark places of the world, to exert the Church's influence, sometimes in ways that may not be done plainly before all men. There are times when I must be wicked to do good. I am the shadow of Innocent III across the earth, and Sinibaldo is the shadow of the shadow.

"I have made many enemies, and many thirst for my blood. Sinibaldo is a man of excellent skills, and he employs them to keep me safe from my enemies. They wish to kill me, and he does not permit that. He is here to fend off attacks; on other occasions he goes forth privily, and reduces the number of my enemies by one and by two. He is my bodyguard and, not to be overnice in my speech, an assassin when such is needed. Come into the light again, my son."

Sinibaldo came easily to his feet, and moved to stand by da Panzano's desk, facing Molly's little troupe. They were ranged in a loose semicircle, seated on the ornately carved chairs produced by the monks of the priory for their own use.

"You could all attack at once, and he could fend you off—he has trained himself to leave his right hand free, and snakes would seem slow beside him. Were he to attack you, you would have no defense against him."

To Sinibaldo he now said, "Show them the coin-and-cord." Here he indicated a tall candle alight on the sideboard; it was set in a heavy silver holder. "Use that candle."

Sinibaldo bowed, and as he straightened, his right hand had acquired a thin cord of gray silk. There was a heavy gold Venetian coin, a hole punched by a square nail in its center; the cord was tied through this hole. Sinibaldo whirled the cord, the coin making glowing circles in the candlelight. He loosened his grip; the coin flew toward the candle, the gray silk slipping quickly through his strong fingers. He gave a clever flirt of the wrist and the coin stalled just past the candle, coiled about the wick, and snuffed the flame. It flew back into Sinibaldo's palm, and he spun it out again, and it severed an inch of wax and wick from the smoking tip of the candle.

"He could do that to a man's neck, even so stalwart a man as your Jack here," said da Panzano, nodding toward the dark man seated between Molly and Nemain.

"He could not," said Molly quietly; in almost the same breath she said aside, in the lowest of voices, "Nemain."

Monsignor da Panzano, his urbane and gracious tone slipping just the least bit, said to Sinibaldo, "Do not harm him, but put a loop about his neck."

The word *neck* had hardly left his lips when the gold coin flew toward Jack's throat. A silver flicker passed before Jack's face and the golden coin thumped against his chest and landed in his lap. Nemain slipped her dagger back into its sheath, and Sinibaldo was left holding a length of limp gray silk cord, now floating down toward the floor, deprived of its stabilizing weight of Venetian gold.

The assassin's face darkened, a snarl sprang to his lips, and his left hand leapt to retract the fold of his coat, his right darting to the leather strap and grasping the small obscure thing in the topmost loop.

"*Lascia stare!*" said the monsignor, in a voice like the crack of close-by lightning splitting the air, and the assassin stopped on the instant, as though frozen, but he left his right hand near the fold of his coat, and as ever he was perfectly balanced, feet apart, powerful legs slightly flexed.

Jack Brown took the coin from his lap and stood. He held the coin out, and two steps brought him face-to-face with Sinibaldo. Jack was a tall man, but so powerfully made that the eye, seeking to render him in more ordinary proportions, was often deceived into thinking him shorter than he was. Looming over Sinibaldo, though, in the small office, the threat implicit in being the largest animal in a confined space was made manifest, and over Sinibaldo's face came an expression, not of fear, but certainly of great wariness. He took a step back and reset his feet, still as balanced as a swordsman before a duel, so that he gave himself a foot of space in which to maneuver. He kept his right hand near the left side of his black linen surcoat and extended his left hand, palm up. Jack dropped the coin into it.

Molly's lover stood there a moment more, dominating the center of the room, seeming to fill a great portion of it, then stepped back and sat; throughout, his expression had been its usual stolid self, if somewhat less amiable than was its wont.

Da Panzano had watched everything with rapt attention, his glittering dark eyes shifting rapidly between Jack and Sinibaldo, as though gauging to a nicety the shifts of power displayed between the two men.

"I begin to see why Sir Odinell has recommended you," da Panzano said, his tone smooth, even caressing. "Perhaps we can agree that neither party is to be slighted, and begin again with mutual respect, the better to see where our common interests lie."

He gestured to the bottle, giving the merest shift of his eyes to Sinibaldo. The assassin removed the stopper and picked up the bottle, again doing everything left-handed, and poured more into each cup, with no least sign of animosity toward the monsignor's guests, as though nothing had happened between them.

The pope's agent went on. "Let me tell you of King John and his astonishing apostasy to his religion, his treason to his country. Two years ago, when His Holiness and the king were at each other's throats, and Philip of France grasping at John's lands in Normandy, and King John at a loss for money to pay his mercenaries, he determined upon a desperate throw of the dice."

Sinibaldo settled back in his darkened corner with hardly a sound.

Da Panzano sipped at his cup. "King John sent an embassy to the Emir of Marroch. In this embassy were two knights, Thomas of Herdington and Radulph son of Nicholas, and a priest of ill fame, Master Robert of London. John Lackland charged them to approach the Emir with this offer: that John would swear fealty to the Emir, and further, convert to the faith of the Saracens, and have all England do the same, if the Emir would but support the king against his enemies."

"Holy Mary!" said Hob, half under his breath; this was astounding. Molly and Nemain, devotees of the Old Religion, were surprised but not much affected. Jack was silent as ever, although he had looked over at Hob for a moment with an expression of surprise.

"*È stupefacente, eh?* It is hard to comprehend, evil on so great a scale, is it not? But wait—even the follower of the false prophet Mahomet had more honor than the king. He refused John, saying that one who turned traitor to his faith could never be trusted, and one who would enslave his people for help must be too weak to be a proper ally, and he sent John's ambassadors away with scorn."

Molly was watching the legate intently, as though trying to read in the play of candlelight over his features the hidden purpose for which he had summoned them. "I'm thinking 'tis dangerous knowledge you're just after telling us, and that to no avail, since the king's plan came to naught, and ourselves all unknowing why we're here atall."

"*Pazienza,* dear madam, patience. King John's embassy had failed; his ambassadors were at a wharfside inn in the city of Tangier, awaiting passage homeward. In some manner Master Robert, a subtle and accomplished man with no great store of virtue, sought out in that port town one he had heard rumor of, a man of the dark arts, and spent many hours in an upper room of that inn, and in short, they came to some kind of agreement. This sorcerer—for he is that, a man of evil power—this necromancer is the chieftain of a tribe of evil men, blacksmiths and, and—what do you say, in English? We say *lupi mannari,* men who, with the help of Satan, change into wolves, but these do not change into wolves. They are men of Marroch, but they have sojourned in the far South, in the lands of the Ethiop, where they were universally despised, and where they have contracted the ability to become not wolves, but—you are familiar with the *hyena?* It is a beast of the far South, below the great deserts that are beneath Marroch and Egypt."

Jack and Nemain looked blank, but Hob, to everyone's surprise, said, "Father Athelstan told me of the hyena—he saw it drawn in a bestiary once. He said they were symbols of those who were slaves to luxury and greed, and so could not serve God with a whole heart."

Molly nodded tentatively, and said, " 'Tis like a mixture of bear and wolf?"

"With perhaps a bit of the cat as well, no?" said da Panzano. "There are smaller ones, striped hyenas, in Marroch itself, but these I speak of are the great brutes of the South, with spots instead of stripes. I have seen them in a menagerie in Rome, at the Vatican; His Holiness has strange creatures brought from distant lands. That day, it was late in the afternoon, the sun just leaving the windows of the room, a room of stone, and no one else there but myself, and the beasts—remarkably unbeautiful beasts—prowling back and forth behind the bars. Signor Hyena spoke: it was like the gibbering of a demented woman, high, with a"—here the papal legate made a wavering motion with a flat hand—"a trembling in the sound. And then it laughed."

"Laughed?" said Nemain, startled.

"Such a laugh, daughter, as the demons in Hell must make. My hair, it was—how do you say?—standing on the edges? On the edge . . . ? No, no—on end: it was standing on end. A coldness is sweeping along my limbs, although I am safe in the room, the beasts behind thick iron bars." He gave a little rueful smile, a shake of the head. "The great da Panzano, the pope's feared right hand! I am ready to run from the room, but I make myself walk. I spoke later with the keepers there. These beasts are not small; at the shoulder they are thus"—here he held his hand out, perhaps a yard above the floor—"and they run in packs, very fierce. They eat carrion, like crows or vultures, but they kill also, and if there are enough of them, and there are no male lions present, they will drive even lionesses away from their feasting, and take the kill for their own. They are very strong in the jaws, and can crush the biggest bones."

Molly leaned forward, a little of her silver mane peeping from beneath her veil, her gaze fixed on the legate's face.

"You're saying that 'tis into such an *arracht* these men can change themselves?"

Da Panzano, distracted, said, "*Arracht*?"

Molly gestured impatiently. "A monster, a monster. They change themselves into these beasts?"

"With the Devil's assistance, I presume," said the legate. "And, whispers of your abilities having reached me, I thought to seek your help, and to offer you mine."

He toyed with the little silver cup, swirling the contents about, his well-kept nails tapping against the side of the vessel with little metallic clicks. "There has been communication between the king and this sorcerer, for the past two years. I have managed to intercept one messenger—it may interest you to know that I have lost two of my own agents in this affair—managed, I say, to intercept one of the king's messengers. We put him to the question, but he revealed only that this sorcerer was to come to England, to do some mischief in the service of the king. Perhaps he knew more, but he perished—a result, I fear, of our methods—before he could tell us of it."

He sighed. "We know this magus has indeed come to England, and we know that John has some evil purpose for this man to accomplish. We have tried prayer and exorcism against him, to little effect. He is not a follower of Mahomet; he is one of those few who hold to the old beliefs of these people, these Moors, or Berbers, who have dwelt along the southern coasts of the Mediterranean for years that no memory can recall. They are ancient, and most are now followers of Mahomet, although some are good Christians—indeed the holy Saint Augustine was Berber himself—and some are unregenerate pagans, like these *lupi mannari.* We hear murmurs, that the Ethiops call them *bouda,* the hyena-men. Among themselves, these devil-men, these beast-men, refer to their group as 'the Cousins,' and they are said to have what the Saracens call *al-Ain,* 'the eye.' They can put you to sleep and bring you under their command, just by looking at you three times."

Da Panzano crossed himself with his right hand and made a warding-off gesture with his left.

"In Venice we call it *malocchio,* the 'evil eye.' It may be that we do not understand these ancient powers as well as we should. You, madam, have certainly done better against this sort of evil than we; you know how disastrously we failed in the exorcism we directed against the vile Sir Tarquin, that Satanist or pagan or what-have-you, and yet you destroyed him. It may be that you are closer to these old practices, and so can aid us as you aided Sir Odinell against Sir Tarquin."

"And for this you will help us in Erin?" said Molly, still sitting back, her expression unreadable.

"That, and this as well—" Here the legate leaned forward, the changing angle causing a shadow to fall across his face, only his eyes picking up the candlelight, glittering under his brows. "If you help us, you will escape the stake."

CHAPTER 4

FOR PERHAPS TWO BREATHS, AN appalled silence fell. Then a rusty growl began in Jack's throat, but Molly put a hand on his thigh and he subsided.

"We can offer no surety that we'll succeed," she said.

"I ask only that you try," said da Panzano, sitting back. A trace of humor crept back into his voice. "If you succeed, I give you my word before Our Father in Heaven that you will be safe from the Church, and even aided by us. If you fail, I suspect that you will be beyond the reach of the stake."

Molly stood abruptly and stepped to the table. She put one hand to the burnished wood of the tabletop and inclined across it toward Monsignor da Panzano. The priest made an involuntary movement back in his chair. Hob was aware that Sinibaldo had come swiftly to his feet, half-hidden there in the shadows, but keenly attentive, tense and dangerous as a coiled serpent. Molly extended her other hand, palm up, toward the papal agent.

"Would you ever give us your hand to see?" asked Molly.

The priest, somewhat bewildered, held out his right hand, and Molly took it between both of hers. She stood for a long moment, gazing steadily into the legate's eyes. Then she released his hand and resumed her seat. The priest, with the faintest expression of wary distaste, reached into his robes and drew out a rough cross—it looked to be made of iron, as far as Hob could tell—kissed it, and tucked it and its iron chain back into the folds of cloth.

There was the slightest rustle from the corner: Sinibaldo resuming his seat.

"There's no falseness to this offer you're making us," she said. "That's what I'm just after feeling, any road; but past that there's naught but veils across your heart, and veils across those veils. There are some men whose hearts are like open fields in summer sun; yours is a hidden heart, and it may be 'tis hidden even from you. Certainly 'tis hidden from me, but in this matter, this oath you're making to us, there's no lie I can taste in it."

"But this is what I have asked you, madam; that you learn to trust me." His left hand produced a white, lace-trimmed cloth from his sleeve; with this he quietly wiped his right hand. He was apparently unaware of his own actions, for he spoke on with no hesitation. "Sinibaldo will come to you with a sufficiency of English coin; in this way you need not concern yourself with how to earn your keep while you act for His Holiness. You will also earn a measure of forgiveness for those acts of unholiness you may be engaged in, that enable you to do these strange things."

There was a subdued but angry hiss from Nemain, but Molly made a small gesture, down by her side, and Nemain fell silent.

"I believe that the king has brought in this sorcerer, and he is in turn bringing in his devils, or devil-men, or whatever they may be, from the Moorish lands, in small groups. He is assembling them in the West, at Chester. But why? King John is locked in struggle with these *ribelli*, these rebel northern barons—among whom, dear lady, let me be so presumptuous as to remind you, are your friends Sir Jehan and Sir Odinell, and"—here he glanced down at a parchment held flat to the table by two iron disks imprinted with the seal of Durham Priory—"the so-frightening Sir Balthasar. Against whom do you think the king will use his monsters, *eh*? So it is for your friends that you act as well."

"One thing there is that's fretting me," said Molly. "I am to understand, from Sir Odinell and others, that the pope's after lifting the ban on the king, and hasn't he transferred it to those who rise against the king—my friends, as you say, and you have the right of that—and Innocent is now steadying John Lackland on his throne. And here you're acting against John, and saying that you're acting for Innocent."

Da Panzano sighed. "King John has very shrewdly put His Holiness in an extremely awkward position. The king has done penance, sent tribute, and made himself a vassal of Rome. The pope cannot leave a vassal unsupported—he would lose all authority throughout Europe. So in the open air he supports John Lackland. In the shadows he sends me to England, and with me Sinibaldo. And we will work against the king, and through us you will also."

THE LEGATE SAW THEM to the door. Sinibaldo glided ahead, opened the door, looked left and right, and stood a long moment, blocking the doorway, a man letting the view, and any anomaly, soak into his senses. Hob thought him somewhat overcautious, since the garth outside, planted to herbs and drowsy with bees, was clear to the encircling wall; then again, Monsignor da Panzano, despite all his enemies, was in demonstrable good health. Sinibaldo stepped outside and put his back to the priory wall, and the others filed out. The monsignor spoke from the doorway: "As we seek to send spies into the West, King John may have his eyes here in the North. Be guarded in everything you do."

"We will that," said Molly.

"Go with God," said da Panzano, and retreated into the priory. Sinibaldo stepped back into the doorway, nodded gravely to them, and closed the door. A moment later bolts clacked into place.

CHAPTER 5

FOR A MAN SENDING US INTO THE West and King John's stronghold, sure he's that careful of his own hide," said Nemain bitterly. Her eyes were bright with anger and two red spots burned on her cheeks. Nemain had a volatile temperament at the best of times, and she was still incensed over da Panzano's speech about Molly and her family earning forgiveness.

"It's unwilling I am to speak my mind here," said Molly, "not knowing what can be heard. I'm not trusting even those bees. We'll speak at home."

Home was the three wagons in which Molly's troupe traveled.

The path they followed through the garth came to the priory's encircling wall; here iron gates were set in a graceful but strong stone archway. A heavy middle-aged monk served as porter. When Molly's group came up to the gate, he bowed, drew a key from the bunch that swung at his waist, and addressed himself to the lock.

Hob looked around. Nearby, two strongly made young monks leaned on hoes, idling for the moment amid the banks and rows of herbs. They did not seem eager to garden, and the Benedictines were not known for sloth. Hob suspected that their presence, and the priory gate locked at midday, were more of da Panzano's meticulous precautions against his enemies.

At last the lock's inwards gave a dull *clunk,* and the ponderous iron gate groaned open. Brother Porter murmured a blessing, which Hob echoed. Jack touched his forehead; the women nodded politely.

They went up the road along the priory wall, passed through the north gate into the square, and now they could see down the wooded slope to the river Wear. It was a day to make one feel that death and the fear of death could not exist amid all this sunlight. Hob tilted his face up a bit as they walked to feel the sun, and took Nemain's hand. He felt content for a moment; then they stepped into the shadow of old maple trees. The sudden chill, the abrupt dimming of the light, recalled da Panzano's parting words: "Be guarded in everything you do."

Perhaps Molly and Nemain felt the same, for they turned, almost as one, and peered into the wooded ravine; down there the river snaked in an oxbow turn around the tip of the peninsula of high ground on which the cathedral and castle stood; and Nemain glanced behind her.

"What is it, culver? Is there danger?" Hob asked his wife.

"Nay, it's . . . it's a feeling that . . ." Nemain began.

"A feeling of being watched, and aren't the two of us sensing it at the same time, but now 'tis gone, for me at any road," said Molly.

"For me as well," said Nemain.

The party walked on, but warily. They crossed the Elvet Bridge with its gates and towers, and the two chapels on the bridge, one at either end, and so down into Elvet Borough. Down by the riverbank the path wound through deep shade: the canopies of riparian trees, the shadow of the high prow of the peninsula itself, cast the way into dappled gloom, but through the tree trunks the sun sparkled where it struck the surface of the Wear. Hob looked back across the river. He could see the grand rose window set in the eastern face of Durham Cathedral, the pride of the Prince Bishops, just rising above the trees of the plateau.

They went on, through winding streets, to Godric's Inn, where Molly had arranged for them to stay, with the wagons that they slept in kept in a yard behind the inn, the beasts stalled in the inn's stables, and a place for the troupe to play music each night for pay and for board. Molly negotiated this arrangement whenever possible; it allowed her to keep her people safe and fed during these troubled days, when England seemed to be slipping toward chaos.

They paused before the inn. Molly put a hand on Jack's shoulder. " 'Tis women's business that Nemain and I will be about. Do you two lads go in and have a draft or two, and then come on to the wagons, and we will discuss this pope's man and his demands."

Hob knew there were aspects of Molly and Nemain's religion, the worship of the Old Gods of Erin, that they preferred to keep private, for the sake of the men's consciences—although Jack was not one to trouble over such things, Hob was more introspective, and inclined to chew over moral conflicts. There were, as well, some aspects of the women's worship that were forbidden to men, and that Hob and Jack's presence would cause to fail.

The women entered the alley that ran down between the inn and its neighbor building, eventually debouching into the innyard with its surrounding wall and wide gate for supply wains to enter. There Molly's three wagons, with wheels chocked, stood along one wall; against the opposite wall were the stables.

Jack and Hob watched them till they turned the corner at the far end of the narrow alleyway, and then entered the inn. Within was the sweet smell of countless spills and spots of beer, and of honey beer, and of wine and cider. With this was mixed woodsmoke; a rich and savory scent of garlic and pork and onions and apples from the stewpot swinging over the cookfire; and a faint earthen smell from the packed-dirt floor.

Windows glazed with oiled parchment admitted a yellowed old-ivory light; an oil lamp, hung on a chain fixed to a ceiling beam, cast a somewhat brighter circle of illumination on the planks, laid across three wine-butts, that functioned as a serving counter. The innkeeper's daughter, seeing the two men approach, immediately poured two carved-wood mugs of gruit ale: Molly's troupe had been playing in Godric's Inn for nigh on a month, and Jack had developed a taste for the strong heather-flavored brew. The increase in custom from folk who came to hear them play, and the fact that Molly's people slept in their own wagons and so did not take up space in Godric's sleeping rooms, made the innkeeper happy to provide free food and drink to the company.

They took their beer to a side table and sat on the bench against the wall. The neck wound that Jack had sustained in the Holy Land—it showed as an oval patch of silver scar tissue, but the underlying damage was greater than it appeared—made it preferable for him to remain silent, and Hob, after long acquaintance, was able to enjoy sitting quietly next to his formidable friend, who was like an uncle to him.

They sat and watched the life of the common room unfolding before them. A few of the Durham folk came and went, many of them workers in the mills driven by the tireless waterwheels that rolled their upstream sides down into the river Wear and heaved their downstream sides dripping into the sunlight. The grain millers wore smocks dusty with wheat flour; other men had clothes smudged with fuller's earth: these worked in the fulling mills, where the waterwheels drove great wooden hammers that pounded wool till it was clean and thick. Some drained their mugs quickly, settled their score, and left; others sat with friends and drank and talked and drank again, the conversation usually becoming more and more animated as the drinking went on.

After a while Hob got up and got them a large fired-clay pitcher of ale, poured for Jack and himself, and resumed his seat. He sat drinking quietly for a bit, and then he began to think about Jack, and the secrets the ex-soldier carried within him, and how frightened the patrons of Godric's Inn would be did they know that such as Jack sat watching them.

At heart Jack Brown was a deeply decent man, by chance drifting into the profession of man-at-arms, which inevitably involved periods of controlled savagery. He had been capable of utter ruthlessness in the midst of battle, but once let the lords conclude a truce among themselves, and he would be the first to sit down in a tavern with his former foes. He had the mercenary's dispassionate violence, and bore no grudges, and generally was cheerful all the long day.

He also had curséd luck: on crusade in the Holy Land, he had been mangled by a turnskin, a shapeshifter, in the hot heart of a sandstorm, and had been rendered unclean thereby. He had begun to change on occasion: to become a monstrous Beast like the one that had so nearly slain him amid the roaring brown clouds of sand, leaving him with difficulty speaking and a lifelong limp. It was like a man, but huge, with long arms and thick bowed legs, a black pelt that on the back was tinged with silver at the tips of the hair.

When he was in this form, Jack was driven to kill and eat of human flesh, to his horror when he awoke in some field or barn, naked and soaked in gore. He was heartsick at what he half remembered having done, and he feared being burned at the stake by the Church should he be found out, and he feared he was beginning to change more often, and he feared that one day he would not change back. He had heard tales of a woman who excelled as a healer; desperate, he had sought her out at the annual fair at Ely.

He had gone right up to Molly and stood before her, hollow-eyed, grim-faced, and found himself unable to speak of what oppressed him—partly because of his ruined throat, destroyed by the bite of the giant shapeshifter, which made communication difficult, but also from shame and from the strange nature of his affliction, so difficult to explain.

She saw a powerfully built man, perhaps eight years her junior, in some form of inner torment. For his part, he saw a handsome woman, heavy but shapely, with eyes that were a startling lakewater blue. Her bearing was as one who expects to be obeyed, but her expression was kindness itself. Even then, eleven or twelve years ago, when she was in her midforties, she had a long thick mane of gray-and-silver hair.

She put a hand to the scar on his neck, a gesture one might use to a restive horse, but also an intimate one; she stood with eyes unfocused, as though listening to something. Her touch was warm, and from it a peace seemed to spread through his body. He closed his eyes and stood there, swaying a little.

After a moment she took his hand, as though he were a child, and led him around behind the booths, to a large travelling wagon, and brought him within, and sat him on a large chest.

When Molly told Hob the tale—one night when the *uisce beatha* was flowing freely—she said, " 'Twas my stoutest chest, and I hearing it creak and groan, the poor thing, as though it suffered. And he not a fat man atall, atall. 'Twas then that I'm thinking he must have bones like a bear, and muscle withal, and I'm swearing in my heart that I'll see him made whole, for he's to be my consort. This in less time than a sparrow can blink twice."

Hob on this night was already a married man, albeit a new one, and yet a bit uneasy at his changed relationship with Molly, no longer a child with his adopted grandmother, but almost an equal, if anyone could properly be said to be Molly's equal. He was fascinated, though, and eased his awkwardness by taking another sip of the fiery liquid.

She looked off into the intermediate distance as people do when they observe their own past. She drank, and said, "I'm never taking to a man so quickly—and I've opened my thighs to whosoever I wanted—him so large and dangerous and yet lost: for wasn't he standing at the lip of his own grave, and the edge of the soil crumbling under his feet? But I'm after bringing him back, I'm *pulling* him back, I'm working like a devil at a forge for a sennight to pull him back. I dosed him till he near died of it, and made bargains with the Horned Man, the Lord of the Beasts, and crafted amulets for him to wear, and potions to drink."

She pulled her gaze from the past and looked at Hob. "I would have helped him any road, Hob, ye ken, for 'twas only the right thing to do, but added to all those potions and amulets is the force of the Artist's will that puts power into those potions and amulets and draws the attention of the Old Gods, and here was my desire for him adding a great strength to that will."

Another drink; another pause; another sigh; and then:

"And the great Queen Maeve, for whom I'm named, swore she would have only a man equal to her as a consort—as she was a warrior, he must be a warrior; as she was a woman of wealth and power, so he must be a man of wealth and power. 'Tis not that he's a match for me in wealth, but he's fierce in war, and has power in the strength of his body, and underneath that, the power of the Beast."

It was the power of that Beast that Molly had unleashed on Fox Night, saving Sir Jehan and all his folk from a terrible foe, and that caused Sir Jehan to send them to his friend Sir Odinell when that good knight found himself in perilous circumstances; Molly's destruction of Sir Odinell's horrid and unnatural neighbors had in turn aroused Monsignor da Panzano's interest, and now that agent of the great pope Innocent III wished to enlist them in yet another eerie struggle. Hob sat and wondered at the strange turns his life had taken from the day Molly, perceiving something about him, had taken him into her wagons as an apprentice.

His parents had been lying dead in the middle of a forest road, and a boy of three or four—Hob—sitting dazed and weeping beside them. The carters who found them had buried the couple, and brought the child away with them; passing through the little village of St. Edmund, they had left the boy with the village priest, who had a reputation as a kindly man.

When he was eleven, Molly had taken him from the quiet of old Father Athelstan's priest house to a life in which one startling event led to another like rooms opening into other rooms in a castle. And in each room was a reward, and in each room was a monster.

Hob realized that he was sinking into a mood of introspection that was at least partly the work of the gruit ale, and he pushed his newly refilled mug—how many had he had?—over to Jack, and stood up.

"I'm off to the wagons, Jack," he said, and clapped the older man on the shoulder. Jack nodded, swept a thick finger in a circle indicating his mug, Hob's mug, and the near-empty jug, and then pointed to himself, meaning that he would finish them and then follow.

Hob stretched, and then walked down the room. He opened the side door of the tavern, stepped out into the squalid alleyway, and threw himself violently to the right.

CHAPTER 6

HOB STARED AT HIS UNEXPECTED ally. Sinibaldo came toward him, coiling the silken cord with which he had broken necks, stepping sure-footed over the tangle of bodies, the sprawl of limbs. The Italian drew from within his coat a square of parchment folded flat, and a leather pouch the size of Jack's fist; he looked back and forth between Hob and Jack, settled on Hob, and handed him the parchment and pouch, saying only, "For your mistress." The pouch was surprisingly heavy. Hob noticed that the body-guard kept a pace or two away from Jack, and seemed to be wary of him, though hardly timid.

Hob loosened the leather drawstrings of the pouch; within was the glint of silver. He placed the parchment into the pouch and pulled the thongs tight again.

Sinibaldo swept his hand in a half circle, indicating the fallen. "I am being sent to give your mistress this message, and a little coin for your journey; I come to the inn, and from across the way I see these *teppistas,* these men of violence, of the gutters and alleys. They are waiting to murder or to rob—I am not care, but I am knowing that they do the work, the service, for Bennett in Souterpeth—you know this street? Is where live the, the, the makers of shoes. Bennett is the eyes, the ears, of the king, this King John, in Durham. Is supposed to be *segreto,* but Monsignore da Panzano is knowing ever't'ing. So I watch, because you are here at this inn, and here also are Bennett's dogs, and I say to myself, what will 'appen?"

The bodyguard's accent was thicker and harsher than his master's, although he seemed fluent enough in English. Where da Panzano's speech was musical, though, Sinibaldo's was grating; it accorded with his habitual stern expression, his abrupt demeanor.

The roughneck who had been pounded unconscious by Jack now moaned and began to roll feebly from side to side. Sinibaldo squatted beside him and swept a hard palm across the man's face; the slap sounded like a branch breaking. The bravo's eyes flew open; he gazed in terror at the Italian's somber countenance.

Sinibaldo turned his back to them, so that Hob could see his former attacker's upturned face, but not what Sinibaldo was doing with his hands. Sinibaldo murmured a question, but the man only shook his head. The Italian reached out; the man's eyes widened and he gave forth a shriek.

Hob, in the midst of knotting the heavy pouch to his belt, looked a question at Jack. The burly man-at-arms shrugged, folded his arms, and leaned back against the inn wall, waiting to see what would occur.

A bit more of this savage interrogation elicited the information Sinibaldo sought: the ruffians were watching the priory on Bennett's orders, suspecting da Panzano's presence; they saw Molly and her party leave; they hastened to the inn where Molly's troupe was known to be playing music on most nights, and they were lurking, intending to seize someone of Molly's party and haul them to Bennett for questioning.

Sinibaldo stood, turned; the desperado lay gasping. Sinibaldo took a pace toward Hob and Jack, and then, as if remembering something left undone, stopped dead. As swift as a snapping dog, his right hand darted in and out of his coat; he twisted from the waist; he threw something backhand at the supine man. It was a little dart, perhaps four inches long, and it stuck quivering in the rough's thigh.

A moment later the man convulsed, his body arching up from the ground, a faint wheezing attempt at a scream escaping his lungs. Almost immediately his body collapsed its arch and he lay still, his last breath bringing yellow froth to his lips.

"Better he is dead, *non è vero*? Now no one runs to Bennett and says, 'Da Panzano has met with the *musicistas* who play at Godric's Inn and they are plotting something.' No, is better this way."

He bent and plucked the dart from the dead man's thigh.

He held it up so Jack and Hob could see: a graceful wooden cylinder, tapered, with pigeon feathers set at one end and a slim steel spike like a needle at the other. Sinibaldo indicated the point: "The *dardo*—I don't know how you say; we say *dardo*—he is envenomed." He held open his coat, and carefully replaced the dart into a leather loop in his baldric; Hob could just see that the loops were plugged at one end with what looked like cork. Into this cork the assassin thrust the point of the dart.

"What—uh, what is the poison?" asked Hob, not because he wanted to know but because he was certain that Molly would.

Sinibaldo smiled and put a finger across his lips. "*Roma* is old, and all things, even the most *segreto* of them, may be found there, and the Church knows all hidden things, and uses them for her power."

He looked around at the corpses. Away at the alley mouth, a small procession of three pony-drawn carts rattled by, each led by a lad with a rope to the pony's bridle. None of the boys even glanced into the gloom of the alley.

"Better you should leave soon; that *cartapecora*—the parzme'—" He shook his head; he leaned forward, tapped the pouch that Hob held, tried again: "That parshmen' Monsignore 'as sen' you, will tell you where is the inn to meet. Monsignore waits for a third man; he does not know just when this man comes to him. Go down to York; one will come to you where you stay." He tapped the pouch again: "He will tell you when to come to that place on the parshmen'."

Sinibaldo began to back away toward the alley mouth.

"But only Mistress Molly knows where we'll stay in York," said Hob.

"We will find you wheresoever you are lodge'," said the Italian.

"York is a very big place," Hob said in exasperation.

"Not so big as 'oly Mother Church, *eh*?" said Sinibaldo. He turned and stepped into the street, and was gone.

MOLLY AND NEMAIN looked in dismay at the mud-stained, bloodstreaked pair as they came from the alley into the inn-yard, Sweetlove streaking across the grass to greet Jack. "By She Whom I swear by," said Molly, with the Celts' reluctance to name their deities in an oath, "can you never step in for a wee drop without starting a war?"

"Let me explain," said Hob, Jack being excused from this duty by virtue of his difficulty in speaking.

"I'm afire to hear it," said Nemain, her eyebrows raised high. "How I loved, back in Erin, to sit of an evening and hear a good storyteller, one that could spin tales from Samhain to Beltane, and each one more fanciful than the last." She leaned back against the wagon wheel and folded her arms, waiting.

"Well . . ." Hob began.

EVERYONE WAS CROWDED into the big wagon, shutters closed against observation and against the evening rain that had begun to fall more and more heavily. Hob and Nemain sat on the edge of Molly's bed, lowered down from its wall mount to its nighttime position.

Molly carefully unfolded the square of parchment and smoothed it out against the top of a tiring chest. Hob bent forward and peered at the fragment, trying to see the crude map drawn there. Molly placed a candle next to it; the wavering light struck silver highlights in her gray mane, and drew forth rich saffron tones from the sheepskin, though it had been whitened somewhat with staunchgrain. Jack stood on the other side of the chest, Sweetlove tucked under his arm.

That little dog, a fell-terrier bitch with her left bottom fang growing outside her upper lip, had been in the wagon with Molly and Nemain, the door open to the late-afternoon air, when she heard Hob's voice and Jack's grunts, and had immediately erupted in a paroxysm of barking, leaped out the door to the grassy ground, dashed across the innyard, and hurled herself into Jack's arms. One of Sir Odinell's ratters, she had adopted Jack, for reasons only she understood, and was happy only when near him. Sir Odinell had given her to the silent man, and except when expressly forbidden to follow, she was always at his heels. Now she was quiet and content, leaning out over his forearm to see what Molly was up to, her expression intent, serious—for all the world as if she wanted to read what Molly was reading—so that Hob could barely keep from laughing.

"'Tis clear enough," said Molly, tracing a route with her forefinger, pausing to make out the traveler's notes da Panzano had jotted beside his simple drawing. Molly could read Latin; she could write it, with difficulty; and she could stumble through a conversation in it with a learned stranger, the old speech of Rome and the current speech of the Church serving as a common tongue among scholars and clerics in a foreign land. "South from York, then we turn west . . . *here* . . . and then on along this . . . and here is marked 'Crossed Roads Inn.' But first we're away to York. We must set out just before first light tomorrow, before that spying spalpeen Bennett is aware we're gone. We'll leave as soon as the city gates open."

Just then a sudden increase in the rain caused a swelling roar overhead; Nemain looked up at the wagon roof and said, "Sure the roads will be rivers of mud tomorrow, *seanmháthair*; and the wagons will be mired just outside the city walls."

"Nay, child, there's a road down to York was made by the old Roman folk; 'tis raised and shod with stone, and we'll bide quiet in York till that churchman's finding us."

She began to study the map more closely, committing it to memory; occasionally she would mention something that Jack or Hob should do before they left, or something for Nemain to remember when they had gotten settled in York; half murmuring to herself. She planned for everything and the others followed her directions. Hob lolled back on his elbows and watched his family through lids that were growing heavy. The quiet fragmentary conversations, the dear familiar faces, the candlelight, the din of the rain on the wagon roof: all conveyed a sense of peace and safety. Tomorrow they might journey toward strange and deadly perils, but tonight Hob was content, here in the snug center of his world.

Chapter 7

They entered York at midday by the Munecagate. At once they plunged into the bustle of city life, the constriction of the streets reinforcing the impression of multitudes. Hob, by virtue of his travels with Molly, was no longer as amazed at crowds as when she had first plucked him from the tiny hamlet where he had been raised, but York was an unending clamor for one's attention.

The wagons rumbled over paving blocks, down streets shadowed by the overhanging upper storeys of the shops. A stream of folk slid down each side of the street: builders, cordwainers, saddlers, men-at-arms, the masons and glaziers who worked on the cathedral and the parish churches, wastrels, cutlers, spicers, priests, housewives and their children, Jews under the king's protection in exchange for exorbitant taxation of their financial houses, Dutch traders, tanners, beggars, the men of the watch with their pole arms. In the roads knights rode single file, slowly cleaving the throng; carters led their oxen-drawn wains. From both sides of the street came the calls of shopkeepers who had opened their horizontal shutters, propping them into counters: woolens, saddles, beakers of ale, hot pies, sacks of salt from the salterns, those drying fields established all along the coast of the German Sea.

Cordwainers displayed the leather, made from the supple skin of Spanish goats and kids, from which they made fine shoes. Urchins, barefoot in this city famed for its footwear, ran across Milo's path from the little walkways, too narrow for cart or beast, that led off between two houses, or between house and garden wall, or between two outside walls. *Snickets,* the city folk called them, or *ginnels.* Here and there the troupe passed a smithy, sparks showering within the darker interior, some bouncing out into the road, winking almost at once into extinction.

Hob led Milo, wonderfully stolid Milo, through this confusion, while Molly called directions—down this street, turn onto that—for there were inns where she was welcome and the troupe would be safe, and less visible to any possible agents of King John. One of these was Bywater Inn, one street away from the staithes where vessels making their way upriver on the Ouse discharged their cargo, ensuring a plentiful supply of saltwater fish for the inn's kitchens.

In a short while they had settled into their usual arrangement, the wagons, where they would continue to sleep, chocked against the innyard wall; the animals snug in the stables; an agreement to provide music for the inn in ex-change for board and a small sum of coin per sennight. Here they would stay for a few days, unnoticed in the bustle of the great city, awaiting Monsignor da Panzano's messenger.

HOB EASED HIMSELF into Milo's stall, third from the end of the inn's long stable. The ox looked around, snorted, bumped Hob gently with his forehead, a greeting, as the young man slipped a rope bridle over his head. Hob pushed at the wide breast, and Milo, grasping after a tiny delay what was expected of him, backed out of the stall. They had been in York for three days, and Hob got him out of the stall every day, to alleviate the ills of being idle all the time. Hob led him out into the sunshine of the innyard, and the two walked several times around the perimeter. Even Milo, that most stationary of beasts, seemed to enjoy his period of exercise, plodding along with Hob, who had particular charge of the ox, as Jack tended to Tapaigh, the mare, and Nemain to the little ass Mavourneen.

Milo exhibited every sign of a devotion to Hob that was more canine than bovine, coming to him across a pasture on the rare occasions that they were guests on a farm, snuffling with pleasure when Hob came to his stall. Perhaps because as soon as Hob, then a boy eleven years of age, had joined Molly's troupe, the lad had fed and cared for him, and had walked beside him when they were on the road, and had shown him affection, the ox regarded Hob almost as a parent or other protector.

Away in the north of Britain lived a race of wild white cattle, too fierce to be domesticated. They were hunted as other wild animals were hunted, and the bulls fought among themselves for supremacy, and the king bulls mated with their harems, while the bachelor bulls circled and waited their time. Some years ago, Molly's troupe had had to wait while a small herd had crossed their road, the king bull standing guard and glaring at the wagons, Hob and Milo in the lead, while the cows and bachelor bulls trotted by behind the monarch.

As with most oxen, Milo tended toward the timid, and on that occasion had actually lowered his head till it was behind Hob's back, perhaps on the theory that if he could not see the king bull, it could not see him, or that if the king bull attacked, skinny young Hob would protect him. This ludicrous attachment, this dependence, on Milo's part, had over the years engendered an affection in Hob, a sense of tenderness toward the great brute that was, unknown to himself, the boy's first taste of paternal love.

At last the young man led him from the warm spring sunlight into the cool darkness of the stable. Hob filled his manger, drew water for the trough, and patted the ox's vast warm side. This brought back memories of Sir Odinell's huge steel-gray destrier. Hob was intended for knighthood by Sir Jehan, and had had dreams of a destrier such as Sir Odinell's.

But Hob's path to knighthood was blocked for now by the barons' rebellion: Sir Odinell and Sir Jehan and Sir Balthasar were among those rising against the king, and were unable to continue Hob's instruction, and Molly had decided that the best way to weather the extreme uncertainty of the times was to revert to their roles of humble entertainers and wandering healers, a concealment even more urgent now that Monsignor da Panzano had ensnared them into this errand of his.

He propped an elbow against the ox. "You are my destrier, Lambkin, at least for the moment. Sir Robert and his magnificent warhorse, Milo!" He began to snicker at himself, and at that moment Milo looked around, put a large soft nose to his hair, and gave a mighty sneeze. At this Hob burst into a bellow of laughter: Could his condition become any more ridiculous?

The stall door opened, and here was his young wife, a thin bar of bright sunlight through the loose board walls of the stable lighting her hair to red flame. She slipped into the stall and stood against the wall, arms folded, green eyes glittering with mischief.

" 'Tis often I've thought what a wit yon ox was—" she began.

"Nemain, sweeting—"

"—but he's only making me smile, or mayhap a wee giggle, now. But yourself—"

He took a step to her and swept her up in his arms and stopped her teasing completely for a long moment. When the kiss ended, she drew breath as though to continue, her eyes laughing up at him, but then said nothing. He kissed her again, and began to explore beneath her shift, not entirely serious, but becoming more and more engaged.

She pushed at him, laughing. "Nay, can you not wait till the night, and our wagon about us; 'tis nigh as busy as the street in here, the grooms coming and the grooms going as they are."

"But look you, sweeting," he said—he had his hand laced in hers, and he raised her arm so that it transected the shaft of sun, the warm golden radiance catching the pale down on her forearm and setting it alight.

"Look you, the light is from the west, that afternoon light, and what is it Herself says of the late sun, that it's 'falling into the Western Ocean, out past Erin'? The grooms are at their table, and Milo always keeps my secrets. What—what is it?" he said, for she had grown still, and the mirth had gone out of her face like the flame from a snuffed candle.

" 'Tis the hour," she said in a muffled voice. " 'Tis the very hour!" Her small square hand bunched in his shirt and she turned, dragging at the cloth, forcing him to follow her from the stall.

A quick glance down the aisle between the two rows of stalls: hard-packed earth with stray wisps of straw, and away down the far end, the door to the stable yard, the daylight glowing outside, the corridor shaded. There was a strong sweet smell of hay from the stores of fodder on the upper tier. Somewhere down the row of stalls a hoof thudded into a wooden door. There was not a groom in sight.

She pulled him farther toward the back, into one of the two deserted stalls on Milo's other side, and began to pull his garments from him, almost in a frenzy. Puzzled but happy, he set in to help, and then they were down in clean hay. Underneath her cool smooth skin, a surprising heat rose to meet his hands, and her legs locked behind his hips, and she made small ferocious noises deep in her throat, and was urgent, and thrashed beneath him, and cried out as her moment came upon her. Later he could never decide if, after her cry, it had been a very long time or a very short time till he felt a stroke of pleasure that was like a buffet from Jacob's wrestler angel—powerful, disorienting, poignant—and another, and yet another, and then the sweet slow rolling echoes, gradually fading to quiet contentment.

They lay panting for a while, and then he rolled on his back and pulled her atop him, and contrived to cover her with his shirt, and held her for a while. He lay, utterly happy, looking up at the underside of the boards that were the floor of the hayloft: bits of hay poking down into the spaces between the planks; the square heads of hand-forged nails driven into a beam; a spider in its web, hanging motionless with a terrible stony patience.

Nemain seemed to doze for a little while, then she stirred. She raised her head from his chest and looked into his face. "Robert the Englishman," she said, so somberly that he had no slightest impulse to laugh. She kissed him, almost formally, and sat up.

Her back glimmered palely in the gloom of the stall, save where it was lit to a blaze by the last shafts of the sun threading through the chinks in the stable wall. He reached up, brushed off a few wisps of straw that clung to one shoulder blade. She stretched, arms up and out to the side, small round bunches of muscle forming at her shoulders.

She slumped again, and sat looking at the stall door. She spoke, very low, perhaps to herself. " 'Twas as Herself said, the late sun, the words coming from your mouth—'twas the very hour!"

He was completely confused now. "Nemain, culver, what is it you say?"

She turned, leaned back, put a small hand to his mouth. "Nay, I should have said nothing atall, nothing atall. I'll be telling you in time, but not this night."

She began to dress.

CHAPTER 8

A ROUGHLY ATTIRED YOUNG MAN came into the common room of the Bywater Inn; his hose were patched and his tunic was of undyed linen. On a broad leather belt, a heavy dagger was sheathed on a slant at his left side, the hilt convenient to a cross draw; a canvas purse was slung by its cords, kept to the front of his body to foil thieves. He looked around for a moment, blinking in the murk of the inn; then he headed for Molly.

"Mistress Molly?" he asked. He loosened his purse strings and plunged his hand inside. Before he could withdraw it Jack was looming over his right shoulder. The man-at-arms had his usual pleasant stolid expression, but he stood very close, and the youth turned a startled face to him, then swung back to Molly. He rummaged in his pouch; finally he found what he searched for. He held it out on his palm: a ring, with the crossed keys of the papal seal, silver and gold, on the face.

"Ah'm to tell Mistress that the time is a sennight hence, and that she knows the place, and ask if there's owt she wishes to answer."

"Just say that it's there we'll be at the appointed time, without fail. And . . . stay a moment, lad—here." Molly pressed a small wedge-shaped chip of silver into his hand: one piece from a penny that had been cut into quarters.

Into the pouch went the farthing; the lad touched his forehead and bowed clumsily, and was gone.

Molly looked after him. "He'll be bringing that ring back where he got it. If he's not having the sense to be afraid enough of da Panzano, perhaps he'll keep silence from gratitude."

She looked round at the other three. "To the wagons, and make ready: we're gone from York on the morrow!"

EARLY THE NEXT MORNING they left York by the Micklegate Bar and headed south. Two and a half days' traveling brought them to the west-trending road da Panzano had indicated, and Hob persuaded Milo to turn through a wide semicircle to the right, and they set off west across England.

A day later they were still trundling westward, somewhere in the West Riding of Yorkshire. The way was level and well maintained—hard-packed earth, but narrow—and when Hob heard the sound of men singing behind them, he stepped to the side and looked back along the line of wagons, to see a troop of men-at-arms striding along in a loose double file, coming at a fast walk.

"Mistress," he began, but Molly was already turning in her seat.

"Pull off the way," she said. "There's no gain in disputing the road with suchlike folk."

Hob led Milo onto a clear place by the side of the road, knee-deep in lush grasses. The ox immediately lowered his head and began to crop the grass, now and then emitting muted groans of pleasure. Nemain and Jack pulled in behind Molly's large wagon and set their brakes. Nemain climbed down from her wagon seat, stretched, ambled up toward where Hob stood by the ox. He put his arm around her, and they leaned against each other, watching as the double column of foot soldiers—mercenaries, by the look of them; perhaps some of King John's Poitevins—came up to them.

They were on their way past, but some of them were looking at the wagons, and some at Nemain, and the reputation of these *routes*, these bands of for-hire soldiers from Poitou, was not good. In any rural setting, a free company such as this—thirty or forty *routiers*—would represent the greatest concentration of force for a few miles around, and was not above some thieving, or worse. Still, the leaders were marching past Molly's troupe and continuing on.

Sweetlove, though, did not have a high opinion of them: she stood up with her back legs on the wagon seat and her front legs on Jack's thigh and burst into a tirade of barking. Jack scooped her up in one hand and swung down from the wagon. He went toward the back; a moment later he reappeared with his crow-beak war hammer and joined Hob and Nemain up by Molly's wagon. He swung the little dog up beside Molly and pointed his finger at her, then, with a sharp downward motion, at the wagon seat: *Stay!* He never spoke to her, speech being as painful for him as it was, but they had evolved a language of sign and gesture. Now Sweetlove sat down primly, but could not resist a mumbled near-bark. Jack looked at her and she quieted.

Now he propped the hammer against Molly's front wagon wheel, so that it was partially hidden behind him, and stood to watch the passing band.

Suddenly the foremost man spun on his heel and strode back toward them. He was a man of perhaps forty winters, strong of body and scarred of face, his scalp showing through thinning hair. He wore a quilted gambeson and frayed wool leggings; a heavy dagger hung at his side; some fashion of club was slung by a strap to his back. Hob straightened and let his hand drop to his own dagger. Jack felt behind him, picked up the hammer, and then to Hob's surprise let it drop. The mercenary, opening his arms wide, walked up to Jack and wrapped him in a gleeful hug.

"Jacques, Jacques!" he bellowed. "Jacques le *forte,* Jacques le *brun!*" The two men were thumping each other on the back, but Jack was silent, and he pointed to his throat, and shook his head.

The Poitevin peered closely at the oval scar that the Beast had made, and clucked. Jack swept his arm to take in Molly, Nemain, and Hob, and the mercenary bowed, not ungracefully, and shook Hob's hand and kissed Nemain's and touched his forehead to Molly, still up on the wagon seat. He was grinning hugely. "Monsieur Jacques and I, we are comrades, long ago—we are young then, so young! I t'ought he was *mort,* dead. I am Jourdain; you are 'is *famille,* yes?" Hob could just follow the thick Poitevin accent, so different from the Anglo-Norman high speech that was still such close kin to French.

"Yes: Jack is my man," said Molly, from her perch. "And this is my granddaughter, and Hob; we are musicians. Hob is her husband." She emphasized this last, for although the rest of the mercenary band had taken the opportunity to sit and rest while their leader was occupied, two or three had come near, and one was openly leering at Nemain. Jourdain, following Molly's gaze, turned and noticed his comrade's interest.

"Waleran, *mon frère,* we are many and they are few, but this is that Jacques I 'ave told you about, when we are sitting around so many campfires, and if you are t'ink to be foolish, he will make you ver' dead before we can stop him." Waleran looked from Jourdain to Jack, gave a shrug, turned, and walked back, with ostentatious slowness, to where his comrades sat by the side of the road, pausing once to spit into the grass, to show that he was not really afraid. After a moment the other two turned and trailed after him.

Now Jourdain noticed the war hammer, propped against the wagon wheel, and once again there were exclamations of delight, and how he remembered when Jack traded with another mercenary for it, and how *dextère* he became with it, and so forth, Jack beaming at him but unable to do more than gargle a word or two. Jourdain unslung from his back the *plançon a picot,* the weapon that he and his men carried, and showed it to them: a long club with a spike protruding from the top, the spike to pierce, the club to beat. "Not so good as Jacques's *bec de corbin* there, but we are experience' with it."

Molly had Hob fetch some *uisce beatha,* and Jourdain and Jack drank a cup together, Jourdain standing with his back to the road, for there was not enough for the whole band, and he did not want to be seen not to share, a sin, if a small one, against the *routiers'* code. Jack, with sign language and with help from Nemain, managed to convey a much shortened version of the adventure in the Holy Land that had resulted in his terrible injuries. Jourdain shook his head and clucked again, and told them of Jack's *très* deep and indeed beautiful singing voice, such a shame and a loss—this was a great surprise to the others, who had not known Jack before he went on crusade—Jack grinning broadly the while, and nodding, and generally enjoying himself.

Now Hob noticed that, among the mercenaries, some of whom, in the manner of experienced soldiers, had stretched out in the grass and were seizing the opportunity to sleep— was a group sitting by themselves: ten or eleven men with swarthy complexions, as though they had labored all summer in the sun, with strong noses and glittering dark eyes. Most wore workmen's coarse tunics and hose; some who seemed to be leaders were swathed in voluminous white or purple cloaks. Almost all had headgear of cloth wound around their heads, the ends tucked cleverly into the folds.

They were clustered around three handcarts, each with an anvil, mallets, tongs, and other tools of the blacksmith's trade.

"And who might those men be, Master Jourdain?" he asked.

"They are blacksmiths, them; come special from across the water, from Marroch; Marroch is the land across from Spain," said the mercenary.

Hob managed to conceal his shock: these were the devil-men that da Panzano had warned against! He carefully avoided looking at the others, and Jourdain did not seem to have noticed anything amiss. "The king, he is tell us, meet them in London, bring them to me at Chester Castle, I 'ave need of many swords, an' these are the finest swordsmiths that live today. We are escort them; they don' speak good English, we are to keep them safe. . . ." He turned to Jack. "You know escort duty, is so tedious, no loot. . . ."

"Are they followers of Mahomet, then, and daring to come into England?" asked Molly; she told Hob and Nemain afterward that she asked in order to make sure that these were the men—not Mahometans, but followers of an older religion—of whom da Panzano had spoken.

Jourdain looked around, moved a pace closer, dropped his voice. "These are not. I t'ink most of them, yes, they are the Mussulmans, there in Marroch, but not these: they are not good Christian men, neither, they. Somet'ing else. The king he don't mind, so Jourdain he don't mind, but they are ver' strange. They say they are all one *famille,* one family, an' they do look this way." He looked around again. "They call themselves 'the Cousins.' This, it is the second group that my *routiers* are the escort for, an' when we camp, I say to *mes camarades,* 'Keep watch: some to look outward, for enemies; some to look inward, on the smiths.' For they are strange."

He cast an eye up at the sun, which was just past its zenith. "We 'ave to be on our way; the king, 'e will say, 'Jourdain, you are picking flowers while I am wait for my smiths?' an' I don' 'ave an answer." He turned and whistled sharply. The mercenaries came to their feet, and seeing them do so, the strangers stood, grasped the handles of their handcarts.

Jourdain and Jack embraced; the mercenary stood back and bowed to Molly. "Come to Chester Castle," he said. He grinned hugely. "King Jean, he is enchant' with the music, and later Jack and I will sit far into the night and tell you, gracious lady, lies about our campaigns." He looked at Hob. "Maybe your fine young man here would like to join my *route,* my free company, and make his fortune, eh?" When Hob just smiled and shook his head, the *routier* shrugged. He bowed again, already backing away, to Molly, and cried: "Jacques, *adieu!*"

And with a wave of his hand Jourdain trotted back to the head of the company. He circled his upraised arm in the air, a signal, and with that the men resumed their march. From somewhere in their midst a hand drum began to sound a rhythm, and gradually the men-at-arms fell into step.

The men of Marroch thrust against their draw handles, and the handcarts began to roll, creaking and squealing. They walked along, clustered together toward the rear of the mercenaries, but one broke ranks and walked toward Molly's wagons.

He came right up to them, a broad-shouldered, long-armed man—his arms seemed almost too long for the rest of him—with an oddly stooped walk. It was not that he was bent over, but that he inclined forward more than seemed comfortable, and—perhaps because of what da Panzano had told them—this stoop, with the man's long arms and his prominent nose and receding chin, struck Hob as eerie, even sinister, although there was no characteristic that could be singled out as threatening.

As he approached, Sweetlove rose, but only into a crouch. Her ears went back, close to her head; her lips drew apart, revealing a thicket of surprisingly menacing teeth, very white, very sharp; from her narrow chest came a murderous growl. Molly put her hand under the dog's belly and pulled Sweetlove against her thigh. The terrier turned and gave her a look of outrage: *Why do you hinder me?* But Molly held her with one hand and stroked her with the other, and after a moment the tension ran out of her and she slumped against Molly, mumbling protests.

The Cousin went to Jack and stood very close, peering into Jack's face. Jack, being Jack, just looked back at the outlander; the big man still had a faint smile on his face from the pleasure of seeing his old comrade, and in any event was not easily put out of countenance. The man came even closer. Hob put a hand to his dagger-hilt, and took a step forward, watching the stranger narrowly. The man's headgear had slipped a bit, revealing dark hair pulled straight back, receding from his forehead in tight waves. He lifted his chin—almost he seemed to be *smelling* Jack, although there was nothing so obvious as sniffing, just a way of steady breathing.

"*Gema!*" he said.

Jack looked at him blankly; smiled politely; shrugged.

After a moment, the man turned away, and began walking after his departing companions. He turned and looked back at Jack, just once; he did not look back again, and in a short while the *route* and their charges were all out of sight.

Molly sat back with a sigh and handed Sweetlove down to Jack, who put the terrier on the ground. She immediately began to run in circles, nose to the ground, picking up what must be Jourdain's scent, and that of the Cousin.

"Let us bide awhile here, and let them draw away. Those strangers Jourdain is protecting, sure they're the very men we're to spy upon. It's an ill-looking bunch they are, these Cousins, with the scent of sorcery upon them," said Molly. Hob looked puzzled, and she said to him, " 'Tis like a thin smoke haze, or very like; Nemain and I can sense it, if you men cannot."

After a while Sweetlove decided that she had learned all there was to learn; she squatted to make water, and then trotted over to Jack and stood on her hind legs, her forepaws against his knee, begging to be picked up.

"Sweetlove has spoken," said Molly. "Away on!"

CHAPTER 9

WHERE A ROAD RUNNING north and south through a village in Derbyshire intersected a road running east and west, a freeman named Averill had established an inn by the simple expedient of acquiring three houses: one on the northeast corner, the one to the east of the corner house, and the one to the north; and then connecting them with passages. Finally he built a stout high fence to enclose a yard behind the three houses; there he placed stables and other outbuildings, backed up against the fence. This was the origin of the Crossed Roads Inn, some three score years before Molly's troupe arrived there, bringing the wagons into the yard and stabling the three draft animals.

Molly set up a variation on her usual arrangement: meals at the inn, the troupe to sleep in the wagons, but instead of offering to perform she paid silver from the pouch that Sinibaldo had brought them. If they were to meet with the papal agent and his two associates, it might be better if their telltale identity as musicians were not remarked.

They settled in to wait for Monsignor da Panzano. The appointed day came and went, and then another. Nemain, ever volatile, began to fret, and thought that perhaps they should travel a little distance away, and camp in some quiet vale, and come each day to see if the papal legate had arrived, for if he had been taken and had betrayed them, the king's men could swoop down upon them at any moment.

Molly agreed, but counseled that they wait one more day. That very evening, the common room mostly empty, the four sitting at a table with beer and bread, the late spring sunlight beginning to fail outside and the innkeeper's son going around and lighting a candle here and a candle there, the door creaked open. In came a traveler, his face concealed by the hood of a cloak, with a walking staff in his left hand. He stepped to the side of the door, perhaps scanning the common room to see who waited there. His right hand, large and muscular, hovered near the opening of his cloak.

"Sinibaldo," said Hob in a low voice.

"Aye," said Molly and Nemain, almost in unison.

Sinibaldo held his staff where it could be seen by those outside and made a small gesture; at once two other cloaked and hooded travelers entered, also carrying staves. Sinibaldo pointed to where Molly sat against the wall.

The three approached Molly's table. "Madam," said

Monsignor da Panzano, bowing courteously and propping his staff against the wall, "allow me to present Father Ugwistan, my colleague and a great help to me in this matter." Father Ugwistan gave a graceful half-bow, handed his staff to Sinibaldo, and threw back his hood.

Molly gestured to the benches on the other side of the table. Da Panzano and the new priest seated themselves. Sinibaldo, having taken the newcomer's staff and placed it with his own and da Panzano's, came to Molly's side and seated himself with his back against the wall, and, as always, took no part in the conversation, but watched the room behind his master's back, tensing whenever anyone came too near.

Beneath their traveling cloaks the men wore the plain robes, the leather scrips, and the knotted rope belts of pilgrims. Sinibaldo kept his cloak on; presumably he had the same belt of darts, the same copper-hilt Italian dagger, that Hob had seen when first they met.

"I have wanted you to meet Father Ugwistan," said da Panzano, "because he is Moorish, or as some say Berber, as are these Cousins, and he can tell you what they say. You will both be at Chester Castle, and he is hearing their so-difficult language, and you are watching their so-strange behavior, and learning their secrets, and how to destroy them."

At this point Sweetlove, who was curled asleep against Jack Brown's thigh and so hidden below the line of the tabletop, decided to sit up and investigate the new voices. Sinibaldo glanced over and then resumed his watch on the common room, but both men across the table started at her sudden appearance. Da Panzano scowled, impatient at any distraction, but Father Ugwistan laughed a little. He put a long arm across the table, intending to pet her, but Sweetlove would barely tolerate the three other members of Jack's family, and certainly would have no truck with strangers. She drew back and gave the faintest of growls, and the priest withdrew his hand, a rueful half-smile on his face. Hob began to think him a good-natured man, in contrast to the suave but rather sinister papal agent.

Jack tapped Sweetlove twice with his index finger, and the dog turned about and slumped into a coil, shifting about in small increments until she was once again hard against Jack's thigh. She sighed ostentatiously; a moment or two later she began to snore in a high tenor.

Molly sipped thoughtfully at her beer. She looked at the newcomer. "Is it a priest you are, then, and a Moor or Berber as well?" she asked. "Are they not followers of Mahomet?"

Father Ugwistan, in whom the pale brown skin and dark tight-waved hair of northwest Africa was set off by light blue-green eyes, leaned forward, his gaze dancing from face to face and a not-quite smile tugging at the corners of his mouth. "I am a priest, madam, and I have the honor to work for His Holiness through Monsignor." Here he put his hand to his heart and inclined his head slightly toward da Panzano. "We are an old people: we are the *Imazighen*—'the free and noble ones.' Some have called us Berbers, but we do not like it. Yes, most have been led astray by the false Prophet, but some are true Christians. The great Saint Ugwistan, for whom I am named, was an Amazigh."

"We are knowing him as 'Augustine,'" put in the papal legate.

"Ah!" said Hob. Father Athelstan had often mentioned Augustine in Hob's lessons. Molly and Nemain, those pagans, looked uncertain, and Jack, that casual Christian, nodded amiably, which meant nothing.

Here there was another interruption, as the innkeeper's son appeared and asked their pleasure. Da Panzano ordered red wine and the lad looked confused.

"We've nobbut barley beer an' honey beer an' apple wine," he said in his thick Derbyshire accent.

The legate closed his eyes as though in pain. "Barley beer, then." He looked at the other two, and they nodded.

"I'll bring ee a rissom o' boohter fra yon, as weel," the boy said, nodding at the loaf of bread.

Da Panzano, his face a mask of utter incomprehension, gave a twitch of the head that might have been a nod.

The younger priest resumed. "We—the Imazighen—were at one time mostly pagan, even after Saint Ugwistan, but then the Mahometans are coming with the sword, seeking to convert, and we are resisting." Apparently da Panzano had told him something of Molly, for he went on: "There was a woman like you, madam, a great queen and a true warrior. She held to the old beliefs. Her name was Dihya, and she fought the Arab armies to a standstill. The Arabs called her *al-Kahina,* the soothsayer priestess; it was said she could see the future. She was a big woman, with very long hair: something like yourself, madam."

He sounded more and more enthusiastic as his tale went

on, while Monsignor da Panzano made a moue of distaste, and grew more and more impatient.

"Tell her what you have learned of the *lupi mannari*," he said brusquely.

"I was in Marroch on Monsignor's business," said Ugwistan, "and I am lurking in some very low places: I make believe I am a beggar, and I sit against walls and pretend to sleep, or in stables, or where men gather to argue and to gossip, and I hear 'the Cousins, the Cousins,' and rumors of this sorcerer, Yattuy—I do not know if this is his name, or only what they call him, for it means 'the Tall One,' and he *is* very tall."

" 'Twill not be his true name," said Molly. "Sorcerers do not want their true names known, for names give one power over the named, and it can be dangerous for them, when they strive against other sorcerers."

"Madam . . ." began da Panzano—tense, unhappy with this direction that the conversation had taken, this veering into casual blasphemy and forbidden practices.

But at this moment there was an interruption: the innkeeper's son returned with three mugs of barley beer, which he set before the newcomers, and a small wooden dish with butter on it, which he set beside the bread.

Da Panzano drew breath to resume his complaint to Molly, but thought better of it—Hob felt that he could almost see the legate's thoughts: *Not now, not now.* The legate reached for the bread, tore off a chunk, and morosely began to butter it.

Father Ugwistan took a sip of his beer, and resumed.

"Finally, I am hearing that King John is sending for these Cousins; they are coming in small groups, not to make the big fuss, and he is assembling them at Chester Castle. The number I have heard is tenscore."

"Tenscore!" said Molly, a bit shocked.

At once da Panzano bent forward, his keen eyes searching her face for portents. "What will you do against such an army, such a macabre army, madam?"

But Molly was not to be prodded into a rash promise. "I'll be seeing them at Chester Castle, and it may be soon or it may be late, but I'll know the way to deal with them when it comes to me, or when the Mórrígan sends me Her aid."

Reflexively the two priests crossed themselves, da Panzano scowling openly at Molly. He might deal with her from expediency, but he plainly did not enjoy hearing of unholy practices.

Father Ugwistan hitched his chair forward. He was younger than da Panzano, and of a more openhearted disposition. Hob thought that, priest or no priest, he had to some extent formed a degree of admiration for Molly: perhaps because of what he had heard of her from da Panzano; perhaps because of the legends of his people, the heroic resistance of the woman called the *Kahina* by the Arabs; perhaps because of the attractiveness of Molly's person.

Now he asked, "This *Mórrígan,* it is a thing you worship?"

"It is the name of the Great Queen, who is also sometimes three queens: Badb, Macha, and Nemain, like my granddaughter here."

"This is away in"—he gestured vaguely to the west, the name in English escaping him for a moment—"Ireland; three queens in Ireland?"

" 'Tis: three queens in Erin," said Molly. "Queens and more. And all of them the One Queen, the Mórrígan."

"It is like the Trinity, yes? Of which our Saint Ugwistan—Augustine, you say—has written so well." He looked around, actually smiling with pleasure at this comparison, only to encounter the icewater stare of da Panzano, a man who thought of himself as flexible and pragmatic, but who was not amused by pagans and heretics and Satanists, and who was convinced that Molly must be at least one and perhaps two of the three.

Father Ugwistan's manner sobered immediately; he looked down at the table, tapped his fingers a moment, and cleared his throat. "So, then," he said, "I have been to Chester Castle—I present myself as a Maltese, which island I am very familiar with, and I stay at Chester, at the castle, with Father Maurice—he is the chaplain to Sir Ranulf, but he is also . . ."

He faltered, and looked to da Panzano for permission. The legate nodded, and Father Ugwistan resumed. "He is also secretly in Monsignor's service. I say to the people of the castle that I have made a vow: that I am to say Mass in as many countries as I can travel to, and I beg my food and lodging, as did Our Savior. This allows me to stay awhile—I say two Masses in the Chapel of Saint Mary de Castro. It is a little chapel in the gateway tower to the inner, the inner—yard?"

"Bailey?" said Hob.

"Yes, yes, it is the bailey. Up the winding stair, to the next level. Two Masses I say there, and in the afternoons I walk in the outer . . . bailey, on the wide dirt. I am walking about but I am also saying my daily office or my beads, so no one is attending me closely. When I walk around, I tell this one and that one I am from Malta, but I dwell in Rome, so everyone is confused, and no one suspects I am Amazigh, not even the Cousins, although they make me fearful, with their noses that seem to be questing in the air, like so many dogs."

That reminded Hob of something—what was it? But now, up at the front of the long room, there were raised voices. Jack looked a question at Molly, but she made a patting motion down by her side with her right hand: *Ignore it.*

She had been pensive for a while: now, obviously troubled, she asked the Berber, "And is it yourself who saw this great number of these *conriochtaí,* these werewolf blacksmiths?"

"Worse than wolves," muttered da Panzano.

"I have seen them; they have their tents set against one wall of the outer, outer . . . bailey, and they have set up forges also, and they are beating out swords and such for King John, but everyone I talk to thinks they are there for something else, and they are much hated and feared. Sometimes a group of them goes out, with a leader, a *bouda* captain, on horseback, and one of King John's men as a guide. They are away for a few days, and they come back, and settle, and in a little while another group goes out. They are doing some errands for the king, I think.

"They keep to themselves, and every day the magus, this Yattuy, comes from his quarters in the keep, and goes to visit them, and stays with them awhile, and speaks to them in Tamazight, our language."

Nemain could tell that Molly was not pleased with the description of the task before her, and the young woman, ever impatient and obviously beginning to become irritated with Ugwistan and his gradual approach to explaining the situation, clenched her hands into fists and sat very straight, the blood suffusing her pale, pale face. She said through gritted teeth: "And what might it be, then, that they're saying in Tam—in, in your language?"

The Berber priest lost his generally amiable expression; he became somber on the instant.

"I dare not approach when Yattuy is there; he is a frightening and powerful man—he speaks to kings and they listen—and I feel he can look once at me and see through my little mask. But later, when he is not there, I go close, my eyes down and my beads in my hand and my lips moving, and I listen. And what I hear—these *bouda* are to be used against the king's enemies. King John, he will invite the northern barons to a parley, and when they are all in one place, these men will change, and pour down upon the nobles, and they will be helpless against them. You know that ordinary weapons will not avail against them?"

"We do that," said Molly grimly.

"There is some uncertainty—Yattuy will tell them when it is time, and they will move as one at that time. Some said it was the midpoint of June, others said it might be later than that. There are many things that must come together, and so there is this uncertainty. But it will be June or soon thereafter."

"Father Maurice also will tell me if he should hear a time discussed, by Sir Ranulf or John Lackland or the kitchen maids or whoever you will," said da Panzano. "I am sending Father Ugwistan back as well, but he—and you, when you come there—must be ready to slip away quickly, for this sorcerer is no fool, and his followers, even in their human form, have senses more keen than ours, and at any time might discover your true nature."

Again something tugged at Hob's memory, something about the conversation that reminded him of—what? It slipped away from him, as when dreams, so present to him just as he awoke, departed when he opened his eyes and saw Nemain—all that beauty, and so close beside him.

"I will have to return tomorrow," said Father Ugwistan. "I am telling the story, God forgive me the lie, that I am going to walk into Wales and there to say Mass somewhere. But I go out and turn away from the Bridge Gate; instead I turn, quietly, and go past the tanners' yards. What terrible odors! How do they endure it? It is between the castle and the Dee, so I fear every moment someone looks from the walls and says to his fellow: 'Ho! There is that Maltese priest; why does he go past the tanners instead of crossing into Wales?' and so I try to scurry like the mouse while looking calm like the cat."

"But were you seen?" asked da Panzano, frowning.

"I do not think so. I hope not." He laughed. "But with

the smell of the tanning vats I know the Cousins could not detect me with their beast noses, even with the breeze off the river."

And with that Hob had it. The way the Cousin had come up to Jack, and seemed to be trying to get hold of Jack's scent. He sat forward and said to the Berber, "Father Augus—Ugwistan, one of the Cousins said something to Jack. Could you tell us—" He paused to get it right, relying on his excellent memory for things once heard. "What does *gema* mean, in your language?"

The Berber blinked at him. "Why, *brother*. It means *brother*."

CHAPTER 10

MONSIGNOR DA PANZANO leaned in, put his forearms on the table, and looked from Father Ugwistan to Hob, and then to Jack. He seemed intensely interested: he was a man who existed to learn secrets, to keep secrets, to discover the truth behind things—and to use what he had discovered to further his power and that of Innocent III. Here was an oddity, and he wanted to understand it.

Hob had felt a chill run through him the moment he had heard the Berber's translation: plainly the Cousin had sensed that Jack was a shapeshifter as well, and perhaps someone who would be an ally. But how had he sensed that? Could the Cousins actually scent that other Jack, that Jack that lurked beneath his skin, Jack-the-Beast?

Hob, by temperament an open and honest person, found it hard to dissemble ignorance, but he made a great effort and kept a faintly puzzled expression on his face; Molly and Nemain, with their great self-control, were the very definition of innocence, and Jack's normal expression was stolid and uncommunicative.

"But why is he saying such a so-strange thing?" asked da Panzano of the table in general.

"Perhaps because Jack is such a dark man, he's thinking 'tis some one of his kin," said Molly smoothly. This struck Hob as less than convincing: Jack was dark-haired and dark-eyed, and even swarthy for an Englishman, but could hardly be said to look like kin to the Cousins.

Da Panzano took a sip of his beer, grimaced, and put down his mug. He drew a white cloth from his sleeve and wiped his lips, then he folded the cloth, folded it again, and sat looking at it, his eyes far away as he worked and worked at the puzzle. At last he sighed and tucked the cloth back in his sleeve.

"I feel that it means something, but what? I cannot think what, but it is an odd occurrence, and I do not like these odd occurrences."

Hob, behind his mask of innocence, was thinking hard. So da Panzano knew that Molly had dealt with Sir Tarquin, and perhaps had heard some rumor about the Fox, but was not aware of Jack's secret. This was important: it was one less vulnerability that the papal agent might exploit.

The noise from up at the head of the room was growing louder—one voice in particular, thick with drink, was raised above the others, a voice of protest and outrage at some ill treatment. The innkeeper and two housecarls were shoving a tall portly man wearing a broad-brimmed traveler's hat, impelling him toward the door. He staggered, recovered, turned and cursed them, and walked backward a few paces so that he could hurl a few more maledictions at his tormentors. Then he strode down the room in a kind of controlled stumble, knocking over a chair here and slapping a mug off a table there, out of rage and spite.

Sinibaldo came out of his chair with a smooth silent movement; he stepped close to Monsignor da Panzano but left the aisle clear for the man to pass. The bodyguard's cloak was open a slit; his right hand flashed inside for a moment, and then was held down by his side. The banished drinker swung a blow at a peasant sitting too close to the aisle, but missed. The papal legate was seated with his back to the center of the room, and his chair withdrawn a bit from the table, so that he intruded, although minimally, into the pathway through the tables. Hob saw what might happen, although da Panzano, mulling over the Cousin's word, did not seem to be completely aware of the ruckus.

The drunken traveler's eyes alighted on the back of the papal legate's head, nominally in his way, and he cocked a fist. From Sinibaldo's side a streak of gold and gray flew toward the man and curled like a live thing about his wrist. Sinibaldo gave a skillful jerk, and the man was pulled off balance by his snared arm. As he fell, the bodyguard gave a sharp and powerful yank, and Hob could clearly hear the man's wrist snap. He yowled with pain, rolling about on the ale-stained floorboards, and the coin was whipped back to

Sinibaldo's side. The bodyguard whirled it thrice to gain speed, producing a momentary illusion of a gray wheel with a golden rim; then it flew out again and struck with surprising force against the man's temple. He subsided, groaning, only partly conscious, and now here came the innkeeper and his men, and hauled the offender to the front door, and heaved him through into the road outside.

Da Panzano nodded at Sinibaldo; some small signal of gratitude passed between them, and the bodyguard stepped smoothly back, seated himself, and leaned against the wall again, immobile, a venomous lizard sunning itself upon a rock.

The incident had had the virtue of distracting da Panzano from his contemplation of the *bouda*'s odd remark to Jack, and Molly sought to move to other topics.

"If you've no more to tell us of these strange men," she said to Father Ugwistan, "perhaps 'tis time we made an early night of it, so to be away in the morning. 'Tis not well for us all to be met here, huddled like plotters—and we are that!— and so to be noticed by John's spies."

"You have the right of it, madam," said da Panzano, "and one more thing—at the castle you are not to know one another. Father Ugwistan will contrive to get word from myself to you: maybe he stops and prays near you, maybe he pets your little dog, but do not be seen to converse. Remain at the castle a few days, a sennight—whatever you need, to plan destruction for these evil ones. When I am near, I will send a young man to tell Father Ugwistan where we may meet, that you may report to me."

"We are off to our wagons for the night," said Molly. "Will you stay here at the inn?"

"A quick meal, a few hours' sleep; we will be off before dawn. Father Ugwistan must return to the castle before there is talk, and you should not come there at the same time, but a little after, a day or so later, perhaps. Sinibaldo and I also must be away: I have affairs I must tend to, affairs in many other parts of this so-rainy land."

CHAPTER 11

THE WAGONS ROLLED ALONG BEneath a darkening sky. The trail, a track of beaten earth winding between stands of yew and oak and hedges sprinkled with dog-roses and red campion, began to show small puffs of dust where the first fat drops of rain heralded the beginning of the storm that had threatened all afternoon. The road veered rightward, to run closer to a stream bank. Reeds fringed the river; a rushing sound filled the air; a sweet cool freshwater mist drifted off the surface toward them.

The rain began in earnest, rattling off the wagon rooftops, spattering on Milo's broad haunches. The ox snorted with annoyance; he shook his head every few paces as the raindrops tickled his ears; he turned to look reproachfully at Hob, a look that plainly said:

Can you not get us in somewhere, away from this? Hob who fed him, Hob who stabled him—surely he knew what to do.

Hob indeed began to pick up the pace. He and Molly looked from side to side, hoping to find a dense enough copse of trees, a cave, even a rock overhang, where they could shelter the animals and retreat within the wagons till the storm blew over. The rain was becoming a kind of slate-colored curtain, and it was hard to see very far. But up ahead, a structure loomed through the downpour: white walls and a darker thatched roof, a yellow gleam in a window.

Hob pulled on Milo's rope, leading the great beast in a shallow curve, off the road and toward the riverbank. Milo could be guided by reins, but was prone to a perhaps disingenuous misunderstanding of what was required. The clop of hooves, the rumble of wheels, brought a man from the cottage, hooded and cloaked, holding high a horn-paned lantern.

"God save you, master," cried Hob. "Have you room for us to stable our beasts for the night?"

"Coom wi' me, young man: theer's a bye in t' cottage."

He led them to a kind of water-meadow between cottage and riverbank, where the wagons might be unhitched. Beyond, through the veils of rain, could be seen the little river; across it a fish-weir revealed itself as a smooth stream-wide curl of silver water. Molly set the brakes and Hob began unhitching Milo from the draw bars.

The cottager was hearty and confident at first, when dealing with Hob, but he became somewhat bashful when

Molly, a capacious shawl over her silver mane, dismounted from the wagon seat—he was perhaps discomfited by her queenly air; and then he seemed distracted when Nemain came up, so beautiful a young woman had she become. But it was when Jack came limping up from the line of chocked wagons, the lead ropes from the little donkey and the mare trailing from his hands and Sweetlove trotting at his heels, that Hob saw a wariness creep into the cottager's manner. It was easy, seeing Jack's size, the facial and manual scars of a lifetime's soldiering, his thick neck and broad sloping shoulders, to overlook the perfectly amiable set of his features, his calm, even soothing, manner.

But then: "This is Jack," said Molly, in her wonderful voice, with her fear-melting smile, and Hob saw the man's drawn-together brows smooth themselves, the tense muscles at the corners of his mouth relax; his shoulders, hunched in unthinking anticipation of a blow, lowered to a more usual position. "Here is Hob, and Nemain, and I am Molly."

"Ah, well," said the cottager, and then, under the sunny radiance of Molly's smile, he could no longer resist smiling back, and Hob saw that once again, somehow, Molly had opened locks that may not be seen by the eye.

"I am called Elias, Elias Weir-tender, and it's welcome you are to stop the night with us, but Jesus save us, let us go in from under this rain."

Molly left the wagons unlocked: in this deserted spot, in this storm, there was no need, and in any event, she intended for them to sleep in the wagons tonight. The women went ahead with Elias; Hob, leading Milo, and Jack, with the other two animals, trudged behind.

Elias led them past a modest structure that stood some little distance behind the cottage. A door on a peg latch, two small windows—it was too cramped for anyone to live there, and Hob wondered what its purpose was, until they came downwind of it and he caught a strong, not entirely unpleasant, smell of fish. A workshop of some kind, then, to clean and store the catch.

The rain now was sheeting down, so that the cottage had all but disappeared; gusts of wind blew the rain almost sideways, so that Hob had to squint his eyes to little more than slits to protect them. And now the cottage reappeared in front of him, and Elias was beckoning them in, holding open a broad door set midway in the rear wall.

The cottage was in two parts, set to take advantage of the slight natural slope of the ground: the larger part, set lower and with a slope to the earthen floor, was a stable. Hob led Milo in several paces and then turned rightward, into the stable's central aisle. This was flanked by a row of stalls on one side, where drowsed a milk cow and two goats; on the other side were bins for hay, pegs where hung tools and fishnets, a milking stool and pails.

The cottager set about opening stalls and moving shovels and stool and pails, pushing things to the corners, to provide more space. There was just enough room to settle in Milo, the little ass Mavourneen, and the mare Tapaigh. The house and this stable shared a common roof, and the heat from the animal bodies helped to warm the cottagers' living quarters; the slope helped in sluicing animal waste away downhill.

Elias led Molly and Nemain into the other half of the cottage. Hob began rubbing Milo's broad back dry with Elias's stable cloths. Jack was doing the same for Mavourneen and Tapaigh, and soon they had the animals watered and fed from the weir-tender's stores. Over the rattle of heavy rain on the roof close above his head, Hob could just hear Elias's introductions, and the murmur of conversation.

The inner door of the stable, with a high threshold to prevent seepage from the stables into the living quarters, led into the cottage's main room. Hob stepped over and through after Jack. A central hearth in the old Saxon style dominated the room: a raised stone platform with a central depression. Here a peat fire smoldered, the smoke rising to exit through a hole in the ceiling; above that a short chimney carried it up to be swept away by the river winds. The arrangement was by no means as efficient as the newer Norman fireplaces; a thin haze hung in the air, and there was a strong smell of woodsmoke that mixed with the undertone of fish—an inevitable consequence of Elias's work.

To one side of the hearth was a crude table; the only other furniture in the room was a large cupboard, with compartments and shelves. Elias had seated Molly and Nemain on a bench by the table. Across from them sat a woman, and behind her were her three children, peering shyly at their guests.

Elias turned to the men. "Here be my goodwife, Cecilia, and there be Wymon and Adam, and this is little Estrild."

Hob, orphaned when he was three or four, looked at

them and thought to himself what a pleasing family they made, and felt a pang of sorrow that he could not explain to himself. Then he thought that one day he and Nemain would have such a family, and his heart leaped up again.

Cecilia was a woman who looked to be in her early thirties. Like all cottagers' wives she worked in her vegetable gardens, and the spring sun had browned her somewhat. Hob thought it a fine sight, her light eyes gleaming in her dark face, an observation that—innocent as it was, and as young a husband as he was—he knew not to mention to Nemain. It was indeed a rather pretty face, its appeal marred somewhat by the lines wrought by long experience of pain, a kind of squint of suffering. Her left arm had been broken at some point in the past, and set badly. The misjoin was clearly visible at the midpoint of her forearm. Hob noticed that she moved that arm as little as possible, and winced whenever she had to move it.

Wymon and Adam were older children, perhaps thirteen; shy little Estrild took shelter behind her big brothers, peeping out from behind Wymon's leg, holding on to his shirttail: a blue eye, a wisp of dark-blond curl, was most of what could be seen of her.

Cecilia began to direct the children, sending the lads on errands and drawing Estrild to her side. Two cauldrons were swung out over the fire, filled with oats and with fresh-caught trout, pounded to fragments, as well as bits of onion and apple, boiled to a slurry. The boys helped with the heavy iron pots, and soon large wooden bowls of the porridge, with a few bits of hard cheese thrown in to melt, were set in the middle of the table. Everyone crowded about on benches, and Cecilia and her daughter put out rounds of hard bread. Elias plied wooden ladles, and saw that everyone had a heap of porridge on his trencher. Hob kept a keen if surreptitious eye on the proceedings, and noted that the crocks that held the oatmeal were being upended, the apple bins emptied: they were finishing the little family's stores.

Outside, the downpour, seen through the partially open shutters, was turning from pearl gray to lead gray as the evening drew on, and the light in the little room began to fail.

Cecilia rose and retrieved two beef-tallow candles from a shelf. One was half the size of the other. She lit them from the fire and set one on the table, the other in a holder fastened to the cupboard. Hob thought that these were probably the only candles in the house.

Molly evidently had the same thought, because she signed Hob to come to her, and when he bent down, she murmured instructions to bring in a handful of beeswax candles from the wagons. He let himself out and trudged through the downpour, squelching a bit in the mud behind the house, to the wagons. Returning across the backyard, he nearly stumbled over a small pile of very large bones. In the dim light, he bent to look more closely: the bones, from some large animals, oxen perhaps, were cracked, broken open; in some cases the ends were crushed, sprays of splintered bone still adhering to the ends.

Within the cottage, the meal was in full progress. Hob

moved about the room, setting up about a third of the candles, lit from the fire. Molly kept up a running flow of conversation in her role of itinerant entertainer and healer: places they had seen, what York and Durham and even London were like, odd incidents in the traveling life. She told an accurate but truncated version of the truth: that she and her granddaughter had fled Ireland ahead of clan warfare, and now lived in England, making their way from fair to market, occasionally staying at inns and even castles, as guest entertainers.

Then nothing would do but she must describe what life inside a castle was like, for the children were intensely curious about it—though Elias and Cecilia seemed just as enthralled. In turn, Molly began to ask questions about Elias, and to encourage him to tell what he did at the weir.

"'Tis most of the day settin' the nets, sithee, Mistress, and then haulin' them in, cleanin' t' fish in yon wee cabin out back, and then into the sack wi' 'em. Tom Carter come by near every evenin', and take 'em up to castle in his wain, sithee. Earl William's man gies me salt to cure t' fish, and string for nets, an' my boys there have learned to repair them nets as is rent. Next year I'll start 'em on makin' the nets fra t' beginnin'."

Hob, happily consuming a large portion of trout porridge, paused long enough to ask, "And what is it, Master Elias, that you use those large bones for—that pile of large bones behind the house? You have broken them with hammers; do you use them to lure the fish in some way?"

Elias actually looked over his shoulder, as though there were a listener in the shadows of the tiny room, and lowered his voice a bit.

"Nay, I've not taken a hammer to 'em; that's how I found 'em. 'Twas like this: there's trouble everywhere, young master, and clashes between the king's men and the barons' men, and there was one skirmish not far fra here. Our pastor, he called us oot to help bury the dead—someone had looted their armor, their weapons—even the saddles and suchlike— already. 'Twere an unco grim task, sithee." Here he glanced at the children, and lowered his voice still more, as though they might not hear, seated at the same table though they were. "Most on 'em had been . . . got at, sithee, and none on 'em was whole, and what we done in the end was, we had but one grave dug for the lot. Them huge horses, them destriers they use, they was mostly eaten, right down to the bone, and the bones—have you ever seen the thigh-bone of a destrier? Great thick bones they were, cracked and crushed as though they was no more than lambs' bones that the wolves have been at. Father Benedict tells us take what you want, after we'd done the buryin', but these bones was all there was, except that Maggie's Wat found a wee dagger. I took the bones for the miller to grind into meal, to spread on our vegetable garden."

Elias looked about once more, a comic sight were his tale not so macabre, and then, his voice hushed so that it was rendered nigh inaudible: " 'Tweren't wolves, neither. I seen their sign in the dirt, paw-marks all about in that damp soil. They'm like to a bear, but wi' one less toe-mark, sithee;

prints like a wolf, maybe, but bigger, bigger—about the size of a large man's hand."

Hob poked at his porridge a bit, and the subject changed, but, as he told Molly later, he was hearing again Monsignor da Panzano's voice: "They are very strong in the jaws, and can crush the biggest bones."

After the meal, Cecilia told the children to prepare for bed, but there was a storm of hushed pleading; they were wildly excited at this wonderful intrusion into their lives, and did not want to miss a moment. Estrild by this time had grown so bold that she was leaning against Molly's knee— children tended to collect about Molly—and Molly was stroking her hair.

"Shall I tell a wee tale or two, and give them something to dream on?" asked Molly, casually. Cecilia put up a hand, a gesture of surrender, but she was smiling.

And so by firelight and by candlelight, in her deep beautiful voice, Molly told stories of old Erin: stories about the Sidh, the tall cruel beautiful folk who lived under the hill, in fairy mounds invisible to mortals; stories of the parti-colored horses, caparisoned in jeweled saddles and gold-embroidered saddlecloths, that the Fairy Folk rode; of mortals who spent a night of love with one of the Fair Ones, and woke to find that a score of years had passed; of a ferocious boy who killed a blacksmith's huge guard dog, and in compensation guarded the smithy till a replacement pup could grow to maturity; of a tree that was one-half in leaf and one-half aflame; of a house that was one-half red-gold and one-half silver. The children, and even the parents, sat with mouths slightly open and eyes wide, afraid to make a sound lest Molly's recitation be interrupted.

At last the children were sent to bed—the boys were blinking slowly and Estrild, who had drifted off into sleep in Molly's lap, had to be awakened so that she could climb the ladder into the sleeping loft.

CHAPTER 12

MOLLY HAD HAD A SMALL CASK of her *uisce beatha* brought in, and the adults sat drinking for a while. A comfortable silence grew, and the fire collapsed into embers. Hob could tell that Molly had been observing Cecilia, although the scrutiny would not have been obvious to one who did not know Molly, a subtle person despite her open nature. It became evident that Cecilia's arm bothered her: a wince, a drawing down of the corners of her mouth, indicated a constant drone of pain, obviously interrupted by the occasional sharp and unexpected twinge, which caused her to start slightly, and once to give a stifled yelp.

At last Molly said, "Is it that your arm troubles you, sweeting?"

" 'Tis not a great thing," said Cecilia, but in a subdued tone.

" 'Tis a great thing," said Elias, "and 'twas set by a scoundrel barber, and he half in his cups at the time." He moved his wooden mug upon the table in an aimless pattern. "She fell from the hayloft ladder, and this lackwit undertook to set it, and she's not had a day of comfort since."

"Well, he's gone now," said Cecilia, "and in the church-yard, and there's nowt to do about it, nor should you do aught but pray for his soul."

Elias gave a small snort, but would not go so far as to speak further ill of the departed barber.

"Is it that you'd trust me to fix it, and I a stranger to you?" asked Molly gravely. "I have some experience in this."

Hob had seen Molly, with Jack's help, re-break and reset broken bones on two earlier occasions. Molly had trained Jack how to re-break a limb, practicing on legs of lamb, legs of veal, and Hob knew that Molly could greatly improve the woman's lot. Still, it was much to ask of the couple, and Hob did not think anything would come of it.

But to his surprise, Molly's manner, her presence, her way with the children, convinced the couple, at a level below speech, that she would do right by them.

But Elias said, "Mistress, I canna pay aught, poor man that I am."

Molly said pleasantly, "I'm not hearing anyone ask for payment tonight, and myself least of all, sitting here eating your fine trout porridge, and my beasts safe out of the rain at that."

Elias looked at his wife. "Well . . ." he began.

"Yes," Cecilia said. Just that, but very firmly.

"Nemain, Hob, go bring what is needful," said Molly.

Hob followed his wife out the door and around the back to the wagons. She climbed into the large wagon and handed out linen, pots of salve, and splints that Jack had whittled around the campfire in idle moments. She went to the little wagon and reemerged with two small crocks of Molly's elixirs: remedies to induce stupor and dull pain.

Inside the cottage again, Hob saw that, while Cecilia remained determined, a certain tension had crept into her manner, and Elias was unconsciously, slowly, wringing his hands below the level of the table.

Making the least fuss possible, but wasting no time and moving with a swift economy, Molly gave Cecilia a draft of thick milky liquor from one of the crocks while Nemain cleared the table and spread clean cloth. Nemain refilled Elias's cup with the fiery *uisce beatha,* and encouraged him to drink it off, the better to keep him calm. Hob casually took station near Elias, to prevent any interference with Molly and Jack at a crucial moment.

Cecilia's head began to loll upon her neck; her eyelids drooped; she breathed heavily. The two women urged her to stretch her upper body across the table. Molly positioned the younger woman's deformed arm so that the badly healed break was just at the table's edge. Molly's strong clever fingers probed for the misaligned bone; she moved Cecilia's arm forward a trace, then back. Finally she clamped both her hands on the goodwife's arm, one hand above and one below the elbow, holding the joint against the table, and nodded to Jack.

The dark man stepped forward swiftly and took Cecilia's wrist in his left hand, keeping the arm out straight and stiff. Now half her forearm was still on the table and half was out past the edge. Almost immediately Jack's huge right fist went up and came down like a hammer, just outside the table edge; there was a muted crack, and Cecilia's eyes flew open. She gave a startled yelp, curiously muted, and at once her eyelids began to sink again.

Elias was half out of his chair, but Hob put a brotherly arm about his shoulder, and urged him to sit back down.

Molly was already manipulating the ends of the bone, lining them up by what she felt beneath her fingertips, while Nemain hovered with splints and bandages. Cecilia mumbled unintelligibly, apparently a protest, but without much conviction, and soon she subsided.

In a very short time Molly was satisfied; she held the bones stable while Nemain splinted and bandaged and fastened with string, and soon the arm was held firm and slung from a shawl knotted about Cecilia's neck. Cecilia herself was snoring gently, and Elias wiped a sleeve across his forehead, damp with fear and strong drink.

With Jack's and Hob's help, Elias moved Cecilia into her bed, covered her, and after a last cup and a promise from Elias to call them if Cecilia was troubled in her sleep, Molly's troupe repaired to the wagons for the night.

· · ·

THE NEXT MORNING Cecilia was indeed in some pain. When the travelers came into the cottage, she was sitting at the table, cradling her arm in its sling and rocking slightly in place, while Elias and the children fussed about getting breakfast. Molly immediately placed a small jar in front of her, told Estrild to fetch a cup, and poured Cecilia a draft. After that the goodwife seemed easier, while Molly and Nemain took control of the kitchen, and soon all had breakfast before them, and were quietly eating.

After they had eaten, Hob and Jack got the animals hitched up, and Molly gave Elias jars of embrocation and of pain's-ease for Cecilia, and instructed him in their use, and murmured words of encouragement to Cecilia, and kissed her and kissed each of the children. Then she said to Cecilia, "Your other hand, is it working well?"

Cecilia, a bit puzzled, said, "Why, yes, Mistress Molly, 'tis well."

"Let us see, child, let us see," said Molly, gesturing for Cecilia to hold out her hand.

The woman put her hand out, palm up, to Molly. Molly took Cecilia's wrist in her hand. "Let me see you close it, *a rún*."

The goodwife did so, her puzzled expression giving way to real bewilderment.

"Now open it," said Molly, and as soon as she was obeyed, she produced a soft deerskin purse from within her robes and placed it on Cecilia's palm. "And now close it, and we're done."

Cecilia closed her hand and Molly released her wrist.

From the way her hand dipped, Hob could see that the purse was rather heavy.

"But—"

"Hush, now," said Molly, and kissed Cecilia's cheek, bent to embrace each of the children, patted Elias's shoulder, and led her little family out the door and to their places on the wagons. She waved to the weir-keeper and his children, standing in their doorway.

"Away on!"

"Did you hear what Master Elias said about that pile of bones, Mistress? It reminded me of what Monsignor da Panzano said, about the strength of those, uh, hyenas; their strength in the jaws," said Hob as they trundled along, perhaps a mile down the road.

"I did, and myself not wanting to show too much interest, but I had the same thought, and 'twas well that you asked, and twice well that you observed the bone pile so closely, and you coming back nearly in darkness."

"Does it mean that the hyena-men are scavenging on the battlefields, then, Mistress?"

" 'Tis worse: it's meaning that they are skirmishing with the Northern barons' knights, and destroying them. The king is winning in two ways: he reduces his enemies, and feeds his monsters the human meat they need, both at the same time. Otherwise he'd have to start feeding them English peasants, and I would think that that would be noticed, surely, and king or no king, he'd be swept from his throne."

They went along for a while longer with no sound but the plodding of the ox's great hooves, the creaking of wood from the wagons, the rush of wind through the trackside trees, and then Hob, mulling over the events of the last days, asked, "Mistress, that leather bag that you gave to Mistress Cecilia—what was in it?"

"'Twas enough coin to make them rich, for they gave to us when they had so little."

IN THE VILLAGES for a few miles up and down the river, years and years later, a tale persisted, a tale told around the smoky comforting warmth of peat fires in the little cottages: how two queens of the Fae, and their handsome prince, and their demon servant, visited a humble cot by the weir, and were given lodging for the night; how they healed the goodwife with their magic; how they vanished the next morning, leaving behind them bags of silver.

CHAPTER 13

THEY CAME TO CHESTER IN MID-afternoon. They had come in on a road that ran slightly to the north of the city, and so had been forced to turn and come down perhaps a mile, and enter the North Gate. Hob was enjoying the walk: the trees beginning to sway in a freshening breeze; the scent of growing things; Milo's steady pace.

Chester was a city as York was a city, but much smaller. The troupe made its way with little hindrance through the streets to the banks of the river Dee. The sun-glare rippled on the surface of the water; swifts skimmed along above the river, then with piercing cries spiralled up toward the high air. Here Chester Castle crouched, a guard against the ever-volatile Welsh. It was the stronghold of Ranulf de Blundeville, the sixth Earl of Chester, one of King John's few loyalists among the nobility.

The troupe's stated business, seeking employment as musicians, earned them admission to the outer bailey, but only after a thorough search of the wagons by alert and professionally suspicious guards. Sweetlove objected to any stranger entering what she now considered *her* wagon, and advanced, barking and snarling, on one sentry as he poked inside Jack's wagon, until Jack caught up with her and scooped her up under his arm, whence she mumbled complaints and maledictions until the search was over.

At last they were waved through into the expanse of the outer bailey, where they were able to find a senior page, a young man named Aubric, to direct them. The stables were backed up against one side of the curtain wall, a complex of three interlinked outbuildings. Molly's troupe was shown where to put the wagons, wheels chocked, nestled against a nearby stretch of blank wall. The draft animals, Milo and Tapaigh and Mavourneen, were settled comfortably in the stables, and Sweetlove locked in the small wagon.

Aubric was distracted for a moment; a young page needed to ask something, and the two conferred a short distance away, the boy's high piping voice carrying indistinctly to the troupe. Hob looked a question at Nemain, but she shrugged. He took a moment to look around: across the expanse of grass with its grazing sheep and milk cows, a carter and his helper, high up on the wooden driver's seat of a heavy supply wain, were trundling up to the inner gatehouse; a small boy with a long cane was herding ducks toward a pond near the inner bailey wall; and there, stretching the length of one wall of the outer bailey, were the white tents of the Cousins. Some lean-tos and improvised wooden huts had been fitted with small brick forges and with anvils, and here there was a constant wheeze of bellows, and a ringing as of many bells, as the swarthy men of the desert made play with their hammers, perhaps thirty at once, fashioning sword-blades, knives, ax blades, the murderous socketed heads of partisans and halberds.

And here came Aubric again, done with his little subordinate. He conducted them through the gatehouse into the inner bailey and pointed them toward an annex where they would be heard and judged fit for the castle's entertainment, or not.

"Ask for Magister Percival," he said; and so, carrying their instruments—the women each with a *clairseach,* an Irish harp, Jack with the bodhran, a goatskin drum, and Hob with his symphonia, all in soft leather cases—they walked over to the indicated outbuilding, a substantial stone-and-timber structure that connected with the keep by a long enclosed walkway. Within, they found themselves in a large hall, with benches all around the walls, interrupted only by the doorway and by two arches: one leading to the passage ending at the keep, the other to a long corridor with smaller rooms on either side.

They sat for some time on a bench, the instruments at their feet. Across the hall floor a troupe of acrobats tumbled and leaped, formed human pyramids, turned somersaults in tandem. Down at one end were five singers, heads leaned together, singing in harmony, each with the vacant look of one listening intently rather than watching, listening to his own voice while following those of his comrades: seasonal hymns, to be sung in the castle's chapel.

A young man, dressed in the Earl of Chester's livery, said merely, "Come with me; bring your instruments."

Down the corridor, its floors of dressed stone still wet from recent washing, to a side room, its walls of wood stained dark and polished with beeswax—a faint honey scent lingered in the air—and benches on two sides of the room. On one sat a man in early middle age.

"Mistress Molly out of Ireland," said the page, and turning to the troupe: "This is Magister Percival; he will hear you play." He withdrew, pulling a heavy tapestry across the archway, effectively muffling the faint sounds of the singers in the main hall.

Magister Percival did not rise. He gestured them to the bench opposite his. Hob saw a lean man, bald but for a fringe of salt-and-pepper hair. He had somber heavy-lidded blue eyes, a strong nose, a mouth whose tight-pressed lips somehow managed to express disappointment with the world. A prominent vein snaked up each temple.

"Play for me," he said.

"What would you hear, Master?" asked Molly.

"What you will," said Magister Percival, and he leaned back against the wall, crossing his legs and lacing his long fingers around his knees.

Molly and Nemain consulted a moment, then Molly

signaled to Jack and Hob to remain silent. She rested her *clairseach* on her shoulder, and began to play. After a few phrases Nemain's harp joined hers, weaving notes in and around Molly's main melody. The piece was a simple Irish country air, which, as the two women developed it, grew more complex; each time they circled around to the beginning of the refrain they added more and more grace notes and connective runs, till at last there was a bewildering rain of notes, all in perfect agreement, all advancing the main melody.

Magister Percival did not interrupt, though the piece was not short, and when they had finished, although his expression did not alter by much, he nodded at them. Then:

"Can you play for dancers?"

Molly signaled to Jack and Hob, and they struck up a dance, Jack tapping and booming, Hob spinning out the melody line of a carola on his symphonia, while his drone strings purred below and the harps gamboled above. After that they performed an estampie, and then Jack and Hob put down their instruments and Molly and Nemain sang in Irish to their harps.

At last Magister Percival clapped his hands, once, sharply, signifying that the audience was at an end. The page reentered and stood against the door, waiting.

"You will be in readiness to perform this evening for my lord the Earl of Chester," Magister Percival said. "Till then you may refresh yourselves—Guillaume will show you to the quarters where the performers may eat and rest. We expect a visit from the king in a few days, and I would have you play before him—I will say to you that I have not heard a better performance in a score of years. If you are well received by the king, there will be quarters for you until you are no longer needed."

"If it please you, master, we have our own travel wagons in which to lodge, over by the stables."

"As it suits you. Only be prepared when Guillaume comes for you to play." He nodded to the page, who bowed to him, then beckoned for Molly and her companions to follow him, and with that, they had access to the castle, and to the bailey where the Cousins worked their forges.

CHAPTER 14

GUILLAUME SHOWED THEM TO A refectory where they were served hare cooked with wine and onions, slices of roast pork, coarse dark bread, and Rhenish wine. The acrobats were there, eating heartily and arguing amiably; gusts of laughter periodically swept their table. Hob gathered, from snatches of their conversation, that they had been accepted as part of the resident entertainers, and had hope of continuing patronage from the Earl of Chester.

After Molly's troupe had finished eating, Jack took out a small cloth and wrapped some of the meat and bread in it, and they returned to the wagons to await Guillaume's summons. The women retuned their harps, and Jack unwrapped his cloth and fed Sweetlove from it, one morsel at a time, the small dog sitting politely beside him on a chest, accepting each tidbit graciously. Hob resined the wooden wheel on his symphonia.

The women changed into the gowns they wore when at castles such as Blanchefontaine or Chantemerle. Jack and Hob had sets of clothing finer than their usual belted linen overshirts and wool hose—Hob's had to be altered on almost a monthly basis, as he came into his full strength under Jack's instruction, new muscle growing to his bones day by day.

They had barely finished, and fitted the instruments into their soft leather carrying cases, when Guillaume rapped smartly on the wagon door, and announced, "Messieurs, mesdames, it is time." They swung down from the wagon, Jack handing instruments down to Hob, and trooped after the page.

They passed again through the gatehouse to the inner bailey. This gatehouse was a squat square tower, its entrance a pointed arch formed from three courses of brickwork; the passage through the gatehouse echoed to the sounds of their footsteps. There was the usual strong smell of horse; the women lifted their gowns, and the men watched where they walked, in order to avoid the occasional horse droppings.

Bored guards ignored the troupe once they saw that Guillaume was conducting them. Twin yetts, iron grilles, one at each end of the passageway, were drawn up in their slots to allow free movement; they could be dropped at a moment's notice if there was an alarm.

The troupe entered the building where they had played before Magister Percival, and Guillaume preceded them down the corridor that led to the keep. Where the passage ended at the keep wall, an iron door of modest size but great thickness was flanked by two hard-eyed guards who, Guillaume or no Guillaume, took their time before passing them through.

The leather cases were opened and the instruments drawn partially out and returned. Jack and Hob were examined for anything larger than their daggers, which doubled as utensils at dinner. One of the guards made to search the women's gowns, but Molly gave him such a withering look that he decided it was unnecessary.

Guillaume said, with a certain asperity, "Magister Percival awaits them; they are to play immediately," and with that one of the guards swung about and fitted a heavy iron key into the bulky lock. It turned with a *clank* and he had to put his shoulder into it to move the door inward. Along a narrow passage, up a winding ill-lit turret stairwell, and here was a short broad corridor with a curtained archway on one side.

Magister Percival stood by the arch, and when he saw them he lifted the heavy door hanging to one side and gestured for them to enter. Once through the arch, Hob saw that they were in a small unlit gallery overhanging the main hall; the three projecting walls were a carved screen of some fragrant wood. The torches of the main hall cast a wavering golden light through the screen's openings, enough for the musicians to play by, but keeping the gallery dim enough to conceal those within from those below. Percival indicated chairs and murmured to Molly a general program of some dances interspersed with soothing music to accompany the diners without distracting them.

Hob, waiting to begin, thought that it was an ideal place for an assassin with a bow to lurk, seeing without being seen. He looked around. Sitting quietly in the corners were two men-at-arms: the Earl of Chester was evidently not one to leave safety to chance.

And now Molly nodded to Jack, and the goatskin drum boomed out, and they were off in a lively rendition of a ductia. After that they played for a long time, Molly calling in a hushed voice to tell them what to play next.

At times when the symphonia was not called for, Hob inclined a little closer to the screen. The openwork design of the screen left many openings, and through them he could see the upper side of the hall and, by moving about a bit, some of the rest. It made a brave sight, with its three hearths, the colorful tapestries and war banners draped on the whitewashed plaster of the walls, the artfully displayed collection of pole arms and of shields with their escutcheons. There was the usual bench and trestle-table seating for the castle folk and those tenants dining there this evening, and on a dais at the head of the room, the high table, where sat the castle's knights and their wives, important guests, and Earl Ranulf himself with his family. On the wall behind the high table was an oversized silk banner with the coat of arms of the Earl of Chester, a shield with three *garbs,* or sheafs of wheat, gold on a field of blue.

The earl himself proved to be a small man in his mid-forties, sturdily made, confident, and, from what Hob could see, an accomplished wit: the table was often set laughing at something he had said.

Soon Hob was called upon to play again; when next he had the opportunity to observe the hall, the earl had retired, and the high table was half-empty. Molly and her troupe were excused for the rest of the evening by Magister Percival, and they returned to the wagons.

THE NEXT DAY Hob and Nemain took a moment to look in on Milo and the other animals. Hob went into the stall, the ox turning his head and snuffling with pleasure; Hob brushed him and inspected his ears, and generally made re-assuring sounds, so that the enormous beast might know that all was well despite the strangers' feeding and grooming him. He felt rather foolish about this, but still—they were not often apart, and the ox seemed to depend upon him in some way. And Jack took good care of Tapaigh, and Nemain—Nemain treated the little ass Mavourneen as though it were a pet. Nonetheless, Hob felt that Sir Balthasar would be scornful of his tenderness. When Nemain opened the stall door, his murmured endearments stopped immediately. He put down the brush and stepped out to join her.

Outside the stables they found Molly and Jack, with Sweetlove slumped against his ankle, listening to Jourdain and one of the farriers.

"There's a mort of Englishmen can swing a hammer, and there's many of us skilled at the forge," said the farrier, who like most of them also did other forms of blacksmith-ing. He was a burly man of perhaps thirty-five with thinning blond hair. He crossed his arms over the long leather apron that shielded him from neck to knee. "Yon wights be devil-worshippers or such, and 'tis a curse they'll bring on us all, living in our very house as 'twere. Mark me, we'll suffer for it later as we're sufferin' for it now, with all the work we could be doing."

"Sure it's a shame," said Molly, to encourage the flow of any information, never knowing when something useful might be said. Jack just made what were meant to be sympathetic noises, although with his broken throat the sounds he produced tended to be more frightening than soothing.

"It is as I 'ave said, they are ver' strange," said Jourdain, "an' here is come the most strange of all." He indicated, by a small lift of his chin, the figure now stepping out of the inner gatehouse.

Hob was instantly alert. He saw a very tall, very thin man, clad in a voluminous night-blue robe that the wind caused to flap behind him. This, then, was Yattuy, the sorcerer. His lean wrists and long hands, his ax-blade face, were the color of the Cousins', a light brown, as dark as Jack's hands after a long summer's tanning. The hood of the robe was pushed back, disclosing a hairline that, by nature or artifice, began a little distance behind the break of his forehead, giving a masklike appearance to his narrow face. He took long strides across the bailey, his head turning from side to side; with his prominent nose and his long thin legs, and with his robes flapping behind him, he gave the impression of a striding, predatory bird.

Men and women alike appeared to be frightened of him; men-at-arms crossed themselves surreptitiously and kissed medals of St. Martin; stepping out of the washing sheds that were wreathed in steam, a pair of laundresses with their heavy baskets managed to drift out of his path, seemingly by accident.

"You see, ever'one is avoid him," said the Poitevin. "He is un'oly fellow, but the king, he like him. He is take his advice; he is consult him as a soothsayer. The king, he want to know what will 'appen, an' Yattuy he tell him. Who knows what he say? They are like two gossips at market, heads together."

The farrier spat on the grass. "Jesus with us!" he said. "Good English smiths put out of their work and yon devil inside the walls! The pope will put England under the ban again—he's done it once, he can do it again. 'Twill end in blood, mark my words."

"They say he is ver' smart fellow, him," said Jourdain. "He is speak seven, eight languages; ver' smooth, too."

"'Tis not everyone who dislikes him," said Molly, watching the sorcerer stride up to the tents. The Cousins came toward him, bowing, kissing his garment; some prostrated themselves. He moved among them, placing a hand on a shoulder here and atop a kneeling man's head. He appeared to be speaking to each one, smiling, patting them: the very picture of encouragement and comfort, the eerie followers crowding about. *He is like a malevolent Christ*, thought Hob, *with malevolent disciples.*

After a while Yattuy sat at one of the campfires, and was handed a cup of something, which he sipped, and all the while talking, instructing, the Cousins around him attending every word.

Molly said, "*Och*, well, we've some practice to do if we're to play again tonight." They had traveled together and played together for so long that no practice was really needed, but as she told them later, " 'Tis not the cleverest strategy to stand and gawp at your enemy, so that he knows that you are aware of him."

They began to move away toward the wagons, and Jourdain called, "Come an' visit us: we are quartered in the inner bailey. Ask the gatehouse guards. Jacques, we 'ave good wine, from Poitou!"

CHAPTER 15

O N THE FOLLOWING MORNING Molly decided it was time that she and Nemain observed the Cousins more closely. To this end the four began to stroll about the outer bailey, skirting the perimeter. They started from the stables, which ran along the west wall, and ambled along, pausing to engage in lively conversation now and then, to dissemble any appearance of purposeful observation. Hob and Nemain walked hand in hand, but Jack, whose social status was obviously not equal to Molly's, was careful to walk a bit behind her and to the side, giving the impression of a servant, and thereby attracting no unwanted interest.

On the whole Jack, a man of action rather than intellect, was content to leave the making of decisions to Molly, as was Hob—Hob had often thought that Molly was always the wisest person in any gathering. In a sense Jack Brown, in relation to Molly, was as a soldier is to his general, or a subject to his queen, except when she summoned him to her bed; for, as Molly remarked one night when she'd had a goodly amount of the *uisce beatha*, "There are times when 'tis better to drop the reins and see where the horse may take you."

At the northeast corner of the outer bailey they turned and proceeded to pace along the eastern wall, outside which there was a strip of land, and then the river Dee, the haunt of salmon and otters, sliding past the castle, curling over its weir with a rushing hiss. Toward the northeast corner a breeze shifted, bringing over the wall the reek of Tanners' Row, where the tanneries for which Chester was famed clustered in a foul-smelling line along the river.

From that corner they wandered idly about the bailey, observing the farriers at work in their forges by the stables, the duck pond with its boy herders and their long flexible poles with which they drove the ducks, and the saddlers' workshops; gradually they wended their way over to the little tent village of the Cousins.

This began just to one side of the duck pond, and the tents stretched away along the east curtain wall to the wall that separated the outer bailey from the inner. It seemed to Hob entirely possible that there were tenscore of them. These men were also at work, perhaps thirty of them at a time at as many makeshift forges, voluminous sleeves rolled up over muscular arms, their hammers swinging overhead and down, ringing upon their portable anvils, the many hammers making a kind of music.

The Cousins made no horseshoes, only weapons, and they kept their attention on their work, and made no attempt to speak to anyone outside the group. According to Jourdain, they lived together and worked together and kept apart from castle life. Their chieftains arranged for the delivery of foodstuffs. In the evenings the Cousins sat around small fires and ate together, boiling wheat flavored with bits of roasted lamb and drinking hot beverages brewed from herbs they had brought from their homeland.

The party walked along, still talking and laughing among themselves, and feigned an interest in the Cousins' work. Molly and Nemain pretended to listen as Hob chattered of this and that, but all the while they were strolling by the tents they were feeling with their fey senses for the power hidden in the Berber blacksmiths.

For a time they stood and watched one of the craftsmen at his anvil as he pounded a glowing length of metal, destined to become a sword-blade. He threw down the hammer he was using beside his anvil, picked up the shimmering steel with tongs, and stepped into the open-faced tent, to plunge the blade into a barrel of cold water, producing a sharp *shush* and a burst of steam.

Molly picked up the hammer that he'd thrown down; she exuded idle curiosity, remarking in Irish to Nemain, but all the while turning the wooden handle in her palm, rubbing it, absorbing some sort of knowledge from the wood itself, so lately under the Cousin's palm. She handed it to Nemain with a laughing remark, and Nemain pretended to be struggling with the weight of it, giggling a bit, but she, too, was rubbing and squeezing the handle.

A moment later the *bouda* came from the tent, saw what was toward, and marched over to Nemain. His face was not precisely hostile, but it was grave, and he held out his palm in an unmistakable gesture. Nemain placed it in his hand, contriving to touch his fingers as she did so. She bowed slightly to the smith, who stood looking stonily at her, and then Molly sauntered on, and the others followed.

When they had completed their circuit of the outer bailey, strolling along the wall that separated inner from outer bailey, crossing before the gatehouse, and so coming again to their wagons standing against the west wall, Hob turned as if casually surveying the open expanse. To his unease he saw that the Cousin whose hammer the women had handled was still watching them. He stood at his anvil, and struck a few blows now and then, but mostly he gazed across the field at Molly's little group.

"Mistress . . ." began Hob, trying to keep the *bouda* in view without being too transparent, but Molly forestalled him.

"Aye, I'm seeing him. 'Twas a chance that needed taking; when you observe a person of Art, you risk discovery of yourself as an adept. There was some tinge of force that I'm feeling in that hammer handle. Nemain, you touched his hand itself; what is it you can say of that?"

"I'm not sensing a great man of Art—there's a flavor of

power, but it's more a feeling of the Beast than of spellcraft."

Jack looked away at this; he was uncomfortable when the subject of the Beast within, of shapeshifters, arose. He walked away to the small wagon, reached up, and opened the door. There was an eruption of small dog, and Sweetlove leaped into his arms, licking his face and emitting high-pitched whimpers of happiness at the reunion. Jack sat down cross-legged on the grass and began to pet and stroke her; Hob suspected that he found Sweetlove distracting and comforting. He knew that Jack, normally stoic and even phlegmatic, became troubled at the thought of what he had been, and the things, terrible things, that he half remembered doing when he was in his altered state.

"You can sense he can change like Ja—that he can change to a Beast?" asked Hob, keeping his voice low.

"Aye, and there's malice as well—he's a man of ill will, and there's little love in him, and a mort of strength," said Nemain.

"And there are two hundred of them," said Molly bleakly.

CHAPTER 16

T HE NEXT DAY THEY WERE AGAIN in the outer bailey. Sweetlove was dashing after the stick Jack was throwing, trotting back to him and, with a flirt of her neck, tossing it at his feet. Then she'd retreat perhaps three yards, hunker down facing him in a tense crouch, eyes fixed on his face, tail wagging, her whole aspect one of coiled expectation. Jack would pick up the stick, wait, pretend to lose interest, then suddenly throw it toward her, but high. She would spring out of her crouch and race in a tight circle, heading out to intercept it, somehow running and looking back over her shoulder. Much of the time she'd pluck it out of the air, and deliver it again to Jack with a smug look. Then they'd repeat the process.

Hob sat with Nemain on a bench set in the sun-lit grass of the bailey. She was in the position she favored, leaning back against his chest with his arm around her; they were both watching Jack and Sweetlove playing. Hob was thinking that Jack had an expression of pure unthinking pleasure; he seemed to take as much delight in it as Sweetlove. A peaceful scene: Nemain slumped a little more against him as she slipped toward a doze.

From one of the two towers atop the outer gatehouse a trumpet sounded, a long complicated call. The call was echoed from the top of the inner gatehouse. Nemain sat up a bit, rubbing a small white hand over her face. There was a bustle from the inner bailey, where the garrison had its quarters, and a gang of men-at-arms trotted through the inner gatehouse and along the grass of the outer bailey. Sergeants blew wooden whistles in a series of staccato notes: signals that had the effect of chivvying the men into two lines, facing one another, each right fist held across each chest in salute.

Now they could hear a fanfare of trumpets from outside the main gate, and the portcullis began to rise. There was the clank of iron and the groan of wood, and then the sound of hooves thundering on the drawbridge outside, the hollow sounds of horses clopping through the gatehouse passageway, and here came a party of knights with the various banners of John, King of England and, at least in name, Duke of Normandy, Duke of Aquitaine, Count of Anjou, and Lord of Ireland. Next came two squads of archers, bows strung but slung over their shoulders.

After that came a cluster of the king's immediate household knights, bodyguards, courtiers, and in the center, on a handsome roan mare, King John himself, a man in his late forties, a man of middling stature but athletically made. His red-brown hair was now touched with iron, but he sat his horse well and seemed keenly interested in his surroundings, particularly in the tents of the Cousins.

Behind came three companies of men-at-arms with pole arms slanted back on their shoulders, supply wagons, more knights, and a swarm of lightly armed mounted scouts.

At the entrance to the inner gatehouse, Sir Ranulf, his family, and his senior knights and advisors awaited the king. King John dismounted nearby, and the Earl of Chester came to him and went down on one knee; John extended his hand and Ranulf kissed the king's ring. John raised him up and embraced him, and then amid a flurry of greetings and introductions they strolled through the gatehouse toward the inner bailey. A small army of grooms descended on the king's entourage and began the process of stabling the mounts and securing the wagons.

That evening, Guillaume the page came to the wagons. The four were in Molly's big wagon, the women discussing possible strategies against the Cousins and making almost no progress, Hob and Jack sitting and listening, Sweetlove mock-chewing Jack's big fingers.

Without warning Sweetlove flew off Jack's lap and threw herself at the door, unleashing a storm of barking, surprisingly deep for such a little dog, but with here and there a yelp of soprano hysteria. A moment later came the page's knock. "I am from Magister Percival," he called.

Jack picked up a loaded stick—a wooden club with the

head hollowed out and filled with lead—that he kept behind the door. He opened the door and there was Guillaume, who bowed smoothly and then, looking up at an angle at Jack in the raised doorway, said, "Magister Percival requires that you come play for the great hall; I will return in but a little while. If it please you, sir, have Mistress Molly and her folk ready with their instruments."

He bowed again and Jack just smiled and bowed awkwardly himself. The page disappeared into the gloom of the outer bailey, and then there was a rush to change to their best garments and to tune the instruments. Hob then had to submit to an inspection by his young wife, *tsk*ing and pulling his collar this way and that, and smoothing his hair.

Jack was an old campaigner, and could have himself ready in a moment, but he would never make a courtier, and Molly made a few adjustments and tucks to his garments, as Nemain had done for Hob.

The women inspected each other, turning in place, but neither could find any fault, and so they stepped out into the night bailey and waited for Hob to hand the instruments down to Jack. Sweetlove had jumped down to be beside Jack, and now had to be swept up and deposited inside the wagon and the door locked, and here came Guillaume, ready to conduct them to the keep.

They came to the gatehouse that connected outer with inner bailey. The outer yett was closed, and a torch burned in a socket set in the gatehouse wall beside the archway. A guard stepped up, peered through the yett at Guillaume, and nodded to someone off to the side. Guillaume led Molly's party to a smaller door beside the yett. This door, of thick oak braced with iron straps, was set in the stone of the gate-house; it opened ponderously, and two guards stood back to let them enter. The men-at-arms immediately closed the door behind them, sliding heavy bolts in place to lock it.

In theory everyone in the outer bailey should be a friend; Hob wondered if there was some lingering distrust of the Cousins that caused the earl to be so cautious, or if it was the king's presence itself, for power engenders enemies, and the greater the power, the more widespread the enmity.

Once again they followed Guillaume to Magister Percival's outbuilding, and thence along the corridor to the iron door to the keep, with its wary guards, and so by interior passage and stairwell to the musicians' gallery.

They withdrew their instruments from their leather sheathing, tuned, retuned, and composed themselves to play. As had been the case for the past few days, when they had played for Earl Ranulf, Magister Percival stayed below in the hall, with Guillaume by his side. As need arose, the magister would dispatch the page to the gallery, to require the musicians to play a lively dance, or a soft accompaniment to conversation, or to hold themselves silent for a space, the quiet serving the same purpose for the ear as a sherbet served between courses, cleansing for the tongue—a Saracen custom brought back from the Holy Land.

For the moment, they were ready, but no instruction had come. Hob looked around; there were still two guards, sitting quietly in the corners at the rear of the little room. He bent toward the wooden screen and peered down at the great hall. The pattern of carved leaves in the gallery screen left, by chance, a somewhat larger opening right by Hob's chair, and he had a clear view of the dais. In the center sat King John, with Earl Ranulf at his right hand, and Lady Clemence, the earl's wife, at his left. The view to Hob's left was limited, but there appeared to be no common folk present—the high table and side tables had been arranged to form a horseshoe shape, and entertainers would perform in the central space, or diners would arise for a period of dancing.

And here came Guillaume, with a directive from Magister Percival to perform three dances: two sprightly, with a stately dance between them. The precise choices the master left up to Molly. Soon Hob was deep in concentration, closely following the rattle and thump of Jack's drum, smoothly turning the symphonia's wheel as the fingers of his other hand danced over the keys.

When the three dances were done, Magister Percival sent word for a spell of silence; then the tireless Guillaume reappeared with a request for unobtrusive but constant music. Molly had Nemain play her harp to Hob's accompaniment, a task at which the young husband and wife were achieving a kind of quiet excellence.

But they had not played for very long before Hob became aware of a rising turmoil in the hall below. Still cranking the symphonia's wheel, he leaned closer to the screen and risked a quick look down into the hall.

King John was pounding the table with his fist. He was clearly in one of his infamous rages, at first addressing Earl Ranulf—as far as Hob could tell, it was about some third party whose actions had displeased him—and then more and more just shouting into the air before him, his gaze the abstracted unfocused look of one envisioning a foe who is not present, his face ruddy as raw beefsteak, his hands clutching at his already disheveled hair.

The music trailed off into silence. It seemed disrespectful to play over the king's tirade. And now, to Hob's great astonishment, the king fell from his chair and rolled upon the rush-strewn floor, bellowing at the top of his lungs, snatching great handfuls of reeds and throwing them in the air, and finally stuffing a fistful of the tubular stalks in his mouth, biting down on them, his eyes bulging and staring at nothing while his fists and heels beat a drumroll upon the floor. This was the notorious Angevin temper, a half-crazed display of rage, with which both John's brother, the Lionheart, and their father Henry before them had been afflicted.

Suddenly Magister Percival himself appeared beside them. "Play the first piece that ever you played for me," he said to Molly, his face expressionless, his voice low but singing with intensity.

Molly gave the "keep silent" signal to Hob and Jack, nodded to Nemain, and took her own *clairseach* onto her lap, resting it on her shoulder. She swept her fingers over the strings, and they were off on the simple Irish air that gradually grew more complex, becoming more and more intriguing as the ear strove to follow, through the rain of notes from the plucked strings, the play between the two harps, and all the while the piece retaining the sweet and soothing quality of the original country song.

Slowly the king's thrashing subsided; he lay for a time gazing at the great beams that upheld the hall ceiling, while the folk, from the earl to the lowest page boy, looked at anything but the king, and strove with wooden faces to seem not to have noticed anything amiss.

Soon the king sat up, swiping rush stalks from his surcoat, running his hands through his hair. The earl offered him a hand, which the king angrily thrust aside. He rose and resumed his seat; he spat out a fragment of stalk; he took a sip of wine. He looked for a few moments up at the musicians' gallery, and spoke aside to one of his aides, who left the dais. John then resumed his conversation with the earl as though nothing had happened. Earl Ranulf had a tight smile upon his lips and seemed to be laboring to maintain his part in the conversation despite the shock of John's spectacle of fury.

Magister Percival signaled for them to stop. "Do you leave us a little silence," he said. "Let speech and jest recover at the table. Yes?" This last was to a page who held aside the heavy cloth that sealed the archway into the corridor.

"By your leave, Magister Percival, a word with you?"

The music master stepped out through the curtain; a few moments later, he returned, and held out a soft leather purse to Molly. She took it, and hefted it; her eyebrows rose somewhat in surprise.

"You are invited to join the musicians at Windsor Castle. It appears the king finds your playing . . . soothing," said Magister Percival in the dryest of voices.

· · ·

SOMEWHAT LATER in the evening, when the symphonia was again silent, Nemain and Jack performing on harp and drum, Hob looked through his spy hole and saw, seated beside the king, Yattuy the sorcerer. The Amazigh was like a shadow in his dark-blue robes beside the king's richly embroidered surcoat. The king, looking out over the hall, leaned toward him, and the tall magus bent to speak in the king's ear, muttering, muttering. Hob could not even hear the sound of the Berber's voice over the music and the general noise of the feast, but the sorcerer's whole aspect, and his proximity to the king, spoke of a desire for privacy, if not secrecy itself. As Yattuy spoke, the king's mouth turned down, but he nodded, and nodded again.

King John straightened, and made a dismissive gesture. The Berber stood and bowed, and made to turn away, but the king stayed him with a hand on his sleeve. Yattuy turned back, and the king drew a large gold ring from his right hand, and folded it into the sorcerer's sinewy brown hand. Yattuy bowed again, and withdrew.

Hob sat back from the screen, thinking of Father Ugwistan's words: "He is a frightening and powerful man—he speaks to kings and they listen." He looked over at Molly, who had set her *clairseach* down while her granddaughter and her lover played. She sat with her usual big-cat composure, but Hob thought to see a faint expression of unease, and the fitful light from the torches in the great hall that struck in through the fanciful carving of the wooden screen, though it set small patches of brightness tangling in her silver hair, yet left Molly mostly in shadow.

CHAPTER 17

HOB WENT TO HEAR MASS IN the chapel of St. Mary de Castro. He reached it by climbing up a narrow winding flight of stone stairs in the gatehouse tower, and then turning left through a doorway of no great size. It was a pretty little chapel; against a side wall stood wood scaffolding, and already one could see the beginnings of frescoes that had been commissioned. Hob stood in the back, listening to the drone of Latin competing with the occasional military call-and-response from the men-at-arms on guard duty on the tower roof reporting to those below at the gate.

He became aware of someone standing close at his elbow: Father Ugwistan. The Berber priest at first seemed lost in his devotions, but then he took a half step back and plucked at Hob's sleeve. Bent over his paternoster beads, Ugwistan began to murmur to Hob, low enough to be mistaken for prayer by the nearest worshipper.

"I have been listening; the Cousins speak of the two women who pay them such close attention, and how they believe them to be witches, and so on. They work at their forges, and they amuse themselves with chatter about this one and that; but this, this is more serious—they wonder are you aware of them. It is a matter of a day or so till Yattuy is again among them, and then the talk will reach his ears, and from him to King John is but a small distance. I have also a missive from Monsignor da Panzano. His business takes him to the north, but he desires to meet with you, for time is short and he wishes to know what you plan to do. So: here is this inn, at these crossroads, marked on this square of parchment."

A small bit of parchment slid smoothly between Hob's left elbow and his side. He took it with his right hand and quietly tucked it into his pouch.

"It is twenty leagues up the coast. Monsignor regrets he cannot meet somewhere closer, but his business is a desperate one, and he cannot always control where he must be. Be there in a sennight, but leave tomorrow, before the women are denounced by these *bouda,* and then imprisoned."

The Mass ended, and Father Ugwistan slipped away to the stairwell before the first of the worshippers turned to leave. Hob was not far behind him, his thoughts in a whirl. He made straight for the wagons, to report to Molly.

• • •

IN THE EVENT, the king and his military entourage were leaving Chester Castle the next day as well, and all was confusion in the outer bailey. Hob and Jack went into the stables, and brought out the three draft animals and hitched them up. With vigilance at the outer gatehouse being much reduced—parties of knights and men-at-arms and supply wagons were constantly passing outward to join the column forming outside the walls—it was easy enough for the three wagons to trundle through the echoing passageway and, skirting the king's growing column standing all along the verge of the road, make off toward the east and, having gone out of sight of the castle, turn north, eventually gaining the coast road.

Part II

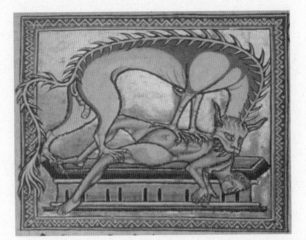

THE EYE OF THE HYENA

. . . It stalks the sheepfolds of shepherds and circles their houses by night, and by listening carefully learns their speech, so that it can imitate the human voice, in order to fall on any man whom it has lured out at night.

. . . It is true that if the hyena walks three times around any animal, the animal cannot move.

—The Aberdeen Bestiary, ca. 1200

I trot, I lope, I slaver, I am a ranger.
I hunch my shoulders. I eat the dead.

—Edwin Morgan, "Hyena"

. . . awful Thing of Shadows, speak to me!
Why dost thou laugh that horrid laugh?

—Byron, *Heaven and Earth*

CHAPTER 18

MOLLY HAD SET A FAST PACE UP the coast road, for twenty leagues was a good way for an ox-drawn wagon to travel at speed, and she did not want to miss her appointment with the papal agent. Still, with effort comes a need to rest, and soon enough she had them pull off the road at a promising spot, with good grazing for the animals, and a fresh breeze from the Irish Sea.

She was generally a person of good cheer and brisk intelligence, and so it was the more striking that she had become quiet, and introspective, and sat that evening at their campfire, after they had eaten, staring moodily into her cup. Hob and Nemain exchanged glances. The silence stretched on for a bit, then Nemain, who was both impatient and outspoken, cleared her throat.

"There's something troubling you and no mistake, *seanmháthair*," she said. "What is it, then?"

Molly looked up and around the fire at the other three, and seemed to come to herself.

" 'Tis these *bouda*. So many of them, and each one a double hundredweight, and none of them easily killed—not by iron, that's certain—and they led by this sorcerer, who is by my sense of him a lion of the Art, and myself not knowing what to say to yon papal spy, nor what to do with these *conriochtaí*—I'm turning it over and over in my mind, and sure I'm no nearer an answer than when I started."

Hob tended not to delve too deep into his family's abilities in the matter of what they called "the Art"—what old Father Athelstan would have called "traffic with the Devil"—for though he could not believe that either Molly or Nemain would be a part of something evil, yet it went against all his beliefs and the teaching he had received. It was easier not to pry, and in any case the women were secretive about their practice. But now he had to ask; he looked from his wife to her grandmother.

"Can you not just slay them with, with, a spell? A curse? Or something like?"

Molly looked at Nemain. The young woman shook her head. "Nay, *seanmháthair*, I'd not know where to begin. He's a grand husband," she said, patting his arm a bit, "but in fey matters, isn't he deaf as a post."

Molly sighed. "Hob, *a rún*, to work the Art against someone, it's requiring concentration, and the force of the will, and sometimes an object or two, to help . . . aim, let us say, the will. 'Twill work against one enemy, or perhaps a few, if they are in one place, and if you know their names—names, as I said to the good monsignor, give you power over the named—and if you are not fighting also in the world of things—the world you know. Have you never wondered why we do not go back to Erin and destroy our foes with our spellcraft? The clan that attacked us has its share of practitioners of the Art, and a mort of wild Irish tribesmen as well, with their short spears and their Dalcassian axes, so that one must fight in the solid world and the spirit world, both at once. When we return, Nemain and I will have to deal with their witches, while their warriors will have to deal with Jack Brown and Robert the Englishman, and others. Aye, let them chew on Sir Balthasar and see if their appetite for war does not wane."

She picked up a thin branch from the ground and poked at the fire. "But that's a trouble for the future. 'Tis this day, and the next, and the next, that I'm planning and scheming for, and, thus far, 'tis all for naught. I'm asking the Mórrígan to show me my path, but I've no response."

"She will answer," said Nemain, in a soothing tone. "When has She ever failed you?"

Hob was now concerned—usually it was Molly who comforted, who advised. He had rarely seen her so at a loss.

Molly stood and stretched. "That's enough keening about my troubles for one day. 'Tis time I were in my bed. Jack, come cheer me up."

She went toward the big wagon, and Jack drained his mug, stood, winked at Nemain and Hob, and followed her.

CHAPTER 19

S UDDEN SHOUTS AND SCREAMS FROM the road ahead. Hob looked back to Molly for guidance. She was already standing up on the swaying wagon seat, balancing easily, pulling open the hatch and reaching into the wagon for her bow. She called to him over her shoulder: "Away on!"

Plainly they were to become involved; Hob turned and pulled harder on Milo's guide rope. The ox stretched his neck out to accommodate the increased tension, then realized that he was to increase speed. He gave the obligatory wheezing groan of indignation, but then began to move appreciably faster.

They came past a last few trees, a final cloud of bushes, and there, so close to the road that most of the gardens were behind or to the side of the dwelling, was a small tenant's cottage. The narrow strip between cottage and road on one side of the doorway was given over to a chicken run fenced with wicker, and on the other side an herb garden, and it was in this latter that perhaps seven men—armed men, mercenaries—were struggling with two women, by the looks of them mother and daughter. In the doorway, an arm outflung over the threshold, lay a man with a gray beard and a deep cleft in his bald head. The doorstep was soaked in his blood.

Hob had a moment to take this in, dimly aware of Molly kicking the brake shut and clambering toward the roof with her bow. In a heartbeat the bandits had the women down, some men pinning each woman's wrists and ankles and the others tearing at their clothing. The herbs were being crushed beneath the women's heaving, straining bodies and the stamping boots of the men, and the savory scents so released, speaking of domesticity, peace, the kitchen, lent a nightmare quality to the horror before him.

Hob was beginning, now that he was a new-married man, to see a bit of Nemain in all women. He had had the experience of a long night's fear for her turning to rage; now he found that same rage ready to hand on the instant. It came surging up, quick, strong, a salmon jumping a waterfall at the Tyne headwaters, the battle fury that would in time make him in Ireland the much-feared "Robert the Englishman," and he dropped the lead rope in the dust of the road and pounded toward the herb garden, drawing his dagger on the run.

There were three men holding the mother's limbs, and

two the daughter's. The two men not engaged turned toward Hob. The nearer clapped a hand to his knife-hilt just as Hob reached him. The young man seized his opponent's wrist and plunged his own dagger into the mercenary's midsection, and again, and again. The mercenary's legs buckled; Hob released him and he began to sink down, gasping and holding his belly.

The second man had unshipped an ax from a hook on his belt, a fighter's ax, polished and keen-edged, and now he whirled it in a swift arc at Hob's head. The young man had just enough time to leap backward outside the range of the gleaming axhead, and then to step rapidly backward to avoid the reverse swing, and as he took another step, now almost in the road, a stone turned under his heel, and he fell flat to his back, directly in front of Milo. For a moment he lay with the wind knocked from him, and then his attacker loomed over him, the ax swung high over his head, beginning the downward stroke, unavoidable, the terrible onset of gleaming death.

At that moment Milo, timid Milo, suddenly came alive, stretched forth his neck, and swung his great head with its shortened, blunted horns, swung it as a king bull would hook at another bull in a to-the-blood battle for herd rule, the power of his thick neck driving a flat horn-tip into the soldier's chest. Hob heard ribs break; the soldier was knocked down, arms flung out; he sprawled breathless, half-stunned. Hob rolled up to his feet, stepped onto the wrist of his foe's ax hand. He bent down, snarling through clenched teeth, implacable, remorseless: with a grunt he drew his dagger across his enemy's throat, and withdrew it, and the man's lifeblood began to pump out into the dust of the road.

He straightened. Jack went past him in a fast limping run, his war hammer at the ready; as he passed he tossed Hob a loaded stick. Hob sheathed his dagger, picked up the heavy stick, and went after Jack. From the wagon roof-walks, Molly and Nemain sent their crow-fletched arrows whistling toward the cottage door, where two or three mercenaries, who had been tearing up the little rooms, the poor furniture, in search of anything of value that might be plundered, now tried to reinforce their comrades. The first out was allowed to get a few paces from the threshold before the women struck him down. The other two had just managed to step outside when arrows sprouted from their chests, the women as usual instinctively dividing their targets: Nemain to the right, Molly to the left.

The five remaining in the herb garden had abandoned their victims and turned to meet Hob and Jack's onslaught, drawing swords and poniards. It did them little good: Jack, with his unusual strength and his long experience at weaponcraft, crashed into their midst, the hammer side of his war hammer smashing into one *routier*'s chest, shocking his heart to stillness, the backswing circling the dark man's head and the crow-beak coming around and down to plunge into a second man, there where the side of the neck joins the body.

Right behind him was Hob, and here tricks he had learned from Sir Balthasar and others he had learned from Molly or Jack were combined in rapid succession, so that even though he was faced with a tall mercenary and he armed with a broadsword, in short order Hob feinted, broke the bandit's shin with the heavy lead-loaded head, and, as the bandit dropped, struck the broadsword from his hand, and with a backhand blow broke his elbow as he fell past him.

Jack was battering his third man to death while Hob faced the last *routier*. A short wiry man with a horribly scarred face—one eye was missing—and grimy hands, he gambled everything on one thrust of his long knife, leaping forward with his right arm out before him, so that his whole body became a sort of spear, with the knife as the spearhead. Hob twisted violently to his left, bringing his club, held with a hand at each end, down at a slant on the knifeman's wrist, forcing the knife to one side. The mercenary, his strike thwarted, now was impelled by his momentum to stagger past Hob, who switched smoothly to a one-handed grip and swung with all his might, the club's murderous head banging into the back of the man's neck, a place so vulnerable that a strong blow meant death. And so it proved now: One-Eye fell and did not move again.

Jack came striding back from the herb garden. The man whose elbow and shin Hob had broken was thrashing about gracelessly on the ground, uttering wordless cries of woe. Jack, that unsentimental soldier, killed him with one blow of the war hammer as he passed, hardly slowing.

Molly was calling orders as she climbed down from the roof. Jack went to the small wagon and came out with a compact chest with powders, ointments, bandage. He carried that into the yard and put it down by the two women, who were pulling their clothes into some semblance of order. Then Hob and Jack went into the house, went room to room to make sure no attacker lurked therein, and discovered the husband of the house, lying in a small pool of blood from his battered head, but still alive.

They took stock. The mercenaries were all dead, and the elderly man was dead. The husband might live. The women were sitting together in the ruins of their herb garden, holding each other and sobbing. Molly and Nemain went into the house and cleaned and dressed the man's head—he had been clubbed several times—and the two men lifted him onto a bed. Nemain found two coarse but clean blankets, and covered him; as Molly said, " 'Tis peril for a wounded man to have a chill come into his bones."

Then they went out into the sunlight and sat with the women and discovered that they had not been greatly hurt, but only terribly frightened. Now they looked round and saw the graybeard, presumably the grandfather, dead by the doorstep, and set up a wail, and the younger woman began crying, "Hugh! Where is Hugh?" She became more and more upset, and her cries grew louder; and now from the goat pen nearby, a boy of perhaps ten crept out and ran to her arms, and then there was renewed weeping, some of it from joy and relief, some from sorrow.

Molly and Nemain prepared calming drinks for the women; Jack and Hob carried the dead grandfather into a back room and laid him out on a pallet there. They sent the boy on a run to the nearest neighbor's cottage, to bring help, and when the neighbors had come, two men with axes and three women, one very old, Molly advised them to send for the shire reeve's men.

And when the neighbor women had clustered about the victims, petting them and wrapping them in shawls and generally making soothing sounds and murmured exclamations of pity, and the axmen had taken up station in the yard, looking angry and determined, and spitting on the mercenaries' corpses and cursing King John and all Frenchmen and especially the *routiers,* Molly had the troupe resume their journey, pulling away quietly, with a simple wave to the axmen in the yard. For, as she said later, "If we're to avoid being taken by King John's men, 'twill not do to be found in the midst of a battlefield, and everyone speaking of us."

THEY HAD GONE a fair distance before Molly signaled that they were to camp for the night. They pulled off the road into a field bordered with a line of apple trees; a little stream provided water, and there was grass for the animals.

They sat around a small fire and ate a simple meal of bread and hard cheese and brookwater, and reflected on the day's events. At some point they were mulling over Hob's near brush with death, and how Milo had saved him, and Hob said, "I think he must have been startled by yon *routier* swinging up his ax, and swung his head to avoid it, the horn by chance striking the man's chest."

And now Nemain, that most hardheaded and sarcastic of their little family, surprised Hob by shaking her head and saying "Nay, nay, 'tis not what I think." She looked out into the meadow, where Milo grazed at the end of his tether, partially obscured by the gathering darkness, the firelight echoing from his thick blunted horns, his large dark eye now and then flashing as it caught the ruddy beams.

She looked back at her husband, and said gravely, "I'm thinking that he's feeling some faint shadow of that passion to protect that you're seeing in bulls—they ranging round the herd and ready to attack wolves and other bulls and suchlike that threaten the cows—and Milo's full fond of his Hob."

Hob said, laughing, "Our Milo, our timid Milo, a king bull, like the king bulls of the wild white cattle?"

"I'm not to be changing my word on this, husband," said Nemain. " 'Tis the way of it; I'm feeling it in my heart."

Hob spread his hands and looked at Molly, an appeal to authority, but Molly just shrugged and sipped at her cup. "When she's so sure, I'm finding she has the right, almost always. And any road, I'm too tired to think more on't."

But Hob was still chuckling. "Perhaps you think he's becoming an ox warrior—I could ride him into battle." At this point Nemain threw a bit of bread at him in mock fury for teasing her, which made Hob laugh harder, and look for a crust to throw back—in some ways they were still the boy and girl who had grown up together—and which provoked him to elaborate on his theme: "Or, or, we could sharpen his horns and use him against those Cousins."

"What?"

Hob, about to pelt Nemain with a pebble's worth of hard cheese, paused, shocked. Molly had leaped to her feet and was glaring at him.

"I, I, said that Milo . . ." began Hob, at this point not sure what he had said, the startling having driven it from his mind.

"He said that we might use Milo against the Cousins," said Nemain, looking at her grandmother curiously. "But 'twas just in banter. Why should that make you so cross?"

Molly looked back and forth, her expression still stern but softening. "Cross? Nay, child, I was startled myself. Hob, you have given it to me, you have given it to me." She pulled Hob to his feet and swept him into a hug; she released him, kissed his cheek, and sat down again. She turned to Nemain.

"Deaf as a post in fey matters, is he? I'm thinking the Mórrígan Herself put those words in his mouth."

Nemain, still with an oddly cautious expression on her face, said carefully, "You are going to use Milo against the Cousins as though he were a king bull of the wild cattle?"

Molly waved her hand dismissively. "Nay, child, think, think! I will use the wild white bulls themselves. I will send them, kings and bachelors both, against these vile hyena-men, and they will trample their blood into the earth."

AND WITH THAT, Molly, much cheered, emptied her mug of water onto the grass, and rose, and began making preparations to retire. Jack pulled down her bed in the wagon and set about spreading blankets. Molly sat on the narrow rear platform of the wagon, her feet dangling, and brushed out the four-foot silver length of her hair.

The others followed her example. Nemain made up their bed in the midsized wagon while Hob watered the draft animals and banked the fire. Jack whistled for Sweet-love; doors were closed and locked; shutters were opened partially on a chain.

Weary as they were, sleep came easily, with the fragrance of green growing things drifting in at the wagons' open windows, and the stream laughing quietly to itself at some private jest.

CHAPTER 20

Up the coast they went, the north–south road that they traveled veering inland somewhat. Several days' travel brought them to the river Lune, at this point a narrow lovely fast-running stream, tree-bordered, pouring between rock gates into pools, rushing over big boulders, dark cold water alternating with stretches of white-foaming rapids.

They crossed on a plank-paved bridge set on stone piers, the planks banging and creaking beneath the wagons, and turned west toward the coast. The next day brought them to the inn.

The inn was known as Warin's Inn, or Fulke's Inn; it had been owned at times by each of these men, and though now the innkeeper was a certain Toly, local custom was stubborn, and insisted on using one or the other name of the two long-dead proprietors.

The inn was set on a side road, not far from the coast. The building nestled amid the deep shade of giant oaks, as though it wished to avoid notice. It was not overlarge, nor did it seem prosperous, but it was a place where people who wished to be overlooked might go for a while. Behind the building a slope led down through wooded land to the shoreline of a large bay, and above the wind in the leaves could be heard the swash of the Irish Sea.

In short order Molly had cornered Toly, halt in his left leg and dour in demeanor, and made her usual arrangements: meals at the inn, the beasts to the stables, but the troupe to sleep in the wagons. Again, in the interests of anonymity she paid in silver rather than barter for their services as musicians.

Jack and Nemain and Hob tended to their respective beasts, Hob taking a little extra time with Milo, so that first his wife and then Jack left the stable before him. There were two rows of open stalls—there was no door at the inner end of each stall. In the stall corresponding to Milo's, across the stable's central aisle, was tethered a handsome rouncey with a small well-shaped head and large eyes. One reason that Hob was slow in settling Milo in his stall, feeding and watering him, and brushing his coat, was that he would stop every now and then to admire the horse. Its coat, in the dull light of two candle lanterns, gave off a rich and subtle chestnut gleam.

And now, at the far end of the stable aisle, a man entered, swathed in a traveler's cloak, his face half-concealed by the tilt of a broad-brimmed hat. He came up to the horse's stall, and Hob, brush in hand, nodded politely. The man, about to enter the stall, turned and faced Hob. His eyes, cast in shadow by the hat brim, by some trick of the farther lantern glittered darkly; he stared into Hob's face. Then he turned, without a word or gesture of greeting, took a saddle blanket from the stall partition, and swung it over the horse's back. The blanket had some sort of complex design—Hob could not quite make it out—and from its edges dangled tassels, each one fashioned of several strips of leather.

The traveler threw a high-pommeled, high-cantled saddle over the saddle blanket, the leather heavily worked with vinelike designs. The horseman settled the saddle, tightened straps, and stopped. He stood a moment with one hand to the pommel, tugged his hat a little lower on his forehead, then turned very deliberately and again looked into Hob's face. Once more little could be seen of his face, but his eyes stared with such intensity they seemed to burn.

Hob, brushing more and more slowly as his fascination with the stranger grew, ceased entirely. He began to become angry: it seemed intentionally rude. The horse already had its bridle on; it was tethered by the reins. The man turned back, untied the reins, and began to back the horse into the aisle. As the horse came out, turning to face the doors away at the end of the aisle, the horseman paused and again glowered at Hob.

But this was too much. Hob was no child, to let this discourtesy pass. His expression grew stony, his hand flew to his dagger-hilt, and he prepared to challenge the lout. Immediately the man's demeanor changed, a smile spread across his face, and he backed away. "Excuse me, young master," he said in the most pleasant tones, tinted with an indefinable accent. He put a hand to his heart and bowed, and walked toward the front of the stables, leading the horse, who followed him at the end of the reins with outstretched neck. Hob, left confused and uncertain after this bewildering shift of attitude, contented himself with a curt nod.

Hob looked after the stranger, troubled; the man left the stable in a swirl of brown cloak, and Hob could hear but not see him mount, and the horse clatter out of the yard. He did not know what it was that had happened, nor what it meant, but there was a sudden weight on his heart, and he hurried through the rest of his chores, crossed the innyard, now sunk in dusk, and entered the common room with its yellow light, its promise of fellowship.

"And here's my hero knight-to-be," said Nemain, with just a hint of mockery. "We were after thinking you'd spend the night in the straw."

Hob was about to tell her of what had happened, but a strange reluctance gripped him. It was almost as though there was a chain on his tongue. He smiled and nodded and sat to his meat, but there seemed to be a shadow between him and his family, and he was moody and silent the rest of the evening.

CHAPTER 21

OB AWOKE BESIDE NEMAIN IN the midsized wagon. The partially open shutter by the bedside admitted a shaft of light from the rising moon, enough to show the fall of her hair that hid her face, the gleam of her shoulder peeping from the coverlet, even a hint of the faint freckles that adorned that shoulder. He absently stroked her hair, which elicited the kind of muffled, enigmatic sound that results when sleepers imagine that they speak.

He could delay no longer: he was summoned elsewhere, for he must . . . he must . . . no matter, it was a summons of some urgency, and right now his task was to get under way. He dressed quietly, and slipped out the door, closing it slowly lest the hinges squeak. A foot to the rope loop, and so to the ground, the steadily rising moon providing enough light to avoid a misstep, and off into the woods.

It was darker here under the trees, but Hob knew he had to follow the downhill slope, so that he could . . . he could . . . no matter, he would know what to do when the time came. From behind him came the sound of a dog barking, faint and growing fainter; he paid it no mind.

He lifted his feet carefully to avoid tripping on exposed roots and the tangle of undergrowth. The slope steepened, so that he braced himself by putting a hand to tree trunks, alternating between right and left. At last there was a push through a tangle of bracken, and he felt a breeze with the bracing scent of salt water against his face. Before him opened a huge empty bay, the tide full out, with the waterline perhaps seven miles distant, the damp sands glistening in the moonlight.

The bay was carved into sections by sandbars—some with the flat rock deposits called *skears*—and by deep gullies that the powerful tides had scoured out.

Hob began to hurry along the shoreline, his legs swishing through the coarse salt-loving grasses. He feared being late for . . . for . . . his appointment, his meeting. He was unsure about it, but just now he needed to concentrate on making all speed.

There was a dark circular mass on the slope down to the beginning of the damp and level sands, and as he tried to make out what it was, his ankle struck against something in the grass, and he tumbled to earth.

"Hob! Hob, where are you?" It was Nemain's voice, right beside him.

"I'm here," he answered, scrambling to his feet. He felt an odd annoyance. Where else would he be?

"What do you see?" Her voice was so close that he turned in a circle, but he was alone on the foreshore, the trees of the forest a good five yards away. Yet she sounded as if she stood next to him.

"I cannot see *you*," he said. "I'm by the bay. Where are you?"

"Hob!" she cried, but now her voice came from farther away, back the way he had come, and he looked up the beach, and saw her burst from the trees and come toward him at a run. Behind her, a moment later, Molly and Jack crashed through the fringe of brush at the tree line and ran after Nemain.

She pounded to a halt in front of him, and peered into his face. "Hob, what were you—" She put a hand to either side of his head and pulled him down to her, looking deep into his eyes.

"Ochone! Hob, you've been—" She kissed him open-mouthed, then stepped back and slapped him hard across the face. Slight as she was, she had trained with weapons under Molly, and a slap from her was no token gesture. His face burned and, shocked, he felt the ground moving under him. A feeling of wakefulness rushed in upon him, a change of perspective so intense that he staggered in place, but at that moment Molly and Jack reached him, and Jack gripped his arm till he steadied.

"What am I—why am I here?" he asked, though he had still a fading sense of an urgent appointment.

"It's for no good purpose," said Molly. She put a hand to his brow. "You're all right now, but there's some evil has called you out here."

From within the forest, directly behind them, came a bubbling falsetto cry, rising to a pitch of hysteria, then falling, then silent once more. A moment later there came a series of yelps, still within the trees, but away to the north; this was echoed by five or six separate voices, yipping in chorus to the south. Finally, from the central voice rose a mad swell of laughter, the mirth of a crazed goblin.

"And there's the ones who've lured you here, and moving toward us, to sweep us up like fish in this fisherman's net," said Molly, and she gestured to the dark circular mass, which Hob, peering in the moonlight, now saw was a round skin boat, over whose tether, hidden in the grass, he had tripped.

Molly was turning in place, looking for a refuge, but they were trapped: the goblin-haunted forest behind them, and before them, the wide sweep of empty sand and then the sea. She was cursing in Irish under her breath as she turned. To run up or down the beach was useless: the line of hunters was too widespread, the gibbering and howling now up and down the curve of bay-bordering forest. There must be a good two dozen of them—hard-to-kill werebeasts, and Molly and Nemain without spell or potion prepared, and even the mighty Jack overmatched.

Abruptly Molly faced the bay. She looked up at the moon, she bent and squinted out at the distant line of water, the edge of the Irish Sea, six or seven miles distant. She whipped out her ring-pommel dagger and sliced through the coracle's tether line.

"Jack, Hob! Take a side of this wee boat and carry it. It's as far and fast as we can that we must run toward yon sea!"

Hob looked out at the expanse of sand, the little pools of seawater scattered at random, and the darker stubs of the skears dotted here and there. They would never make it to the sea; already the devils' choir behind them was perceptibly nearer.

"But, Mistress, we'll never make—" he began.

"Go!" said Molly, pointing to the skin boat, and Nemain put a hand to his back and pushed. Two steps took him to the left side of the boat, and Jack took station on the right. Hob grasped the boat's rim, a roll of skin about a wicker framing rail, and the two men stood with the boat, which was far lighter than it looked. They began to trot, then to run, the women running easily beside them, Nemain beside Jack and Molly beside Hob.

Down the slope of dry sand and coarse marram grass, and onto the flat wet surface of the bay. The outgoing tide had left this soft, unstable surface, which grew alarmingly shifty as they progressed. Hob concentrated on matching stride with Jack, and they fell into a rhythm, not an all-out sprint, for the boat hindered them, but a good steady run. A paddle in the bottom of the craft rattled and rolled with every step. Hob felt the alternating slurp of wet sand and the splash of the shallow tidal pools; once he had to spring up and run on a low rock upcropping, then down again, sinking to the ankle in the viscous sands beyond.

He had to make an effort to free his ankle, and then the run turned to nightmare as the treacherous and clinging surface slowed them to a dreamlike stagger. The moon cast a sheen across the whole waterlogged surface, making distances hard to determine, and once he slipped and lost his hold on the coracle. A wasted moment: getting back into position, picking up speed, and then regaining the rhythm with Jack, the two running like yoked oxen.

All at once there was a change in the chorus behind them. Hob risked a glance over his shoulder. They had covered perhaps a half mile, and he could just make out the hunch-shouldered, misshapen brutes emerging from the forest line, their huge round eyes glinting in the moonlight like Satan's own pack of hounds.

Hob faced forward and tried to coax more speed from his legs, already aching. Behind him there was a continuous gobbling, a sort of ghastly mewing. The sound broke: there was silence and a rough barking. He looked again, just a snatched peek, and turned back with a picture of the pack lifting paws and shaking them, and trotting back and forth sideways, reluctant to advance into the muck. Seen in profile, some, with heads held high, showed the slant of their bodies down the long neck, to the sloping hindquarters and short hind legs. Others had their heads held low, lending them a ghoulish high-shouldered skulking appearance.

Saint Nicholas, make them fear to follow us, he prayed silently, addressing the saint who was known to save travelers *in extremis.* But even as he thought this, the eerie shrieking resumed, and a third glance behind showed the monsters venturing out on the sands, their thick pawpads and blunt claws doing surprisingly well with the unstable footing.

He ran on, his legs beginning to burn, his fingers cramping where they clutched the coracle rail. He looked over. Jack ran easily: where physical effort was called for, he had few equals. Molly and Nemain were keeping pace, the women looking back from time to time to judge the distance between themselves and their pursuers.

For a time they stayed ahead, then the advantage in traction and stability of four legs over two began to tell, and besides, the hyenas were not burdened with a boat, however light. Hob wondered again—did Molly think they could reach the sea and float to safety? They had barely covered half the way to the water, or perhaps even less—the moonlight, the struggle for strength and breath, and the shimmering sands made it hard to tell how far ahead their goal was. Perhaps they had come only a couple of miles from the shore.

He looked back again. The pack had halved their lead and were running full out with their rocking gallop, tongues lolling out over their teeth, disturbingly like monstrous human teeth, a wide semicircular grin with huge fangs set in the corners, rows of smaller teeth in the front, and two lines of craggy tearing teeth along the sides. Their heads swung from side to side as they loped; their powerful legs bounded over the sand; their round eyes, sloping down at the outside corners, gave their expressions an odd melancholy that contrasted with their demented smiles. They were creatures sprung from the tales told to frighten children into obedience.

Molly was looking up and down—up at the moon, and

quickly down to avoid a misstep. Finally she slowed and stopped, as did Nemain. The men slid to a halt with their burden. Molly looked behind, coolly gauging the oncoming threat, then up again at the moon, then out to sea.

"A wee bit farther," she said, and set off again. They ran for a few hundred more paces, and then she stopped again and said, "Here!" She made a patting motion at the boat: *Put it down.* They dropped it with a moist thump.

"Everyone in," said Molly, stepping into the boat. The others followed suit, and sat when she sat. Hob looked back along the way they had come, somewhat farther than he had thought before, and said a quick and silent paternoster. He did not see how he would live through the next hour. He had the utmost faith in Molly, but they were sitting at ease at ground level while a dogpack from Hell lolloped toward them.

He looked over at Nemain. He said in an anguished voice, "I have led you into this."

"Hush; you're after being snared by that *geasadóir*'s spells, and there's no blame to you in that," she said.

Molly was looking up at the moon, and now she said, looking at the hideous creatures running awkwardly but swiftly toward them, "We will come to no harm this night, Hob. Wait and watch."

Perhaps two breaths later, the hyenas appallingly close, Hob became aware of a hissing rush of sound. He looked over the side of the coracle. Beside the boat was a groove in the waterlogged sand, and now there was water in the groove, and it was flowing like a tiny river, foaming toward the shore. A shushing roar began to rise around them, although he could not place its source. The hide boat shifted a little under him.

He peered at the sands around them. There were patches that now shimmered with a skin of water. The boat began to rise and spin in place: they were afloat! Molly handed Jack the paddle and the dark man attempted to scull with it, heading them away from the land, and from the onrushing pack. The water was still too shallow to paddle in, though, and Jack began to use it as a pole, shoving against the bottom.

Water was filling the empty bay at an astonishing pace. Rushing landward through channels beneath the sand, gouts of water erupted here and there in spouts, and rather than proceeding only inward from the Irish Sea, the tide rose all about them. From the beginning it came in faster than a man could run; now it was pouring in faster than a fast horse could run, rising before and behind and all around the pack, which had halted in consternation.

Already the surface was up to the fur on their underbellies, and almost as one they turned and made for the shore. The water tangled in their legs; the weight of the water slowed and fatigued them. Now they began to leap in bounds toward safety, coming almost free of the water for a moment and then coming down, snorting and choking as their snouts dipped beneath the rippling tidewater.

But the speed and weight of the water, the irregularities of the bay bottom, began to generate whirls and eddies, irresistible currents that swept the pack from their feet and swung them in great circles, exhausting even their unnatural strength. The coracle was spinning as well despite Jack's efforts to exert control, but the light little craft rode safely over the ripples, secure as a seabird floating on the ocean swells.

There was a deeper note now in the roar of the waters. Hob looked out toward the Irish Sea. A great wave, stretching from side to side of the broad bay, was thundering toward the shore: the tidal bore, the main edge of the waters dragged upshore by the all-conquering moon. After what seemed a long time, but was not, the wave reached them and loomed over the coracle. Hob had a moment to say another unvoiced prayer to St. Nicholas, patron of sailors, and one to the Blessed Mother, and then the skin boat slid with not a bit of fuss up the ridge of seawater; the crest passed beneath them, smooth as cream, and swept away shoreward.

With the hyenas it was not so kind. Hob saw the heads, like parodies of dogs or bears, bobbing in the swirl of water, and then the wave trod them under, and the surface was clear. They had been pushed under and, caught in the storm of underwater currents, did not resurface.

With the disappearance of the hyenas that had dotted the water, there was no need for Jack to keep fighting to put out to sea and the safety of the deep waters. He turned the boat and began to scull toward shore. The tide pushed them shoreward, increasing their speed; the trees of the forest, at first but a dark mass on the shore, rapidly grew closer with every stroke of Jack's paddle. In a very short while they were pulling the boat up the strand, the coracle's leather bottom sliding with a crunching hiss over the damp sand.

Molly had them carry the boat to where its broken tether

was still floating in the shallow water about its anchoring stake. They set it down where they had found it, and she retied the severed halves of the tether, her nimble fingers fashioning a stout clever knot.

She stood up, brushing damp sand from her hands. She bent again and gave a hard pull at the tether, satisfying herself that it would hold. "For I'll not be having a fisherman come down to the bay, and find his livelihood missing," she said. "Although the ancient laws of Erin say: 'When fleeing from an enemy you may borrow a horse, a weapon, or a boat without permission of the owner.'"

CHAPTER 22

THEY MADE THEIR WAY BACK TO the wagons, where Sweetlove, sleeping with Jack—curled on top of Jack, in fact—in the small wagon, had detected Hob's departure: her acute hearing noticed at once the closing of the middle wagon's door, the creak of the rope loop, Hob's fading footsteps. Dogs are averse to unusual occurrences, especially at night, when all the pack should be denned up till sunrise. She had broken out in insistent objection, and Nemain, disturbed, feeling sleepily for Hob and encountering nothing, had come sharply awake, quickly ascertained that Hob was not merely outside relieving himself, and had run for Molly.

Between them they managed to arouse Jack, peacefully snoring through Sweetlove's din, and set off, following what the two women could barely describe to Hob: a sense that he had brushed this tree, or pushed this shrub aside, a sort of psychic scent left on things he had touched. All the while Nemain was calling to him with her thoughts, along the thin thread of soul that connects husband and wife, useful to such an adept as Nemain was becoming, and so strong had she become in the Art that even Hob, that least fey of men, heard "Hob, Hob, where are you?" as though she were beside him.

Now, arrived back at their wagons behind the inn, they released Sweetlove from the little wagon, and after her usual paroxysms of joy at greeting Jack anew, as though he had been gone for years, they took stock of their next move. It was decided that they were too tired to go on by night, and besides, Molly could not detect any lingering threat in the immediate vicinity. Jack, that old campaigner, insisted on setting a watch, and so he climbed up on the big wagon with some bedding and his war hammer, and then went down and scooped up Sweetlove. He could sleep lightly when he knew it to be necessary, and he had a good vantage point on the rooftop, and it would take enemies a moment to climb up there, at which point they would find Jack and his hammer waiting for them.

THE NEXT MORNING, they held a council of war at breakfast. Molly waited till the host's mother, a silent woman in her middle years, had deposited the creamy Lancashire cheese, dark bread, onion, and jacks of small beer, and had retreated from the common room, disappearing into the kitchen, before she began to speak. "Sure they're knowing of us now, and trying to lure Hob away by enchantment, and so perhaps to snare him like a coney."

"But, *seanmháthair*," said Nemain, "why seize Hob and not ourselves?"

" 'Tis no shame to you, lad," said Molly, "but consider: 'tis that sorcerer who's setting them on us, and he will know that Nemain and I will be the most powerful to resist his *bouda*'s spellcraft. And Jack—well, they sense that Jack is more than he seems, and that pilgrim blacksmith calling him 'Brother,' and he's dangerous enough as he is before he changes."

"If he's the least dangerous to them among us," asked Nemain, "why choose to kill him and not us?"

"I am not of a mind that they were to kill him at all, but to take him living, and crush every secret out of him: what we are doing, what it is that we know, and the like. We may have destroyed the war band they sent after us, and be safe for some little while till they realize no one is coming back to report, but we cannot stay still for long. They will come again; early or late, they will come again."

Hob roused himself from his lassitude, a lingering effect of last night's horror. "But, Mistress, we are to meet here with Monsignor da Panzano. . . ."

"I will give him one more day," said Molly, "for he may have news for us, and 'twould be good for him to know my plans, but those plans are laid, and not to be changed, and any road 'twill all come to naught if we are cornered here again, and with no tide to help us. We must call a meeting with the chieftains of the wild cattle. I've a hid-away meadow in mind, down a small boreen that runs through the forest, and we must be there soon, for time is running through our fingers like sand, and it may be that we'll be too late, and here is my appetite near destroyed with fretting."

Hob was watching her clever fingers building up, on a chunk of bread, a layer of rich cheese and a layer of onion. She lifted the slab to her mouth and took a hearty bite.

She hardly seemed apprehensive; indeed—except, perhaps, for her recent transient doubts about how she might defeat the *bouda*—she always seemed to know what to do.

This brought Hob to another question. He sat up straighter, frowning. "Mistress, how did you know what would happen, and even to the moment when it was safe to sit down in the boat and run no more?"

"I am after making it a concern of mine, these years past, to learn somewhat of every place I pass through, and this coast is known for its sudden and mortal tides."

"But to know, to the moment, when that tide would come roaring in—"

Molly looked at Nemain. The young woman took her husband's hand. "There's much that we're not allowed to say to a man and that's you as well, even you, sweeting. But we are priestesses of Herself, the Mórrígan, and we . . . feel . . . *feel* the moon and it pulling on the tides all the while, and we are guided by that, and that's all I can say to you of it."

CHAPTER 23

I T WAS THE VERY NEXT DAY THAT Monsignor da Panzano arrived with Father Ugwistan and, of course, Sinibaldo. The men seemed weary, and thinner than when last Hob had seen them—even the Berber, whom they had left less than a sennight ago; when they removed their cloaks and hung them to pegs, the garments engendered small clouds of road dust that hung in the air a moment, and slowly settled to the floor. They sat down wearily—Sinibaldo, as always, with his back to the wall—around Molly's table, eyeing the earthenware jug of barley beer with its beads and trickles of condensation.

"I am most pleased to see you, madam," said da Panzano. "From what I am hearing from Father Ugwistan—he is telling me this so-troubling tale, and we are rushing to come here, he is gasping as we are going along the roads—I am thinking, we will find them dead or taken."

The host himself, almost as silent as his mother, appeared and, unbidden, set mugs before the newcomers, and withdrew to the kitchen. Jack reached over, effortlessly lifted the heavy jug, and poured for the three.

Molly said, " 'Tis a fine place for food, and we about to eat, and you looking thin as a blind wolf. Will you be having a wee bit o' scran before we speak?"

"You do not comprehend me fully, madam. We all must away within the hour. A mug of this wretched beer, and—I will let Father Ugwistan tell you, that I may hear it twice, and note what I may have missed."

He sipped at his beer; Sinibaldo had not even touched his. The Berber priest, on the other hand, drank off half the mug, set his elbows on the table, and began. "The first and most urgent thing I must say, madam, is that the accursed Yattuy has set a group of these *bouda* on your trail; they are to kill or capture you."

Molly sat up straight and put both hands on the table. "And how large is this group, and when will they arrive?"

"I am walking in the outer . . . bailey, and I am telling my beads, and I hear three speaking together, one is beating iron flat on the anvil, so I miss a word here and there, but—"

"Swiftly, Father, swiftly!" hissed da Panzano.

"Ah, yes, yes. I have told you this part before, madam, when I warned you to flee the castle: the *bouda* are suspicious of you and your granddaughter. These three are saying that they heard that—I don't get the name, the forge is banging—one of the *bouda* is working and the two women from the wagons have come by, and looked at them immodestly, and touched their tools, and"—he nodded at Nemain—"the young one touched his hand, and he feels a shock, the feel of witchcraft, and then he sees them for the witches they are— they burned the tools you touched, you know—and he tells Yattuy, as I said he would. The Cousins are monsters, but Yattuy, he frightens me more. He sends a, a, *squad,* there are two twelves—four and twenty—and a leader; they are to find where you have gone, and to learn what you know, and who you have told. And then—well, then to do what they must.

"These leaders of the squads, they are not common *bouda.* Yattuy, he has captains, they are more trusted, they can control themselves, they control the *bouda* when they change to the hyenas, but they themselves do not always change. They have brought over some of their horses, and the leaders, the captains, ride them, so they may keep up with the other *bouda* when they are on four legs. When they are hyenas, they do not think so well; the captain tells them what to do, and when to change back. Then, after a bit, they are men again, they can think. They change back and forth easily, I think. But they need ashes from their forges to begin the change."

He had been speaking in a rush and now he had to pause for breath, and then he drank more beer.

"This Yattuy, is he ever changing to a hyena himself?" asked Molly.

Ugwistan looked at her for a moment as if she had asked the difference between the sun and the moon.

"No, no—Yattuy is not *bouda*." He spoke slowly and distinctly, tapping his forefinger on the table with each word: "He is a man who can control tenscore *bouda* with a word, with his eyes; he is like the centurion in the Gospels, he says to this one 'Go,' and he goes, and to that one 'Come,' and he comes—this is why I fear him even more than these terrible beast-men."

Hob asked him, "These horses of theirs—do they have tassels on their saddlecloths?"

"Yes, yes, in Marroch horse trappings are very beautiful; many ornaments, many. Tassels, yes."

"And 'twas only the one group the wizard sent after us?" asked Molly.

"One group, yes. And when I have heard all this, I haste to my meeting with Monsignor, and we come here."

"And we must go, now, all of us," said da Panzano in a grating voice.

"We must go soon, but 'twill be a day or two before they can get another . . . squad . . . after us."

Da Panzano said through gritted teeth, "They are *already* after— Excuse me, is it that my so-poor English has made me misunderstand you? Are you . . . did you say 'another'? Another squad? *Another*?"

"Sure I've destroyed the first one, so I have," said Molly, and Hob felt his face go stiff with the effort not to laugh. *She is quite enjoying herself,* he thought.

"Christ save us!" cried da Panzano. "Destroyed!" Father Ugwistan was gaping at Molly, and even Sinibaldo glanced at her before resuming his vigilant survey of the common room, the archway to the kitchen, the door to the outside, and around again.

"But how?" asked the Berber priest.

"I drowned them," said Molly quietly. The two men sat back a bit, as though to put some slightest distance between them and this woman; only now were they beginning to realize how dangerous she was, and they were beginning to be somewhat frightened of her. Sinibaldo did not move. It was hard to know what Sinibaldo would be afraid of, thought Hob.

"Then you can destroy the others?" the papal agent said eagerly.

"I can," said Molly as though it were a thing done every day. "But in a different way, and I'll be needing some help. Not much—a few horses, a place to put our beasts and wagons while we're about your task, a refuge afterward. But I can destroy the others."

Hob was trying to emulate Sinibaldo, and let nothing show on his face, certainly not amusement. He was thinking that it was only the other day Molly was in despair at what to do. And then if not for that skirmish at the cottage, and Milo acting so strangely, and that poor jest of his, she would still be at a loss, and without a proper answer to da Panzano, and perhaps of no further use to him, and perhaps again in peril from the Church. A string of good fortune, letting her stumble onto the answer.

And suddenly it all turned over in Hob's mind, and he saw it differently: they had stopped at the cottage to interfere, because Molly was a good woman, and would not skulk past, and then Milo's odd courage, and Hob's own jest, not typical with him—one could as easily say that the Mórrígan had guided them in each step, had impelled Molly to rescue the cottagers, Hob to fly into a righteous rage, Milo to save his Hob, Nemain to defend Milo, Hob to begin teasing. He stopped himself—he was drifting into . . . apostasy? Was he losing his faith?

I will be as Jack, and not trouble myself any more with this, he said firmly to himself, and resolutely rejoined the conversation, which had turned to specifics—Ugwistan had found the location where the hyenas were to gather on the eve of the attack, and Molly and the papal legate were deep into the planning of all that must be done that night.

And now Father Ugwistan had produced a rough map showing an obscure valley, awkwardly placed between encircling and very steep ridges, thickly wooded; part of the king's forests, and yet not so very far from the Thames-side meadow where the proposed meeting between king and barons would be.

"This map nearly cost me my life, madam," said the Amazigh. "Three of the Cousins were discussing it, and I nearby; by the grace of God the Angelus had just rung, and I sank down on my knees and pretended to say my *Ave*s, while—God forgive me—I am straining my ears to hear. They are of Yattuy's inner guard: chieftains of the *bouda,* and they are bending over a map that he has drawn in the dirt with a stick. The map shows where they meet, and they are speaking of when, and when they must leave Chester to arrive there, and the like.

"Yattuy has been there earlier, but is gone by now—I have told you, I dare not go near him! So: they are on the other side of the . . . anvil, yes, the anvil, and I am on this side, with my ear straining to hear, and there is a cry from inside the tent, they need help with the barrel in which is the water to quench the steel—that much water becomes very heavy, and—"

"Yes, yes, Father, please do come to the point," snapped da Panzano, a man not fond of distractions from the business at hand.

"Your pardon, Monsignor," said Father Ugwistan, his good nature quite undaunted by the rebuke. "The bell has ended, and I stand up and pretend to stagger a little, from kneeling, and I take a step behind the anvil and put a hand on the anvil to steady myself and bend to take a long look at the map; I tell myself, 'Ugwistan, seize this map with your eyes and forget nothing,' although I am terrified that they will return, and then I step back to the other side of the anvil—I am still holding my beads, you understand, and at that moment they step back out from the tent.

"There is an angel that must be guarding me, for another moment and I would be found; I am sure they would have dragged me into the tent and killed me on the instant. But now they see me, I hold my beads, I am where they last saw me, and I am looking off at nothing. Then I wander away. But I am not certain that some other *bouda,* in one of the other tents, has not seen me, and so I come away the next morning, and seek out Monsignor da Panzano."

"And when will this all come to pass?" asked Molly.

"A little more than a fortnight and a half from now, madam, a day past the full moon," said the Berber.

Molly turned to da Panzano. "I'm after mentioning that we'll need a refuge: Is there a place near this valley that you know, where we can meet with you, and where we can leave our wagons, and our beasts, in safety?"

"There is a Benedictine monastery a few miles away; I will arrange that the guesthouse is empty, and I will be there myself." He spoke to Father Ugwistan. "As for you, Father, I am concerned to have you return to the South—I would not have you taken at this hour, and the plan forced from you; you are to journey to Durham, and remain there, unseen for the moment."

"We will need four horses to ride," said Molly.

"I will have them ready for you at the monastery," said da Panzano. Drawing a stick of fine charcoal from his pouch, he took Father Ugwistan's map and added the direction and distance to the monastery. He looked up when he had finished and asked bluntly, "But how will you destroy these so-many evil ones?"

"Nay, I'll not be telling you that, for I'd not be wanting to trouble your sleep, nor do I want you to interfere in any way. Do what you must do, make ready what you must make ready." She raised her mug to da Panzano: " 'Tis what you said to me the day we met: 'Listen for a short hour. Learn to trust me.'"

CHAPTER 24

A DAY LATER THEY WERE ON THE road north, for most of the wild cattle were in the north of England and the south of Scotland, and while Molly did not feel they need venture so far, she also felt that it did no harm to get somewhat closer before making her summons, and at any rate she had the very place in mind.

The wagons descended a gentle grade, and the road leveled out. Here it went between two low hills, green with long grass, bright with pink lady's smock, said to be sacred to the fairies; close by the road were meadowsweet and the white flowers of cow parsley. Hob could see bees moving from blossom to blossom, and there was a perceptible buzz that hung in the air. The road curved around the hill to the right; the buzzing increased in volume.

As they came around the hill the view widened; the road ran away to the horizon. To the left forestland came up to the very edge of the trail. To the right was a meadow, in which clouds of flies rose and fell, rose and fell, about the remnants of bodies: both men and horses. There had been a small vicious battle here: perhaps twelve dead men and half as many horses lay amid the grasses and the wildflowers, but it was hard to tell. None of them was whole; animals had been at them. Bones, most of them crushed to the point of splintering, and pieces of meat and bits of offal lay everywhere, covered with flies. Blood soaked the grass. Scattered here and there were discarded weapons; an untouched hoof and another that had been shattered between monstrous jaws; a mailed glove, a hand still within.

The knights had been despoiled of their armor, their weapons, even their clothes, save for those pieces of steel that were too mangled to be of use, those bits of clothing too torn and bloodied. Even the horses had been stripped of saddles, bridles, saddlecloths.

Hob drew a fold of his shirt across his nose, and began to pull strongly on the guide rope, urging Milo to greater speed, for the odor of corruption now struck them with brutal intensity. For once the ox needed no urging: his large and handsome eyes rolled from side to side in fear; he snorted his alarm at the scent of death; he quickened his pace.

"Hob, 'ware the road!" cried Molly sharply, and Hob tore his eyes from the carnage in the meadow to the path ahead. Metal glinted here and there in the beaten dirt of the road. He halted Milo with some difficulty, and Molly set the brake.

Hob went a few paces ahead, and bent to retrieve a curious piece of iron. It was twisted into a tangle by the smith, a knot that sprouted four sharpened spikes, so cunningly arranged that however it was thrown to the ground, one spike always pointed upward.

Hob made to throw it aside, but Molly said, "Nay, *a rún*, bring it here." He handed it up, and she turned it over and over in her strong white hands. She looked away, her eyes unseeing, but her hands feeling over each twist and branch and point of the iron.

"But what is it, Mistress?"

" 'Tis a caltrop, a cruel way to stop a horse and its rider, the poor beast stepping on the spike and falling crippled to the ground."

And still her hands went on tracing its convolutions. By now Nemain and Jack had set their brakes and come forward to see why the caravan had stopped.

"Should I clear the road, Mistress?" asked Hob, but almost at the same time, Nemain asked, "What is it you're seeing, *seanmháthair*?"

"There's something—'tis faint, 'tis faint—but I'm thinking that we'll have need of these one day. It's a sense that they have some place in our lives, and though that's all I can tell, I'm loath to pass them by, as one would not walk past a gold coin and leave it in the dust. Nemain, give your man here one of those stout sacks from Jack's wagon, and Hob, do you gather every one, and we'll be bringing them with us."

Nemain trotted back along the line of wagons, and Molly reached down to hand Hob the caltrop. Hob went ahead down the road, gathering the vicious things, walking from one side of the road to the other. There were many more than he had at first thought, and in the end he had to tie off the bag and jog back for another one from Nemain, and he filled that one too.

He was walking back with the second one when Molly stopped him. "Would you ever let us hold it a moment?" she asked. He handed it up. She placed the bag on her lap and closed her eyes. Nemain came up beside him. He looked a question at her. She whispered in his ear, "She's having more of the second sight than anyone I've even heard tell of; far more than myself."

Hob did not know what to say to that, so he just nodded.

Molly opened her eyes. "Sure it's holding that great lot of them that's making it clearer. They're to be important to us."

"In what way, Mistress?" asked Hob.

"At this moment I know not, but they'll be, in some way, the tipping of the balance of life and death to one or more of us, lad; the balance of life and death."

CHAPTER 25

ON A ROADSIDE BOULDER, MOSS-covered, set amid gorse bushes and backed by an old oak, sat a red squirrel, nibbling at something held between its delicate hands. When Hob and Milo came up the road, the ox's hooves thudding on the packed dirt, the wagons creaking and rumbling behind, the squirrel put its meal in its mouth, turned, and sprang to the trunk of the oak. It ran lightly up the wood to its drey; the twig-built nest was snug in the angle where the first thick branch left the trunk. It disappeared into the dome-shaped structure, then reappeared in the drey's round portal, emitting a series of scratchy barks: it was scolding them.

"Stop a moment, Hob," called Molly, and Hob pulled Milo to a halt, and down along the line the other wagons came to a stop as well. Molly was looking around her.

"Sure, there was a squirrel the last time I passed yon stone," said Molly, "years ago, and this one—perhaps a descendant!—reminding me of it, so that I'm looking at it, and seeing that familiar boulder, and that oak behind it. . . . There should be a branching road just ahead, around that stand of beech, and down that road. . . . Well, let us see."

They set forth again, and it was as Molly remembered: a road led off to the east, a smaller, rougher road, but wide enough for the wagons.

"Turn off on this path, Hob *a rún*," said Molly, "and we'll see if my memory's not gone amiss, and then we'll see . . . what we'll see."

Hob was swinging along at his usual pace, just the right speed to match Milo's steady but not overswift plodding, when without warning he stopped. Milo went on a pace or two before he stopped as well, the big head swinging around to see what Hob was about.

Hob was looking at a configuration of three birches in an otherwise grassy field; they looked familiar. And that low rock outcrop: surely he had seen that before. A flood of memories poured through him, things he had long forgotten—a group of boys up on that outcrop, struggling to push one another off onto the grass a few feet below, the winner to be the last boy on the rock.

And over that next hill should be St. Edmund, the village where, from the age of four to the age of eleven, he had been raised by old Father Athelstan. He turned and looked at Molly but could not speak for the moment, overwhelmed with a tide of conflicting emotions.

"Father Ugwistan's telling us that the meeting with the barons, 'twill not be so soon as we'd thought," she said. "And then I'm realizing where our footsteps have brought us, and thinking 'tis a visit you should have made before this, and—well, 'tis hard not to feel one's meant to go to see Father Athelstan again."

They went on, and in the distance, Hob could see a boy running down a hill toward the village, and soon thereafter the church bell began to toll. They passed fields planted by the villagers; wood-rail fences began; and a young man with a hoe, already looking along the road at the sound of the bell, came walking briskly over to the fence. He put a hand on the top rail, nodding in greeting. Hob looked at him closely: this sturdy young farmer, could it be—

"Dickon!" exclaimed Hob, halting Milo and going to the fence. Here was one of his playmates, one of the very boys whom he had striven to push from the top of the rock, as they had striven to throw him down.

"Hob? Is it ye, i' truth?"

"Yes, we've come back to see Father Athelstan, and, well, everyone! Is, um, is Father well?"

"He's well, he is, but verra old. We heard you were away to do grand things, 'tis what Father said, any road, and then we thought ye might be dead. And we've had a bit o' trouble here as well, that's why Sexton is ringing the bell: we've a boy on watch, and he's announced ye ahead of time. But come and see everyone. . . ." His face fell a bit. "Well, owd Wybert has died, as well as Gammer Madge, but I'm thinking most o' the others ye knew are still on live."

He propped the hoe against the fence, and clambered over. He embraced Hob and clapped him on the back a few times, and was introduced to Molly, who immediately brought out a streak of shyness in Dickon, which only increased when he was introduced to Hob's lovely wife. He shook Jack's hand, the dark man reaching down from the wagon, and the whole group set off for the village, perhaps a quarter mile down the road.

As they came into the tiny main street, with its few wattle-and-daub houses, and the little rectangular church of St. Edmund, built of stones dug from the fields so long ago, the bell ceased ringing in the squat church tower. Folk were coming out from their houses and in from the fields, at first fearful and then delighted at this harmless relief from the sameness of village life.

"Eadward! Margaret! Beatrix! And here's Michael!" The young men and women crowding around Hob were reaching out to touch him, to shake his hand, to pat his back: his former playmates. And somewhat more restrained, standing back a bit, were those who had been older when he left. Seven or so years had wrought some changes. Those who had been unmarried men and women were now young fathers and mothers; those who had been middle-aged were now becoming elderly, and those who had been quite old were now frail and ancient, or had been carried through the lych-gate into the little churchyard.

The wagons were halted, with their brakes on, in the

village square, and Molly and Nemain and Jack were down from the wagon seats, and stretching a little, just standing there with Hob amid the gathering villagers. Hob was kept busy introducing the village folk to his new family. Folk initially in awe of Molly's unmistakably queenly appearance were soon thawed by her sweet smile and her pleasant manner; Nemain drew admiring glances from the young men and somewhat less enthusiastic ones from the young women; and everyone was a little afraid of Jack, even with Sweetlove under his arm.

One side of the village square was given over to the church, and next to it, set back from the road a little, was the priest house. The door opened and out came a young priest, supporting Father Athelstan with a hand beneath his left elbow and another about his shoulders. Hob stared. Here was the man who had been as a father to him. Hob had, as children do, thought Father Athelstan to be very old, when he was merely old; now that the priest was somewhat older, somewhat frailer, he did not seem so very different to Hob.

"God save all here!" he cried as he approached the wagons with small stiff steps, the young priest matching his gait.

He came up to Hob and Hob by sheer instinct put his arms around him; the priest patted his back and pulled away to look at him.

"But look what a tall man you have become, my dear child!" He turned to Molly and took both her hands in his. "It is as you said, dear lady; he has flourished in your care. Many a night I have asked Our Lady to take special care of him, and I cannot help but think you have acted in her place."

Molly smiled at him. " 'Tis the truth: he's after growing into a fine young man, and married to my granddaughter no less, and it's promised by more than one great knight of the North Country that they will see him knighted."

The old priest regarded Hob again. "I had hoped for a quieter path for him, perhaps a scholar, in the bosom of Holy Mother Church." He turned and put his hand on the young priest's shoulder. "This is Father Eustace, whom the bishop has sent to help me, and he is like my own right hand; I could not care even for this little flock without him. He is also a keen scholar, and I hope one day to see him advance in the Church."

"God and Mary with you," the young priest said quietly, looking around at the newcomers.

Father Eustace had a pleasant, open Saxon face, thick-fingered hands, and the general appearance of a farm la-borer; Hob thought he did not look much like a scholar, but then again Father Athelstan would often counsel against giving too much importance to appearance instead of virtue.

Here was kindly old Father Athelstan, with a mild-faced assistant, his "right hand" whom he hoped to sponsor in the Church; what a contrast, thought Hob, with the urbane and sinister da Panzano, and his even more sinister assistant Sinibaldo, to whom he also referred as his "right hand."

"But come in, and refresh yourselves," said Father Ath-elstan, turning toward the priest house and tottering a bit, as one whose balance is unsteady; Father Eustace put an arm about his shoulders for a moment, till the old man was secure, and then they made their slow way back to the priest house. Molly went after them, leaving the disposition of the wagons to the other three.

Dickon showed them where they could pull the wagons to the other side of the little square, which bordered on the commons; Milo, Mavourneen, and Tapaigh were turned out to graze on tethers in the field, and the wagons were chocked and their doors secured against mischievous children.

Dickon leaned close to Hob, punched him lightly on the arm, and said low, " 'Twill be a grand excuse for a feast; there'll be no more hoeing today, God be praised; and we've had two prosperous years, so there's bounty for the table."

"But you spoke of trouble?" said Hob.

Dickon's face darkened; he looked away, toward the hills that rose beyond the bell tower of little stone St. Edmund.

"I'm thinking that Father Athelstan will tell you of it; 'tis not my place to be discussing such matters, but your mistress—oh, Father told us much about her, after she took you away—will want to be told, and yourself—nearly a knight, our Hob!"

Hob gave him a little shove, as if to say, *You make too much of it,* but his friend's open admiration touched him, and for an instant he considered how it would have been to stay here among these friends, and live quietly without striving against monsters, and rise in the Church, or perhaps marry Beatrix, whom he had thought quite pretty till he saw Margery atte Well, his first brief love, and, of course, Nemain herself.

At last Hob and Nemain and Jack were free to join Molly in the priest house, while Dickon went off to organize a celebration. They crowded into the little house, Sweet-love at Jack's heels, and Hob looked around in wonder. All these familiar sights: the small rooms, the simple, even spartan, furniture, the old smoke-darkened crucifix over the fireplace.

He peeked into the little room that had been his bedroom; there was a larger cot there now, for Father Eustace, but the room looked much the same as it had during the years when he had lived there, an orphan dependent on the old priest's kind heart, and suddenly his eyes grew moist, and he surreptitiously swept a finger along one eye and then the other. Sir Robert the ferocious knight, he thought, mocking himself, and then it *did* seem humorous, and he felt better. Still, he looked around one last time, and then rejoined the others in the central room.

While Jack and the young couple were tending to the animals, Molly had taken the opportunity for a little privacy to consult with Father Athelstan about his health, and now she sent Nemain out again to fetch various remedies from the little wagon—jars of this and crocks of that—while she dictated proper use to Father Eustace, who wrote everything down in rapid Latin, scratching letters into the soft inner surface of a section of birch bark with an iron stylus. When he was done he rubbed charcoal into the scratches to darken the letters and make them stand out against the pale birch.

Nemain also had brought back a small cask of the *uisce beatha,* and when Father Athelstan suggested some wine for his guests, Molly countered with an offer of the fiery drink. Father Eustace produced small pewter mugs, and a health was drunk round. Almost at once there was a change among the six people gathered in the tiny room, an increased ease and sense of intimacy. They sat about on Father Athelstan's few chairs and a garden bench that Father Eustace had brought in, and Sweetlove, having determined that Jack was settled, and that no one was having anything to eat just yet, sat quietly at his feet; grew drowsy; slumped more and more; and finally turned around twice and lay down, placing her chin on Jack's foot. Soon she began emitting small high snores.

Outside there was some commotion: the sounds of crude tables being set up, and a bonfire being laid, by the men; the bustle of the women bringing out dishes and food and jugs of home-brewed ale.

Within the priest house Molly was giving a highly edited account of the last several years. She *did* manage to convey the eerie quality of some of the enemies they had faced, and touched upon Nemain's dispatch of a foreign swordsman and cowing of three drunken men-at-arms; and Hob's killing of a near-seven-foot knight who wielded a huge hand-and-a-half claymore, and Hob armed only with a dagger; and Jack's various martial exploits—all without once mentioning the Old Gods of Ireland or that Jack had been a shapeshifter. The two priests hung on her every word: no matter how uncanny her tale, no one would ever think Molly would lie.

"These are troubled times," said the old priest. "When folk go to market—folk here go to Little Bridekirk, 'tis our market town—we hear murmurs of unrest and rebellion, and skirmishing between the king and the barons, and mercenaries roaming the countryside . . . and worse, worse than mercenaries."

He sighed, and regarded his cup, and seemed disinclined to continue. A silence grew.

"Dickon spoke of trouble you had had," said Hob, to encourage the old priest to speak.

Father Athelstan looked up.

"Yes; we have had our experience with what I believe are demons loosed upon the countryside."

"What is it that you are telling us, then?" asked Molly.

The old priest made as if to speak, then paused and took a sip from his mug, and another.

"This is wonderfully good," he said, examining the amber liquid. "The Psalms tell us that wine cheers the heart of man. . . . Ah, well. We had a boy herding the village's goats—this is Thurstan John's-son. Hob may remember John's marriage to young Adelina; this is their child. Thurstan was up in the hills to the south with the goats, and he saw a bunch of men in hoods and cloaks on the road, and two on horseback, and they scattered things in the path, metal things, for they shone silver, and they went up and down the road strewing them as the farmers strew seed, and soon there were these metal things that covered the road from one side to the other, so that nothing coming around the curve of the path, and especially coming fast, could avoid encountering them.

"The hooded men then pushed into the deep bushes to one side of the road. And soon thereafter a party of knights and men-at-arms came along the road from the other direction, all mounted and riding fast around the bend, and the horses stepping on the things in the road, and screaming and falling, so that all was terrible confusion.

"And now from the bushes come these terrible animals, like none that the boy has seen before. There begins this horrid slaughter, the strange beasts irresistible, killing knights, soldiers, and their horses. Thurstan quickly turned the flock and went down the back slope as fast as he could, ran to me, and blurted out his story.

"Now this killing—one could not call it a battle—was out of sight, over the hills, but the road the knights were on, if you keep on it, is this very street outside the door. The nearest castle is two hours' ride from here; the shire reeve is also far; and after Thurstan had seen what he had seen, what use would either be? Old Wybert had just died, and between Wybert and myself we had guided the village, and so now 'twas up to me alone. Should I ring the bell, and summon our people to safety, or would that bring the devils down upon us?

"At last I decided to bring all the people in; I had Sexton ring the bell, and we brought in all the folk and even the goats and sheep, all that we could, into the church, and James Carpenter came with a great leather bag of nails and his hammer and also his little hammer and his old hammer—the head was sturdy but the handle broken in half, but one could use the head by itself. . . .

"Where was I? Ah, James gave out nails and sawn boards and short lengths of logs split in half, and all the young men under his direction nailed up every door and window. We lit candles and I said Mass right there, and shrove everyone at once, and gave Communion. And then the laughter began."

Father Athelstan paused to rub his eyes with a blue-veined hand. Hob thought it was a beautiful hand, in its way, despite the irregular spots and discolorations of age: so gaunt that the tendons stood out like a net along the back, and the knuckles, slightly swollen, were as clearly articulated as a hawk's claw. Father Athelstan drank again: Molly's *uisce beatha* always lifted up the heart.

"Outside it was night, and that night, children, was filled with demons. We saw none—only Thurstan saw them, those strange animals, from a distance, but who else could it be? A storm of laughter, but the laughter of souls in torment, and at the doors, buttressed as they were with James Carpenter's planks and half-logs and the iron nails that Isaac Smith makes for him—you remember Isaac Smith, Hob: his daughter, Big Rachel Smith, would watch you while I was saying Mass, or hearing confessions, or—God bless me, where was I?"

He *was* very old, thought Hob, and a bit forgetful, and talkative, but he seemed still the alert and intelligent man who had been chaplain in two Norman castles when younger, and who had taught Hob all his lessons.

"At the doors, I was saying, even through all the wood of the doors and the further wood that had been nailed on, we could hear the *whuff* of creatures sniffing at the joins, and horrendous scratching at the planks, like the dogs of Hell, and laughing and tittering, very high, and growling, very low. I cannot think what they must look like, but the sound was the sound of Satan and his vassals.

"The women were crying, which set the bairns crying, and all the men talking in loud voices. I said to them—I was rather stern, I am afraid—'Be still! The Lord God will not desert you in your hour of need: you know this, so be comforted, and pray rather than making this unseemly noise in church,' and we prayed together, and after a while the men and women were calmer, and so also became the babes. And so we passed the night.

"But there were screams from outside: they killed all the horses and oxen, for we could not bring them into so tiny a church, and then, and then, they . . . left."

"Left?" asked Hob.

"We heard these terrible noises; they seemed to go on forever, and then they ceased. The next morning James and two of his apprentices climbed into the bell tower and removed the boards from one of the arches; the village was empty outside. Folk worked to open the doors, and found not only had every horse and cow been killed, but they had been eaten down to the hooves and bones, and these were cracked and splintered as though by giant wolves, or giant bears—or by Satan's dogs.

"We lived in terror for many days; horses and cows were lent to us, for the plowing and for milk and cheese, by the bishop and by the castle, and we were just able to have enough. The bishop thought it might be demons, but sent as punishment for the village's sins—my little Saint Edmund's!—and he dispatched Father Ronald, known for his piety, to cleanse the community. Father Ronald said Mass, and prayed all around the outskirts of the village, and blessed everyone, and left.

"The castle thought it was wolves, and sent a hunting party to sweep the valley: three knights and a group of men-at-arms and a huntmaster, as well as beaters and dog handlers. They found nothing, although we showed the hounds the prints, to give them the scent. Giant doglike prints, but not dogs, unless they were the Evil One's dogs. Yet the knights were scornful, I could tell, though they hid it beneath their courtesy. Still, as I have said, both church and castle saw fit to lend us the horses and cows we needed to live. Certes, this is excellent liquor, my dear lady."

This last was said after another sip. Father Athelstan was calm, even telling this tale of horror, and Hob could very easily envision him, by example and chastisement, quieting a churchful of terrified villagers. Now, looking at the old priest with adult eyes, Hob could see him, not as the mild and boring teacher of Norman English and Church lore, but as a remarkable man of force and intellect invisible to a child, a man capable of leading others during a crisis, a man who did not lose his nerve, even surrounded by devils. And, thought Hob, he lived simply, but he was a man who seemed to take a keen enjoyment in life.

Sweetlove chose this moment to waken, and to sit up, yawning, jaws wide and pink tongue curling at the tip. Father Athelstan put a hand to Father Eustace's shoulder, and heaved himself up; he shuffled across to Sweetlove, and bent to pet her.

"Father," began Hob, intending to warn the old priest that Sweetlove did not care for attention from anyone but Jack, but Father Athelstan put out a bony hand and placed a palm alongside Sweetlove's face, his thumb caressing her ear. She tilted her neck and leaned into his hand, and he remained bent over, and petting her, for some little while, and she gave every sign of pleasure.

It might be from sleepiness that she's so docile, thought Hob, *but I believe that there are some people that one senses one can trust, like Father Athelstan, or like Molly, for that matter, and she just trusts him. She'll let Molly pet her, and sometimes Nemain, and once in a fortnight she'll let me pet her, but no one else but Jack, till now.*

"A lovely little dog," said the priest. He straightened with a groan, and resumed his seat.

"Thank you, daughter," he said to Nemain, who had refilled his cup. "But I fear to think of you all, our Hob and his new family, traveling the while these monsters stalk the king's roads."

Hob looked at Molly: he desperately wanted to reassure the old priest, but he would not dare to say a thing lest it put the others in danger or, worse, cause their quest to fail.

But, as she so often had, Molly surprised him.

"These demons that you heard . . ." she began, and paused.

"Yes, my lady?" said Father Athelstan.

"This is not to leave this room," said Molly. "I would have you swear not to speak of it."

Puzzled, Father Athelstan nodded. "I swear by my hope

of salvation." This was as serious an oath as he could have uttered.

"And young Father Eustace as well," said Molly.

"I swear by the Cross," said Father Eustace.

"It's hunting them that we are, and soon we'll be destroying them, and ourselves having destroyed more than a score of them so far. I tell you this that you do not live in fear. Be cautious for a fortnight or two, and then you may live as before."

The priests sat in astonishment for a bit. Father Athelstan looked from Molly to Hob.

"Our Hob? You are hunting demons? God bless my soul! I . . . I cannot picture it. But you tell me this young woman has killed a swordsman? And our Hob has killed a giant knight? You are as creatures of legend, sprung from the shadows!" He beamed at them.

And yet, thought Hob, the old priest, strong of mind, clear of thought, secure in his faith, received tidings of the strange doings of Molly and her troupe with far less difficulty than the worldly da Panzano, or the martial Sir Odinell. He saw Molly for her essential goodness and honesty: he did not doubt her tale, nor did he doubt that she was out to do good and not to do ill.

"We came upon the place of that battle," said Molly. "There was not much left for burying, and all the bones, no matter how big, broken; this sits well with what we know of these creatures."

"But what do they here?" asked Father Eustace. "Have they broken out of Hell?"

" 'Tis that I know, but may not say," said Molly. "To tell you would be to entangle you in matters dangerous to you and your flock, and 'twould not help against this evil atall. Be content; be wary for a fortnight; be discreet. Reassure your villagers, but vaguely. Caution everyone not to speak of this with strangers."

There was a diffident knock upon the priest-house door. Father Eustace went to answer it, and they could just hear Dickon's voice murmuring outside: the words "Our Hob," and the word "feast."

CHAPTER 26

FATHER ATHELSTAN CALLED OUT to his young assistant, "Tell Dickon we'll be there in a moment, and tell him tomorrow there'll be twice as much hoeing for him to do!" But this last was said with a chuckle.

He turned to Hob. "I cannot think how you are to go about destroying these things, that so completely overwhelm belted knights. If I need be so discreet as not to mention our assault by these helldogs to any outsider, should I then be bold enough to inquire about your methods? Advise me, Hob, now that you are a grown man, and a husband, and a knight-to-be at that."

Hob thought a moment. "Perhaps it would be better were you not to ask, Father."

"Then will I not," said the priest. "Let us see what mischief Dickon has stirred up." He struggled to his feet, and Father Eustace handed him his staff, a length of wood elaborately carved by James Carpenter, with vines and leaves climbing up the barrel. Father Athelstan had told his parishioners the story of the martyred St. Edmund, the patron saint of England, and how the Vikings of the Great Heathen Army had tossed the saint's head into a forest, and how searchers for it had found it, undecayed, held between the paws of a wolf who called, "Here! Here!" The cunning James had terminated the staff with a knob in the form of this wolf, with the head of the saint peering out from between its paws.

Armed with this staff, the old priest was more agile, and led them to the door, Sweetlove trailing at Jack's heels, and out into the square, where tables had been set along one side. On the tables stood the contributions of the entire village: large tureens, steaming gently, some filled with a slurry of turnip, garlic, and pork sausage, others with hard-boiled eggs, and still others with a porray—leeks and ham seethed in milk; loaves of dark bread; and from the various alewives, seven barrels of ale from as many households.

To one side of the square was a bonfire that had been constructed but not lit—it was late afternoon, and the day pleasant. At sundown it would be lit for light and warmth, for here in this little valley, surrounded by wooded hills, the air tended to be cooler than the season would indicate.

The priests, the visitors, and then the villagers took their places to either side of the line of trestle tables; the benches filled rapidly, and the boys and girls of the village served rounds of bread to be used as plates, and ladled portions from the tureens onto these trenchers, all under the direction of Gammer Agnes, the village's senior woman, white-haired, bent, and keen-eyed as a peregrine falcon. As with Father Athelstan, to Hob she did not appear in the least different. She circled the table with the aid of a cane, also whittled by the carpenter, and came up to Hob, who kissed her hand and introduced her to Nemain, which prompted the old woman to treat his wife to a flood of reminiscences about Hob-the-boy. Of course Hob-the-husband could foresee a lifetime of teasing from the mischievous Nemain based on his boyhood trespasses.

"But sit, sit! Your wife is hungry and you stand here prattling," Gammer Agnes said to Hob, who had hardly said a word. "Geoffrey! There are empty trenchers down there— are you dreaming, child?"

Hob sat midbench with Nemain on his right, and a boy whom he did not know ladled a heaping portion of turnip and garlic and pork sausage onto his trencher, while a girl— could that be Osanna, Richard's baby sister?—filled the carved-wood mug at his elbow with barley beer.

Jack regularly plucked pieces of pork sausage and other delicacies from his trencher and held them down below his knee, whereupon Sweetlove would emerge from under the bench and delicately pluck them from his fingers. At some point three of the village dogs, rambling around the table soliciting alms, discovered her and objected to her presence, barking at her and snarling.

Terriers are often unaware that they are small, and Sweetlove was no exception: she stalked forth from the shelter of the bench, stiff-legged, her nose wrinkled up, exposing her formidable teeth, while a hideous grinding snarl came from deep in her chest. The village dogs, startled, retreated three or four paces out of sheer prudence. But they were much larger than she, and there were three of them, and so Jack's big hand came down and swept Sweetlove from her feet.

He set her firmly on his lap, stuffed pork sausage into her mouth, effectively distracting her and not incidentally silencing her snarl. Behind him, the trio of dogs, unable to see her, sheltered as she was by Jack's broad back, lost interest and wandered away.

So the afternoon wore into evening, with stories and jests and memories traded back and forth. Molly, always eloquent, told stories of their traveling life, tales of inns and castles, as she had at the weir-tender's cottage, and wide-eyed children—and their parents as well—hung on every word.

Gradually the tureens emptied, and the fourth butt of ale was finished and the fifth broached. The sun hung low above the forested ridges to the west, and dark-gold shafts of light shot between the trunks of trees, black against the blaze of sun.

Five men left the square and returned with instruments: a large and a small drum, two wooden whistles, and a wooden flute. A bench was dragged from the tables to the other side of the square, and the five sat to play. The large drum began the simplest of rhythms: *boom boom boom,* to which the rapidly tapped small drum added complexity. Then the whistles began together, and finally the flute, and the men and women formed circles, the women within, and joined hands, and danced in opposing directions to various lively country airs.

Hob and Nemain joined them, dancing in different rings, and after a while Molly got up as well, and made her way to the inner ring and took a place there, as lively and graceful as one a third her age.

The sun sank beneath the backbone of the western ridge, and darkness flooded the square. Here came Dickon with a blazing torch lit at his cottage hearth, and thrust it into the pile of dry logs and branches the men had constructed. It burned there for a moment as if nothing would happen, a glowing yellow-red heart in the darkness of the pile, and then branches caught, and there was a rapid bloom of flame, and suddenly the pile was afire, and the square lit from one side, and the dancers' shadows thrown against the Saxon stone of the old church's facade.

There was a pause for the dancers and musicians to rest, and to drink more ale. Molly had Jack and Hob bring out their instruments, to the villagers' intense curiosity. They sat on the musicians' bench; each woman tuned her *claírseach*, retested, and retuned. Then Hob tuned his symphonia to Nemain's harp, and Jack tightened the goatskin on his drum's frame. The troupe struck up a lively country dance, and almost immediately folk quaffed off their mugs and returned to the hard dirt of the open square. By now the ale was having some effect, and the more formal circle dances were dissolving: there began smaller rings of five dancers or so; pairs of sweethearts swinging each other about in a whirl, both hands clasped; and the occasional solitary twirler, exalted by the music and the ale.

All this while Father Athelstan presided at the end of one table, in a chair brought out from his house. He seemed in the best of humors, and not at all disapproving. Hob wondered what the dry and desperately pious Father Baudoin, chaplain of Sir Jehan's Castle Blanchefontaine, would have thought of the raucous scene.

After a while fatigue and ale led most of the dancers to return to the benches, and it was then that Molly gave Jack and Hob the stand-down signal, and after the slightest amount of retuning the two harps to each other, she and Nemain began to play. Hob reached down beside the bench and retrieved his own mug of ale, drank deeply, and set it down, prepared to enjoy himself. At one point or another in their performances, the two women played without the men, and it was one of Hob's greatest delights to hear what beauty his wife and her grandmother could coax from the Irish harps.

Nor did they disappoint on this evening that was so pleasant: the air delicious with the fragrance of growing things, the pungent aroma of woodsmoke; the sweet scent of spilled ale. The firelight lit the fronts of the tiny cottages and the ancient church, and the sides of Molly's three wagons across the square. In the open commons beyond, the three draft animals showed as shadowy bulks amid some of the village goats and sheep.

The harps launched into an Irish air, played in unison, one of those ravishing melodies with unexpected drops at the end of a stanza, so different from the yeoman-like English strains. Then the harps diverged, one providing accompaniment to the other, building to a sublime complexity. The villagers sat in something close to stunned silence; all except Father Athelstan, who left his chair and hobbled down the length of the tables to sit nearer to the music.

The instrumental piece drew to a close, and without stopping, Molly and Nemain swept into a song in Irish, Molly's dark contralto and Nemain's bright soprano weaving against each other, their separate but complementary notes now crossing, now drawing apart. Hob sat sideways on the bench, the better to watch Nemain's fingers flying along the strings; Jack, his bodhran beside him on the bench, had taken Sweetlove up onto his lap, and was listening to the music, head bent and eyes closed, while his hard brutal hand stroked along the little dog's back with the most tender of touches. At last the voices swelled to a crest and then plunged to end on a thrilling prolonged low note, Nemain's bright descant holding true, while below it Molly sustained a tone deep and fateful as the drone on Scottish war pipes.

Hob looked over. Everyone was silent, all eyes on Molly and Nemain; a descent of angels could not have produced a greater effect. Father Athelstan was sitting at the end of the outside bench at the nearest table. The aged priest was bent forward, hand on chin, elbow on knee, staring intently at the harps, a look of joy on his face, his eyes bright and alert despite the amount of ale and, before that, of *uisce beatha,* that he had drunk. Once again Hob was aware of how little he had understood of this man when he had been a child in his care: how much more formidable he was than suspected.

The storm of applause finally broke, and the villagers abandoned their seats to cluster around the musicians' bench, to tell Molly and Nemain, shyly, how wondrous was this night to them. Many of them had never heard anything like this, even on holy days in St. Bridget's church, with its large choir, over in Little Bridekirk. After that the two drummers clustered about Jack, examining his bodhran, and asking questions. He was unable to tell them much, of course, although Nemain translated some of his curt answers, but he was willing to demonstrate, with gestures, and short runs on the drum, some of the skills he had learned to employ, and after a while the small-drum player got his instrument, and attempted to copy some of Jack's effects, even though the drums were constructed differently.

At one point Hob, who had drunk quite a bit of beer and was seeing this village sprung from his childhood through a pleasant haze, found himself sitting on a bench next to Beatrix. She was now a pretty young woman, with a billow of thick black hair, Saxon blue eyes, a scattering of freckles.

On her other side sat the rangy towheaded Eadward, with whom Hob had had a long-standing but friendly rivalry: the two fleetest boys in the village. Sometimes Hob won, sometimes Eadward: footrace after footrace failed to establish who had the primacy. Now Beatrix's right hand, Eadward's left, were on the table, fingers interlaced.

They were engaged. "Father's read the banns twice now," she said in a happy voice, while Eadward grinned at him from her other side. For a moment it felt to Hob as it had when they all sat together down by the little stream in the heat of the summer, cooling bare feet in the current and teasing one another.

"God and Mary with you both! I wish you joy of your marriage," said Hob, filled with a strange emotion, perhaps born of the firelight, the half-lit buildings and wagons, the music; perhaps born of the realization that, choosing a path in this life, one must abandon another: a three-strand emotion, that mixed contentment with his own lot and happiness for his old friends, while below these feelings ran a note of sadness, deep and strong as Molly's voice.

HOB AWOKE BESIDE NEMAIN. The ale was still singing in his blood, and he felt pleasantly heavy and sleepy. Nemain lay flat on her stomach with her face crushed into her pillow, the head-cloth disarranged, her breathing deep and regular. He propped himself up on one elbow and reached across her back to push the shutter partway open. The moon was up, but far from full; the bonfire had been banked to embers, with stones placed around it; the square lay ghostly in moonlight, in starlight.

Directly across was the little church, built in Saxon times and still sturdy after several hundred years. Hob remembered how, when he was a child, the one little window in his room afforded a view of the side of that church, toward the rear, and the fields behind them, running away to the dark mass of wooded ridges beyond, everything faint and silent under the moon; on nights when he was wakeful, he would kneel at that window, and spin dim dreams of future glory.

Beside him Nemain's hand fluttered. She turned half on her side, opened her eyes a slit, closed them again, and batted at him blindly, feebly. She mumbled something—low, distracted, thick-tongued—that might have been: "Lie down, sweeting; lie down."

Hob pulled the shutter closed and lay down again. He ran a hand gently across her back—silk was never so smooth—and she gave the slightest gurgle of pleasure, and then began to snore lightly.

He closed his eyes. He had just time enough to consider by how much the vivid joys of adulthood exceeded the muted yearnings of childhood before he sank beneath on-rushing waves of sleep.

CHAPTER 27

THE NEXT MORNING FATHER ATH-
elstan was up soon after dawn, and
shortly the bell rang in the little
church tower. Hob and Jack went to hear Mass;
Father Athelstan officiated and Father Eustace at-
tended him. The old priest, with the remarkable
vitality that some elders display, did not seem much
the worse for his robust drinking the night before.
When Father Athelstan had dismissed the congre-
gation and the villagers had filed out to begin their
daily tasks, he came up to Jack and Hob and said,
"Come see this."

He led the way to the church doors, folded back
into the narthex, and pointed at the door on the
right. Hob bent to see better, squinting in the dim
light within the church.

"Wait," said Father Athelstan. He swung the

door closed, so that one-half of the entrance was shut. Now, with the sunlight falling full on it, Hob could see the deep parallel grooves scored by the hyenas' blunt claws.

"Christ protect us!" said Hob, exaggerating his surprise a little—he had already *seen* the hyenas, loping toward him over moonlit sands—but only a little. It *was* shocking, to see what these things could do with their claws, and to know that their jaws were worse.

"You know, my son, most of the churches built before the Normans came to us were of wood, and many of those old Anglian and Saxon churches no longer stand. We are fortunate to have this church, built in stone, as a refuge: we cannot be burnt out, and even Satan's hounds could not claw their way in. Ah, here is Father Eustace."

The young priest had finished setting the altar to rights, and putting away their vestments in the tiny sacristy. Now he took station beside Father Athelstan, ready to support him should he need it.

"Come, Father," said the old priest, "let us show our guests the print. This way, Hob, Jack."

The two priests set off around the church. Halfway down the right side Father Athelstan pointed to the ground. There was an impression the size of a big man's palm, with four thick toe-prints tipped with the holes made by their claws, and a squat palm-print behind them.

Father Athelstan said, looking down, "I have never seen anything that looks like this; it is like a dog's print, but thicker, broader—and a bear would have more toes."

Here was another side to the old man. One expected

Father Athelstan to know his Gospels, his Latin, his Norman high speech, but not a tracker's knowledge. Hob could not remember the old priest entering the surrounding woodland, or even leaving the village.

But Hob had no intention of introducing the concept of a hyena, much less a *bouda*: a small village is no place for secrets, and one slip by a villager at market in Little Bridekirk could bring John's agents down upon the little place, thirsting for answers, ready to torture for answers, about Molly's troupe and where they had gone. And of course no one would be able to provide that knowledge: their only hope would be that death would end their torment. Suddenly the morning seemed chill, despite the sunlight.

"It's good that you have a stout stone church to retreat to, Father," said Hob. "And you should maintain a watch for a fortnight at least, as we have said. Perhaps it would be wise to keep James Carpenter's lumber in a corner of the church, and the nails, and perhaps one hammer, in the event that they come at you suddenly?"

Father Athelstan considered. "Yes, we have been watching the roads from the hilltops, but you are right: we might not have so much warning the next time—pray God there is no next time!—and it would be well to have the lumber ready, and perhaps a butt or two of fresh water in the church. Father Eustace, see if you can draw up a list of needful things, and send for James, and Isaac."

A small boy came running up to them.

"Yes, Thomas?" said Father Athelstan, putting a hand to the boy's head.

The child hesitated; he frowned in concentration, seeking to deliver his message correctly. Then: "Beg your pardon, Father, but, um, Mistress Molly asks that you excuse men—um, excuse the two men with you, for that she needs them. And Mistress, Mistress—um, the other one, Father—says her husband is just trying to get out of doing work."

The priests smiled, Hob laughed, and Jack made the sounds that passed for laughter with him, but earned him a frightened look from the boy.

"Come say farewell before you leave, child," Father Athelstan said to Hob, and patting Jack's shoulder, he turned to go. He staggered a bit, but only a little bit, the turn making him somewhat dizzy. Father Eustace steadied him; the old priest waved backhanded; and they set off toward the priest house.

THEY SPENT AN HOUR OR TWO putting the wagons in order, watering Milo and Tapaigh and Mavourneen, and hitching those three to the wagons, all with a small crowd of children and those adults who had no chores that could not be put off gathered around, watching every move of these visitors, who might have dropped down from the stars, so different were their lives from the quiet round of life in the village.

Molly called Hob into the big wagon. She shut the door behind him, to speak out of earshot of the army of witnesses standing in the road outside. She handed him a leather pouch, heavy, the drawstrings pulled closed.

"Hob, *a chuisle,* here's a great deal of the silver da Panzano's after giving us. I'm thinking 'tis only right that you help your old priest, who took you in when you were a helpless bairn, and raised you up—and a fine job I've always thought he did of it—and help also this village that sheltered you, and they with borrowed horses and cows struggling to plow, and to have milk and cheese—sure with this they'll be able to replace their animals, and have some beside. He's a good man, and knows how to live, and that without greed, and I'm trusting him. But it's you should make the gift."

"But 'tis not mine, Mistress—da Panzano gave it to you."

"He gave it to us, lad, to the family, and you a part of it—'tis yours as much as it is Nemain's, or Jack's, or mine, and any road 'tis you should be our family's representative in this."

"Yes, Mistress." Hob found himself smiling, happy: he was not sure why, but as an orphan, the thought of himself so embedded in a strong family lifted up his heart, in ways he could not have explained, even to himself.

He swung down from the wagon and strode across the square to the priest house. Father Eustace opened the door to his knock, nodded pleasantly at him, and stood aside. Hob went in, to find Father Athelstan struggling to his feet. Hob put the pouch down quietly as he walked by the table. He went up to the old priest, and embraced him.

"I came to say farewell, Father," said Hob. A sadness swept over him, and lodged in his throat, and in the corners of his eyes, so that he had to struggle to speak without a quaver, and to keep his eyes from filling with tears.

"I hope 'tis but for a while," said Father Athelstan. "The

whole village has had joy of your coming, and that of your excellent family." His eyes took on the unfocused look of recollection. "Those harps! Still they play in my memory. I hope to hear such music again in Heaven."

"I will see that we make every effort to return, as soon as we may, even if only for a little while."

"I hold you to that, child," said the old priest. "But what is in that pouch that you so slyly leave on my table?"

"It is a gift from us, Father—for you, and also for Saint Edmund's folk, that you may replace the horses and cattle you have lost."

The priest moved painfully to the table; he held to the edge with one hand and with the other loosened the pouch strings. When he had widened the opening, and placed a hand therein, and ruffled the coins somewhat, he turned to Hob.

A shadow flickered across the old priest's face. "But how could you come by so much—" He threw up a thin hand. "Hob, child, I must beg your forgiveness: of course there is some perfectly correct way you and Mistress Molly have acquired so much wealth. You are two good souls. There was a moment when I thought—Satan was whispering in my ear, I believe."

Hob was having trouble following what Father Athelstan was getting at, and then understanding burst upon him so precipitously that it brought forth a peal of honest laughter, perhaps the most convincing demonstration of innocence that he could have made.

"You thought we were brigands?" Hob cried, and set himself off again; it was so absurd that he could not become offended either for himself or for Molly, and his laughter diminished only gradually, slowing to chuckles and snorts of mirth, wiping his eyes.

"Hob, I—" Now the priest really was embarrassed. Father Eustace, in a chair by the door, busied himself with his paternoster, looking down determinedly.

"Oh, Father, 'tis not so strange that you should think such—we might be quite successful brigands: my little wife, for example, is more dangerous than any of the men in this village, and how could musicians and such ever earn such pouches of coin?"

"Well—"

"Mistress Molly is a wealthy woman in her own right, and a queen away in Erin; she chooses to live simply to avoid notice. Yet she is hunting those things from which your village hid away, and—this comes under your oath of silence of last night, are we agreed?"

"Yes, child."

"Father Eustace?"

"I consider myself bound to secrecy, Master Hob."

"She is summoned to do so by His Holiness himself. Do you think the Church would not be grateful for someone who can contain these devils; or that Sir Odinell, whose people she saved from a horrid fate, would not reward her; or that Sir Jehan, whose castle folk she kept from being slaughtered, would not be her partisan?"

"I, ah, had not considered . . ."

"There is no taint to that silver, Father; use it for your flock with an easy conscience."

For a moment Father Athelstan considered him very seriously, though a small smile played about the old priest's mouth.

"For someone who spent so many summer hours gazing out the window while he was supposed to be practicing his letters, you have grown up remarkably well, and I trust God will permit me my great pride in you."

"Father," said Hob simply, and hugged the old man again. Fearing to stay longer, he went quietly to the door, bowed his head as Father Eustace signed a quick blessing above him, murmuring in Latin, and left the house in which resided his earliest memories.

THE LITTLE CARAVAN SET out from the square; every person in the village had assembled to see them go. Hob, walking in front with Milo's lead rope in hand, had to stop every few steps to say good-bye to someone else: hugs, kisses, handshakes, claps on the back. Afterward the one clear memory of that raucous leave-taking was of Father Athelstan: Hob turned around, walking backward a few paces, for a last wave; and, standing in the middle of the road, the villagers from respect leaving him a clear view of the departing wagons, was Father Athelstan, matching Hob's childhood memory of the rather forlorn priest waving good-bye to the child he had raised. Now, though, there was Father Eustace to lean on, and there was the knowledge that Hob had done well in the wide world, and there was the hope that Molly's troupe would one day come through again. If it was possible, Hob swore to himself, they would do so.

He turned about and walked on, setting his face to the road ahead; to the future; to unholy peril.

Chapter 28

MOLLY LED THEM FROM A WELL-traveled road running north, onto a smaller, less-traveled road running to the northeast. After a bit some trees appeared amid the cleared land on Hob's right hand, and then more trees, and finally they were dense enough to constitute a forest: some lord's untilled, uncut hunting preserve. An eastbound trail struck off into these woods, and Molly bade Hob turn the ox onto the track. The wagons shouldered aside branches that overhung the way; twigs squeaked along the wooden sides; their leaves, scraped off by the little caravan's passage, carpeted the trail.

After some time moving through deep woods, with the view to either side showing shadowed gloom relieved only by shafts of sunlight that managed to pierce the leafy canopy, they came to an area of increasing light. The track opened into a nearly circular meadow, sunlit and knee-deep in fragrant bent, bisected by a tiny gurgling stream.

Molly looked around, pleased; she drew a deep breath of the perfumed air. "There's a fine dispute over who holds these lands, one earl supported by the barons and the other by the king, and the matter at law, and none hunting through them till 'tis settled. So it's privily we mice may come, and nibble our crumbs, and none to disturb us."

For years, Hob had seen Molly stop and talk with every tinker and every one of the traveling people that they encountered, casual good-humored conversations that somehow yielded information about the road ahead, the sort of lore that wanderers share—where was danger, where was shelter, who was hostile, who was kind. There was never a tavernkeeper on their way whose confidence she did not gain, and she would come away knowing what he knew. So Hob was not surprised that Molly knew of this secluded glade in which they were unlikely to be discovered, let alone troubled.

She directed the wagons to one side of the meadow, the wheels crushing a path through the stiff grasses; here there was a slight swell to the land, the wall of trees climbing up its face. Nestled into the hillside was a huge irregular boulder, higher than Hob's head, part embedded in the ground and part thrust back into the hill. The stone showed a fairly flat side to the meadow; the lake of grasses washed up to the boulder's front and halfway around its sides.

They secured the wagons and unhitched and tethered

the animals, letting them graze at the ends of long ropes. Nemain disappeared into the midsized wagon. Molly went up to the stone and ran her strong smooth hand over the level surface. Hob and Jack trailed after her, Hob wondering at Molly's intent inspection of the granite surface.

"I'm after thinking that I remembered such a stone here," she said to them. " 'Twill be a good place for the Lord of the Beasts to dance."

Hob, a little behind her, looked a question at Jack. The man-at-arms pointed to his shirtfront. Hob nodded: Jack Brown carried an amulet Molly had made for him, a little leather bag with small bunches of dried herbs bound with locks of Molly's silver hair, and a tiny statuette, carved from wood, of an antler-headed man: the Lord of the Beasts.

"Is it a fairy stone, Mistress?" Hob asked, peering at the boulder.

" 'Tis but a stone," she said, "and yet a stone is never just a stone. Here, come close, look hard; feel of it; tell me what you can learn."

Hob, unsure of what was being asked of him, approached the stone, put his face very close, and looked, and looked. There was a fine grain to it that he had not noticed from a few paces back, and there was variation from gray to light gray-brown to dark gray. He put his palm against it: it gave back the warmth of the sunlight that had been playing upon it. He traced an indentation with a forefinger; there was a slight roughness to the surface, but not so rough that he could not slide his palm across it, a small sensuous pleasure.

"And what does it say to you, Hob?" she asked.

He looked from her face to the stone and back. "Say—? It *is* interesting, Mistress. Perhaps I feel now, a bit, what masons feel for stone; and certes I never thought to look so closely at one—but say? It is a stone, and does not say aught."

Molly sighed. "Well," she said, "there's a world behind the world, and some are seeing it, and some are not. But you are a true man of this world—'tis why you're so clever, and are forever riddling things out with your wit, and are so much a man of your hands. But there are those who are seeing or feeling into another world, the world that's made of the shadows that *this* world's casting, and so they're working the Art. So 'tis that I remembered this stone, and knew 'twould be the very place to build my fire, and pray, and sing a calling-up song. I'll be calling up the Horned Man, and won't He send me every king bull of the wild white cattle that is on this island, and won't I be speaking to them, and so assemble my army."

At this point Nemain came clattering down the wagon steps, a cauldron hanging from one hand and a sack of dried peas in the other. She dropped the cauldron to the ground and came up to them.

She swatted Hob on the buttocks. "And where's my fire, husband? Are we to fast tonight? And you"—pointing at the widely grinning Jack—"'tis a shameful example you're setting, standing about, and your great limbs idle." But all this was said with mock severity, and Jack and Hob generally enjoyed this mood, of which Jack, with some difficulty, had once gargled the comment: "Little mother."

"Nay, 'tis my fault," said Molly. "I thought to see if there was some echo of the Art in Hob, but there's nary a bit of it."

"I'm destroyed with astonishment to hear it," said Nemain, in a voice dripping with lemon, and with that she set off to the stream.

CHAPTER 29

THEY SAT TO A LIGHT MEAL OF peas seasoned with chunks of dried venison sausage and dark bread studded with bits of onion. The somewhat stale hunches of bread were softened by the simple expedient of holding them on twigs over the steaming cauldron, swaying gently on its tripod of branches, and there was clear water from the brook to quench their thirst.

After sunset Molly had Jack build up the fire again, and she had him place a stone, a cubit high, between the fire and the great boulder. She and Nemain went into the woods and returned, each with an armload of small bare branches—they had stripped away all leaves.

Hob went to help, but Nemain warned him not to touch the wood. There were aspects of the women's Art that must remain free of male influences—even a touch could compromise the delicate web of unseen influence woven of prayer, spoken or sung spell, certain elements drawn from nature, and the relentless application of the will.

Molly set up a miniature forest of the bare branching stalks in a circle around the rock, thrusting the ends into the soft earth so that they seemed to have grown there. From the large wagon she brought forth a carved wooden figure, perhaps a foot in height, of the Horned One: a man depicted as sitting cross-legged, antlers sprouting from his head, in his left hand a writhing ram-headed serpent and in the right a torc.

Jack had spread cloths by the fire for them to sit and recline upon. Molly had cups of the *uisce beatha* filled for everyone, and cautioned the men to keep strict silence. Then she and Nemain, without further ceremony, drained their cups, stood on either side of the fire, facing each other, and started to chant in Irish.

The incantation, which began to soar and glide, moved closer to song; as the voices rang out over the firelit meadow, Molly reached into an interior pocket in her skirts, and drew out a handful of powder, which she cast into the campfire. At once a burst of varicolored flames twirled up and frayed into sparks. A scent as of spice reached Hob. Molly did it again, and yet again.

Hob abruptly became aware that the firelight, passing over the statue and the stone and the bare branches, was making a shadow show upon the flat face of the great boulder. Because the flames were twisting, were flaring up and subsiding, the shadows of the branches and the antlered man seemed to move upon the stone.

Suddenly the shadows seemed to coalesce into a larger shadow, the outline of a standing man, antlers tossing high, legs astride. Hob blinked, forced himself to concentrate: no, there was only the shadow of the branches and the statue upon the stone. Molly and Nemain sang; Molly tossed powder into the fire again; the chant reached a crescendo.

Beside Hob, Jack gasped. He gripped Hob's shoulder with a large hard hand; he rose to a crouch; he pointed wordlessly at the stone, shaking Hob the while. Hob looked wonderingly at Jack's expression, one of deep awe, and he peered again at the stone, but there was nothing, only the shadows of branch and statue, writhing in sympathy with the shifting flames. Nothing else, nothing else.

Jack sank back down and drew a sleeve across his damp forehead. His other hand still held Hob's shoulder in a near-painful clamp, and now he became aware of this, and let go.

Molly and Nemain were each down on one knee, heads bowed, and Molly spoke in Irish, her tone matter-of-fact but subdued enough to be respectful, and just like that it was done. Molly and Nemain remained immobile for a moment, silent, lost in thought; then the women were regaining their feet, dusting the skirts of their garments, pulling up the branches, carrying the figure back to the wagon.

Hob was unsure what had happened; only that everyone had seen more than he. Even stolid Jack was finishing his cup of strong drink, his mighty hand shaking a little. Hob reflected that Jack Brown wore an amulet containing a small representation of the Lord of the Beasts, and had been a Beast himself at whiles. Jack was as much a Christian as Hob—what had the burly man seen, to shake him so?

Molly came back, poured herself another draft of the life-water, and, holding cup and flagon, lowered herself without using her hands to a sitting position, graceful as a young girl despite her heavy bosom, her womanly hips. She sat cross-legged and leaned back against Jack's shoulder.

"What happens now, Mistress?" asked Hob. He had been prepared to see a herd of the feral cattle come thundering into the glade.

"Now I'll have another cup, and watch the stars, and then to bed, for it's weary work speaking with these Powers, and taking good care to give no offense, for it's prideful They are, and so 'tis perilous work as well."

CHAPTER 30

FOR A SENNIGHT THEREAFTER, folk awoke from sleep, hearing the beat of heavy hooves in the earthen village street or the crackle of underbrush crushed beneath powerful limbs, followed by a storm of barking from the dogs; in the day, farmers turned quickly from their work in the fields, seeing a glint of white in among the bordering trees. The chieftains of the wild white cattle made their way south by privy ways, keeping to unspoiled forestland where it was possible, and where it was not, crossing open plowland, crashing through wood fences with their great bodies, moving at dawn and at dusk and even by night. Their brides, their offspring, and the young bachelors, all remained for now in the North Country, while the king bulls, moving to an irresistible compulsion, fared ever southward, guided by—what? Buried lines of magnetism, or the stars, or the pointing hand of the Horned Man, not to be denied? Few women, no men, can say for sure.

ONE DAY MOLLY ANNOUNCED, " 'Twill be tonight." She told the troupe to bring the draft animals in from where they grazed. She had them hitched up, and then directed the rearrangement of the wagons, so that they formed a rough triangle near the great boulder. Unhitched again, the beasts were tethered tightly within the space defined by the chocked wagons.

"For aren't they all king bulls, and used to their own lordship, and inclined to attack any other such, and yet under the Horned Man's command to come and go in peace. Each of them will be like a haystack in a dry summer—ready to burn at a spark, and I'm not wanting poor Milo or one of the others to be in their path when they're milling about."

They ate early, and the women made preparations, setting up the small stone with the statue of the Lord of the Beasts, warning the men to stay by the wagons and say nothing. Sweetlove was put into the large wagon, Jack urging her by signs, in their private and wordless language, that he wished her to be silent. Most of the time she comprehended his intent; most of the time she was obedient.

The night fell; the half-moon rose, huge against the horizon of treetops. The green meadow showed as a colorless carpet. Hob and Jack sat on the ground with their backs against a wagon wheel. Molly and Nemain stood a few paces into the meadow, hazel staves in hand. Nothing happened for what seemed to Hob a very long time; there was no sound except for the random calls of night birds. Then he became aware that even that had stopped. In the blackness beneath the trees there was movement: something pale, something big.

Then he saw it clearly. Out from the rampart of trees, out from the pool of shadow, came a huge white bull, its horns rising up and outward and then recurving toward each other. It walked slowly into the open, its coat gleaming as the moonlight struck it. The bull broke into a trot, coming at Molly and Nemain, its great musculature moving it lightly over the ground, gaining speed; the cruel points of the horns could now be easily discerned as it drew nearer and nearer to the two women, and Hob involuntarily came to his feet—he felt the need to be nearer Nemain, to protect her in some way, although he had no idea what he would do. But Jack seized his arm and pulled him back down. The man-at-arms just shook his head, then put a finger to his lips.

The great beast stamped to a halt before Molly and Nemain, and lowered its neck. Molly came forward and embraced its head, and stroked its nose, and spoke into its ear, too softly for Hob to hear. The king bull stood in place, as docile as Milo, and now Nemain came and caressed its neck, and spoke to it also.

Hob's attention was drawn away to the circling wall of trees: there was movement on all sides, pale shapes that appeared and then disappeared as they moved around the perimeter. And now the bulls entered, from this side and that, pouring into the meadow, snorting, ripping up the soft earth with their sharp hooves, their massive bulk, as they trotted across the moonlit grass: ghost-white animals, *courant,* on a dream-gray field.

They milled in a circle that slowed, and then stopped. They were all facing the women, the small stone, the statue of the Horned Man. Save for the snorts of exertion, they made no sound, no lowing, no bellowing. They stood, each with a little space about it.

Now Molly and Nemain began to move among them, patting them, murmuring in their ears. In this way they moved all through the throng. You could not call it a herd, thought Hob, each one a separate chieftain, and untamed, unherded, by any human man. Yet the women moved among them, speaking to them, speaking to them, telling them what they must do. In what language, thought Hob, in what language? Perhaps two hundred bulls were facing him, patient as so many soldiers, and far across the meadow, his wife and her grandmother were telling them things in a way he could not understand. All at once the strangeness, the silence except for the breathing of many large animals, the moonlight, washed over him, and he shivered. The hair rose on his neck, and he crossed himself. He looked at Jack, and the soldier, sensing something of his distress, patted his shoulder.

Hob became angry with himself. That he should doubt these two good women, one that he respected completely and one that he loved and had sworn to, and they working their Art with the purest of motives—it felt like a betrayal on his part, and he shook off all doubts. The women were returning, and there was movement here and there among the great white shapes. Slowly the herd began to circle, and here and there individual animals slipped off into the woods on this side and that, the great herd at the half-trot, circling and circling the meadow, and bleeding off, one by one, into the forest.

Jack went to the large wagon, put a foot in the rope loop that hung from the back platform, and pulled open the door. He fought his way inside past the determined efforts of Sweetlove to leap up and lick his face, his hand, anywhere she could get at him. Finally he caressed her a few times, and then pointed at her and at the wagon floor; she sat immediately, but with her tail wagging furiously, brushing the floor in a tiny arc. Hob could hear Jack rummaging about and then here he came, a crockery jug that he held by the neck in his left hand; four pewter mugs were strung by their handles on his left thumb; he grasped the rope handhold with his right hand and swung down easily to the ground.

There was the slightest, most discreet whimper of protest from the wagon and without looking around, the man-at-arms made a "come-along" gesture with his free hand. Sweetlove shot out the door and landed behind him in what seemed one continuous arc; she hit the ground with a thud and trotted behind him, and here came Molly and Nemain, in time to be handed a mug, into which Jack poured a generous draft of the *uisce beatha*. He handed a mug to Hob and filled it partway, and then served himself.

The women were plainly very tired, and the strong drink was welcome, but there was underlying their fatigue every appearance of satisfaction. They sat side by side on a log that Jack and Hob had dragged from the forest when first they camped. Hob sat down beside his wife and put his arm around her, while Jack went back and forth to the wagon, bringing hunches of bread and a cured ham and a cloth to spread on the grass. The women were almost too tired to eat, but Jack urged them to do so with gestures and grunts, and Hob cut dainty slices and fed them to Nemain, and finally Jack sat down on Molly's other side, and bit happily into a piece of ham.

Sweetlove was running back and forth, nose to the ground, a few yards away, on the torn-up field, a jumble of clods of soil and ripped-up clumps of bent. She was plainly reading the tale of vast bodies and sharp hooves from the all-pervading scent of the wild white monarchs of the North. She began to drift away toward the center of the field and Jack clucked twice at her. At once she spun about and trotted over to him; a quick leap and she was on the log beside him and curled into a circle, her back pressed against his thigh.

"She's a good little dog," said Molly in a dreamy voice, a voice half-drunk with fatigue. She leaned against Jack's shoulder.

Hob, relieved that the strange night was drawing to a close, but as always intensely curious about the hidden powers of these two women he loved above all else, said, "Mistress, how is it that these beasts can take direction from you? How can they understand Irish when I cannot?" Nemain had been teaching him Irish, and although Hob was a quick study, keenly intelligent and with a remarkable aural memory, he found Irish to be a subtle and difficult tongue to master. He made progress, but it was arduous.

" 'Tis not that they understand Irish," began Molly, "but that, that—*och,* 'tis like telling of the sunset to one blind from birth! Nemain, is there an understanding you can bring to him? For it's destroyed I am with fatigue and barely able to chew for wanting to sleep." She drank from the mug of fiery liquor. Jack bent and cut a large chunk from the ham and handed it to her, and she bit a good-sized piece from it and sighed with pleasure.

"If you paid half as much attention as yon cattle, you'd be the great bard of Erin by now," said Nemain in the mock-severe tone Hob remembered from when they were both children—she a teasing little girl and practically his sister. "We tell them what they should do in Irish, for 'tis the language of our Art, but they're not understanding the words. 'Tis that the words are fixing our thoughts on what we want them to know, and us touching them and petting them the while, and . . . and . . . passing our understanding from our thoughts to theirs, which are very different thoughts, sure, but understanding can be passed from one to the other. They know that they must come to us, and we tell them *when* by the moon—they can see the moon wherever they are, and they are linked now to my grandmother through the Horned Man—they will know from Him where she is, and will come *near* her in the sennight before, and will come *to* her on the very night they are needed."

Hob drew breath to ask how the Horned Man would

know where Molly was, thought better of it, crossed himself unobtrusively, and subsided.

Sweetlove, curled happily next to Jack, her nostrils full of the rich scent of the king bulls, belatedly became aware of the ham and, sitting up, put one paw to Jack's thigh, and looked in his face with an expression that could only be interpreted as a plea. He began feeding her morsels of ham interspersed with dark bread, and so all sat, quiet and fairly content, until Molly roused herself and said, "Sure it's time we were all abed," and that got them all up, stretching and yawning. Hob watered the three tethered beasts, and soon all were safe in their various wagons, and the camp was quiet, save for Jack's heroic snores.

CHAPTER 31

AWAY UP THE SLOPE THAT formed one wall of the valley that Father Ugwistan had marked on his map, Molly and her little family crouched among the trees, and looked down on a small meadow: a flat oval, floored with grasses, ringed with wooded chines. The wagons, the draft animals, and Sweetlove were three miles away, in the Benedictine monastery where Monsignor da Panzano awaited them, hoping to hear of the destruction of Yattuy's hyena-men; the four horses the legate had supplied Molly with were tethered far down the backslope, out of earshot.

The moon was just peeping over the rim of the opposite ridge, when a confused murmur arose; it swelled; it became more distinct. From the narrow pass at one end that gave ingress to the meadow, the tramp of feet, the rumble of many voices, came drifting upslope to Hob's ears. More light spilled onto the grass as the rising moon, a day past the full, began to win free of the hillside. The valley stood revealed, almost as clearly as in daylight, and a company of Poitevin mercenaries came marching in from the mouth of the pass, their officers ahead of them on horseback.

Behind them came a disordered mass of the *bouda*, walking with heads down, sacks on their shoulders, all wearing hooded cloaks that seemed gray, though this might have been a trick of the moonlight. In their midst, swathed in a striped cloak, seated on one of the beautiful large-eyed arch-necked horses of the desert-dwellers, rode the sorcerer; the *bouda* who were nearest him walked with a hand to his boot, his cloak edges, the tassels that depended from his saddlecloth, as though to draw strength or some other blessing from contact with him.

Behind the mass of *bouda* came another band of *routiers*: the rearguard. The swarthy men spread out across the meadow till they were more or less equidistant from one another. They dropped their sacks where they stood, and turned to watch the sorcerer as he rode to a little prominence on the far side of the meadow from where Hob watched. A squad of ten or so *bouda,* presumably the sorcerer's inner circle, climbed up the hill and stood behind him.

The mounted officers of the Poitevins began to set up a perimeter guard, and soon there was a loose ring of mercenaries facing outward, ready to guard against any interruptions.

The sorcerer dismounted, came to the lip of the little rise

he stood upon, and raised his arms. All the *bouda,* save the group that stood behind him, at once went to one knee. The sorcerer's voice rang out over the crouching throng, but came faintly to Molly's folk on the hillside. In any event, thought Hob, they could not have understood the strange language.

Hob and Jack stood behind stout tree trunks, peering cautiously down at the bizarre scene. There was little chance that any of the Poitevin pickets, looking up into the blackness beneath the trees, could see them, but Molly had warned that the sorcerer, and the shapeshifters as well, might have unexpected powers. Jack had his war hammer with him, propped head down against the tree. Longswords were awkward in heavy woodland, and so Hob was armed only with a sax, one of the old-fashioned single-edged heavy knives, a cubit long and sheathed horizontally at his belt, as well as the war dagger Sir Balthasar had given him.

Each of them, on instruction from Molly, had a sack filled with the caltrops Hob had gleaned from the road. The slope down to the valley was steep enough, but for the last twenty yards or so it fell sheer to the valley floor. There were only two ways up from where the Poitevin picket line faced outward to their position here amid the ridgetop trees: deer trails that led up more gradually through clefts in the rock face at the valley floor. Jack pointed to the trail that ran up past Hob's tree, and to one perhaps fifteen feet to Hob's right; then he indicated Hob, and the trail near him; then himself, and the trail to the right. Hob nodded, and opened the bag of caltrops by his feet. They did not dare throw them now, but the time for that was near.

Now Hob became aware that Molly and Nemain had moved back a few yards, where a small declivity open to the moonlight gave them light while shielding them from the eyes of those below. The women were quietly setting up the figure of the Horned Man, and arranging stones and twigs in odd little patterns. They were working with a combination of care and urgency, Molly placing things here and there and murmuring prayers in Irish, Nemain drawing little sealed pots and bottles from a poke slung by a strap over her shoulder.

A shout drew his attention back to the meadow. The sorcerer was leading the *bouda* in a kind of call-and-response, the mage's powerful bass echoing from the ridges around, then a deep-throated staccato roar from the gray-cloaked men. The Poitevins, facing outward, seeking any sign of exterior threat, kept turning around to see what was happening, and even at this distance Hob thought to detect uneasiness in their demeanor. The officers' horses were less ambiguous, fidgeting and stamping and turning in place, tossing their heads; the Poitevin captains were pulling harshly at the reins, trying to keep them facing outward. Only the sorcerer's Arab was unaffected: it stood quietly where he had left it with the richly embroidered reins, twined with ribbons and tassels, tossed over its head and trailing to the ground, a signal that it was to remain there.

Now the calls grew more frenzied, the responses more savage, and all at once they ceased. Hob was startled by the immediate silence, which stretched on for several heartbeats, the only sound the snorting of the *routiers'* horses, or the occasional click as a hoof struck against a bit of rock, the mounts dancing beneath their riders.

At a bellowed command from the wizard, every *bouda* emptied his cloth bag at his own feet: ashes from their forges, an essential part of their sorcery. A knee-high cloud of ash roiled up into the moonglow as some of the ash rebounded, further enhancing the dreamlike atmosphere in the meadow. Off came the cloaks; beneath them the men were naked.

They dropped to the ground and began to roll in the ashes, as some dogs will roll in carrion. Hob stared, transfixed: in the low ashy cloud, the forms of men rolling about began to alter, subtly at first and then with increasing clarity. The straight limbs of the *bouda* became crooked, and thickened; their jaws lengthened; smooth skin developed a coarse pelt. Here and there began to stand up the nightmare forms of hyenas, shaking themselves like dogs coming out of the water, lifting broad black muzzles and dark round eyes to the moon. A cacophony arose, yipping and howling and the characteristic blood-freezing titter, multiplied tenscore, the demonic forms milling around in the ashy cloud, the *routiers* turned about and gaping at the spectacle, their horses frantic with horror, till Hob thought: *This is what the floor of Hell must be.*

Gradually the shapeshifters fell silent, settled down, turned, and faced the sorcerer. He gave one last call, but faced with beasts incapable of speech, there was no response. Instead they turned as one and fell upon the Poitevins, an explosion of savagery that in one burst swept those hardened soldiers under, only the horses able to scream once, twice at most, before being torn asunder. The powerful jaws and strong necks of the hyenas now came into play, two or more beasts at each side of a corpse, whether of man or horse, tugging, growling, ripping limbs from sockets and stripping great hunks of flesh away from the bone, rib cages left glinting like ghastly harps in the silver light.

Suddenly Nemain was beside him, her hand on his arm, her breath in his ear. She spoke so quietly he could barely hear her. "Herself is nigh to beginning, and it may be that they'll become aware of us when she does. Be ready to flee—or fight."

He turned to her. "They are killing their own guards down there," he murmured.

"When they change, they need their meat, and while they'll eat horse, 'tis human meat and blood they must have, like all shapeshifters." She spoke very softly, and glanced at Jack, to reassure herself that he was out of earshot, for such talk was troubling to him. " 'Tis not till tomorrow that they are to kill the barons, and eat of them, and so I'm thinking yon *draíodóir* has asked the king for a sacrifice, and yon hireling swords were what he gave them, and they thinking they were guards of these monsters."

She slipped across to Jack and whispered in his ear, presumably the same warning she'd given her husband, and then went back to Molly.

Below, the unnatural hyenas were stretched out like so many dogs before a fireplace; they were working at cracking open the bones with their terrible jaws. Here and there was a sharp snapping noise as bones broke beneath their teeth; there was an undertone of grumbling and growling, an indication of their savage pleasure; and now and then, a peal of eerie, hackle-raising laughter would ring out over the blood-soaked field. It was such an evil sight, that Satanic feast, that Hob crossed himself. Almost it seemed a sin just to watch two companies of men and horses being devoured in contentment by these devils.

Hob began to be aware that there was a murmur in Irish behind him, growing louder and louder by barely perceptible degrees. Molly had Jack's goatskin drum, and began tapping her fingernails on the center, a sound like tiny hooves, slowly at first and then faster and faster, suggesting a herd of cattle in full stampede. Without warning, the murmur and the tapping both ceased. He tensed. There was a moment's sense of hushed imminence, then Molly and Nemain together gave a great shattering cry, a savage animal wail that seemed to pierce the clouds, and then silence.

Hob heard this without turning around; he had expected something similar, although the suddenness, the prodigious din of it, had made him jump. But he was watching those below: the sorcerer's head came up immediately, and he threw out a long narrow arm and pointed upslope—to Hob it seemed that he pointed to the very tree he hid behind.

The hyenas reacted more slowly, but as one the ghastly heads swiveled toward where Jack and Hob crouched, and those lying full length in the ashes and splitting bones began to come to their feet, a smooth and ominous motion, their eyes never leaving the slopes above them.

Jack seized his bag from the ground and heaved it in a

long spill of shining metal down the trail nearest him. Hob did the same, and the caltrops, aided by the slope and the pull of the world on all things, rolled downward for perhaps a third of the way to the bottom.

Some of the hyenas nearest Hob's slope had reached the rock wall that ran along the bottom border; questing this way and that, one or two had discovered the trails, and had begun to scramble up them, their paws, with their broad pads and blunt claws, giving them traction and stability on the soil of the path.

A low roll of summer thunder came to Hob's ear. He was watching the first hyenas start up the trail, when he became aware that the majority of the huge pack below had begun to turn away from his slope, and to look toward the pass through which they had entered the valley. Some confused milling began, the two hundred or so animals kicking up the ash from all the bags that had been emptied on the ground. A low cloud of gray powder enveloped their legs, and all the while the thunder grew in volume. The sorcerer gave a great cry, his booming bass bringing the pack around; his lanky outstretched arm, his pointing finger, directed their attention to the entrance to the pass. Hob realized that he was not hearing thunder at all, but the drumming of many hooves.

With an effort he tore his gaze from the throng of monsters: there was a more immediate peril scrambling up the trails toward them. Jack picked up his crow-beak war hammer and set his feet, ready to deal with the first shapeshifter to arrive, and Hob drew his sax, although he had little hope that either weapon would avail against these unnatural beasts. He remembered the Fox, a shapeshifter who, in its Fox form, could not be seriously wounded by steel.

The beasts diverged, one coming up fast toward Hob and two, one following the other, mounting toward Jack. They drove upward in half-leaps with their powerful hind legs, scrabbling for a foothold with their forelegs. Hob, looking at the mad eyes, the jumble of spiky teeth, coming ever closer, decided that he was about to die, and that he would sell his life as dearly as he could, to buy time for the women to complete their task, to protect Nemain as long as he could move his limbs. With the thought came a swift and unexpected peace, a cessation of all fear. He held the sax down at his side, and braced himself with one arm around a young tree, ready for one desperate blow. He did not think he would get a chance for a second stroke, and given their resistance to steel, he knew that he would not kill his attacker; he only hoped to delay it for a while.

Iron might not kill them, but they could be hurt by it, apparently: the hyena coming for Hob, bounding up the path, had reached the patch where lay the caltrops. It sprang forward and three of its legs landed on the bitter points of the twisted iron stars. It shrieked and performed a violent leap up in an effort to avoid coming down fully on the points. Hob watched it twist in midair, a movement like that of a trout bursting free of a river and turning about before landing. But the hyena, in its effort to save its feet, came down on its shoulder, scrabbling wildly at nothing with its paws, and began to roll back down the slope.

Its speed increased, and although one caltrop fell from

its flesh, a forefoot and a hind foot were still impaled, and it could not arrest its downward roll—rather, it fell faster, and at last, near the bottom, it bounced over a small embedded boulder and fell the last dozen feet to the valley floor, where it lay stunned.

Jack's attackers made inexorable progress, by some miracle avoiding the caltrops, of which they seemed to be little aware, and reaching almost to where the burly man-at-arms, hammer at the ready, stood stolidly awaiting the shock of their charge.

But now, almost at the top, the lead hyena's fortunes took a turn for the worse, and it stepped on a caltrop with one foot and then with another. It tottered about just below Jack Brown, trying to avoid putting weight on its injured feet, until he swung the blunt end of the hammer with all his considerable might, catching the thing in the flank, and it lost balance completely and began to roll back down, sweeping its follower off its feet as well, the two beasts rolling and tumbling in a tangled heap all the way down toward their doom.

Now that Hob was free from immediate threat, he became aware that the drumming of hooves had swelled into a roar, and that the hyena-men below were all trotting back and forth, always facing the portal to the pass, and adding a vast chorus of giggles, barks, and growls, as well as their characteristic arpeggios of laughter, to the overarching sound of thunder. The sorcerer seemed to be exhorting them to take some action, but even his commanding voice was lost in the storm of noise.

One of the squad of Cousins who stood behind him, in

human form and hooded and cloaked, was now holding the Arab's reins; considering what was happening, the horse was still amazingly calm.

Hob took all this in at one glance; he paid special attention to the wizard, for he expected him to guide the others as a general commands his army. Then there was movement at the right edge of his vision. He turned instinctively in that direction; he gasped.

A wide front of white, broad as the tidal bore that had swept up the bay to tread down the swimming hyenas and just as powerful, now burst from the narrow pass and fanned out into a valley-wide wave of thick-based needle-pointed horns and iron-hard hooves, driven by heavy muscle and massive bones. The king bulls and the young bachelor bulls of the North Country had come with rolling eye and foam-flecked mouth, pouring into the flat meadow, the outliers spilling a little way up the slope and running on a slant.

And then they reached the shapeshifters, who were running this way and that and giving the laugh that can signify excitement but also fear, backing and snarling just before the white giants bowled them over, trampled them to ribbons, impaled them on those inswept horns and tossed them back over the sea of heaving pallid shoulders and bunching haunches, so that the horn-stabbed hyenas vanished under the hooves of the following bulls.

To the roiling low cloud of ash was now added clots of mud and wetted ash, thick with blood that was black in the moonlight. The bulls thundered to the far wall of the valley and, as though performing an evolution long practiced, the first rank turned widdershins and the second rank followed, and the whole herd turned as a snake turns its body, and roared back down the field, sweeping up those few hyena-men who had escaped the first charge.

In perhaps a half-dozen places, shapeshifters had suc-ceeded in bringing down a bull, one hyena with its terrible jaws locked in a bull's throat, impeding its breathing, while four or five, working in concert, tore their victim to pieces, the bull kicking all the while. These few victorious hunt packs looked up, muzzles painted with gore, to see doom thundering down upon them, as the vast herd came back along the valley.

The uproar was deafening, and even here, so far above, Hob felt stunned by the bellows, the snarls, the maniacal laughter, the thunder of heavy bodies bounding at full tilt along the ash-strewn dirt. He shook his head a bit to clear it, and saw, across the gulf of air separating his slope from the Berber mage's promontory, the sorcerer mounting his Arab steed, and riding up into the trees on the far side of the valley, his personal squad of *bouda* trotting behind him.

Back to the valley entrance the huge herd ran, stabbing and stamping at what was left of the Cousins, turning again instead of entering the pass and beginning another traverse of the valley. But now they were slowing, and Hob realized that he could no longer see any sign of the *bouda* lifting above the curtain of ash that hung knee-high in the meadow.

The giant bulls slowed to a trot and the whole mass moved in a valley-wide oval that tightened as it slowed, slowed, and finally came to a halt. Their heaving sides were dripping foam, rivulets of sweat making patterns in the ash and blood that covered their flanks; their breath came snorting through widened nostrils; they stamped heavy hooves. Some stood with hanging heads, weary from the long trail south and the exertions of running and battle.

Across the moonlit plain, hundreds of the wild white bulls stood, more or less motionless; they shifted in place, but did not move from where they had come to rest, all facing the slope where Molly and her granddaughter had worked their Art. The natural hostility of bull for bull had resulted in a certain distance being maintained, so that the great beasts, all facing the same way and more or less equidistant from one another, resembled an army assembled for review by their general. This was not far from the truth, thought Hob, marveling at the order of the ranks and files set out before him.

The ash cloud kicked up by the slaughter was slowly settling, and, save for the inevitable noises of such a great herd, the valley was quiet. Any night birds in the circle of wooded hills around the meadow were surely cowering in their nests, after that Satanic battle. The scene was now one drawn from some dream, and a dreamlike peace prevailed.

CHAPTER 32

Molly and Nemain came up to stand beside their men, and to look out over the valley. Although still there came to their ears the sounds of a great number of large animals breathing, the dull indeterminate hoof-thuds of those big bodies shifting a bit in place, the occasional low groaning call, particularly from the younger bachelor bulls, it seemed almost like silence after the hideous din that had prevailed only moments before. As Molly stood there, the bulls seemed in some way to become aware of her; gradually they shuffled about till all were facing the exact spot where Molly stood.

"It's down to them Nemain and I must go," said Molly to the men, "and free them to return to the North Country. You lads stay here the while, for I'd not have you distracting them."

Hob looked at Jack, who shrugged. Hob felt unwilling to see Nemain clamber down that perilous slope, so to stand amid those hooves, those incurving bitter-pointed horns. Yet the two had summoned these giants in the first place. Hob sighed and nodded, and said only, "Beware the caltrops."

Molly and Nemain were barefoot, clad only in white linen shifts: when they worked their Art they kept in contact with the soil, the trees, as much as possible. Now Molly leaped down the slope, landing four or five feet down and immediately jumping again, staying just to the side of the trail to avoid the caltrops, checking her fall with a strong white arm slapped against the nearest tree trunk. Nemain jumped off next, planting a foot at the base of a tree and then leaping for a small upjut of rock, so that each bound never turned into an uncontrollable fall.

Once past the zone of caltrops, they hewed to the trail and made better progress, although it was still necessary to snatch at trees to either side to keep their downward course from becoming a headlong tumble.

Finally the women sprang down among the pale giants, and walked through the herd, placing a hand to a bull's neck here, or patting a sweat-lathered flank there. Hob could not hear them at all, but he could see that they were speaking to each bull they passed, sometimes murmuring in its ear.

Molly had said that this would be necessary, a kind of praise and dismissal of the herd, but he winced to think of what ghastly surface the women walked upon with their bare feet, down there on what was a vast shambles. There was also the matter of the sorcerer's escape with his personal guard: Where had they gone, and what mischief might they do?

At last the women were done. They went up on the promontory where the wizard had stood, and gradually the wild bulls shifted position till they all faced the grandmother and granddaughter, their backs now to Hob and Jack. There was a rather long pause whose purpose was opaque to Hob, then both women threw up their arms in unison, and in unison gave a piercing cry.

There was an immediate increase in sound from the herd: snorting, a few groaning calls, and the sound of many hooves shuffling in the mudlike mixture of soil and ash and gore that carpeted the valley. The herd began to move toward the pass that constituted the exit from the field, and Hob felt a hard painful grip seize his arm just above the elbow.

"Lurgh!" said Jack: *Look!*

His mighty arm stretched toward the pass, where the moonlight through the leaves cast a pattern of black and silver just under the trees. For a moment it seemed to Hob as though it might be the shadow of a brawny man of giant stature, crowned with great antlers, and then it collapsed into meaningless patches. But Jack still gazed with a reverence, and perhaps a little fear, into the trees over there beside the valley's gate.

The bulls at that end of the valley now began to move into the pass, and as they disappeared from sight and room began to open up, the herd moved faster and faster, till they were trotting out at an increasing rate.

Molly and Nemain had recrossed the valley, the bulls that were still moving toward the pass carefully avoiding them, and now they were mounting the slope, bent forward and helping themselves by grasping roots and saplings for handholds. When they came to the caltrops they moved aside into the woods beside the trails, and so eventually won to the top, where Hob seized Nemain and held her for some time. Molly stood with Jack's arm around her waist and watched until the last bull disappeared into the darkness of the outleading defile.

She took a deep breath. "Sure, now, that's done. Now we've to tell that scheming churchman that we've destroyed the king's unholy army, but their chieftain is still prowling the night. Nemain, we must collect our things."

She turned and went down the back slope to the declivity where they had set up a temporary altar. She and Nemain soon had the statue of the Horned One and various incenses and amulets packed away in the large leather poke, and Jack's goatskin drum slung from Nemain's shoulder. Molly stood up and brushed her hands together in a dusting-off gesture more symbolic than practical.

"Away on!"

Part III

THE MUTTERER

*Then the king commanded to call the magicians, and the astrologers, and the sorcerers [*mekhashphim, *"mutterers"*], and the Chaldeans, for to shew the king his dreams.*

—Daniel 2:2

the necromancers who chirp and mutter

—Isaiah 8:19

CHAPTER 33

A CLOISTER GARTH PLANTED TO flowering shrubs, fragrant grasses, and medicinal herbs, surrounded by the usual columned arcades, had on one side the Benedictine monastery that had given Monsignor Bonacorso da Panzano refuge while the veiled chess game he played against King John drew toward its close. Opposite was the guest house in which he and Sinibaldo were lodged; the other two sides of the cloister were formed by the chapel and the workshops on the north, and on the south a long closed corridor that connected the monastery to the guest house.

Molly and Nemain had gone out to the garth, to pray under the stars. " 'Tis folly to receive help from Powers such as the Horned Man and not to render formal thanks, for They are prideful and dangerous when slighted."

Da Panzano had turned white as chalk when she said this, and even the stern and taciturn Sinibaldo crossed himself, drawing a little medal of St. Anthony from beneath his coat and kissing it.

"Daughter, do not invoke these forces of darkness in the house of God," said da Panzano.

"And any road," Molly continued, not the least deterred, "this lodge has harbored so many, and they all male, that it will interfere with our prayers; 'twill all go more smoothly out there, the sky over our heads and the earth under our feet and where among growing things and moving things there are females as well as males, not as 'tis with this strange and unnatural tribe of yours."

Now da Panzano truly was in a rage, although the urbane schemer and diplomat showed it only in the thinness of his lips, the clenching of his hand on his paternoster. But Molly had just by dint of great effort destroyed an army of monsters, and was in no mood to cater to the cleric's sensibilities.

HOB AND JACK SAT with the two papal agents at a long table in the guest house, sipping at goblets of wine. This was a communal dining room, paneled in oak from floor to ceiling; the floors were bare oak plank—polished with beeswax rather than laid with rushes. Although this night the papal legate and his bodyguard were the only guests, the monastery's guest house could accommodate a score of travelers.

The guest house had its own lay servants, who had put out wine and bread and cheese, laid fires in the hearths against the unseasonable damp chill of this June night, and retired to the monastery proper for the evening.

When first the women had left for the central garden, passing through an inner door to the arcade that ran around the open square, there remained a certain awkwardness, a tension, in the room. Stolid jovial Jack seemed unaffected, happy with a cup of wine before him, and not inclined to be a respecter of persons other than Molly. Hob, though, was rather at a loss for conversation, and da Panzano spent some moments gnawing at his lower lip and gazing into a corner, while his left hand fidgeted incessantly with the carved-bone beads of his paternoster. Sinibaldo, as always, sat, wary and silent; if there was something to be said, his master would say it.

"*Eh bene*," said Monsignor da Panzano, rousing himself. "So this *Mauro,* this sorcerer of Marroch, is somewhere out in the so-dark, so-secret night, and with a band of these *lupi mannari* to aid him. I do not say anything against your mistress; she has done what is very near the miracle tonight, yes? Although, *è vero,* she has placed her soul in peril with her so-blasphemous words"—here he made a little moue of distaste—"yet she has kept faith with me, so I say to myself, 'Da Panzano, hold your tongue awhile.' But I am concerned for this band of demons, with this man of power to lead them. Let me ask you, young man: What do you know of her ways? Can she complete this task, and destroy the rest of them?"

"Herself can do what is needed, Monsignor; I have never known her to fail at anything," said Hob, realizing with a bit of surprise that that was absolutely true.

"Of course, it may be that King John, he will be angry at this sorcerer for failing, no? Then it might be prudent for him to make his way back to Marroch with his followers, and not to risk the fury of the king." The legate sighed. "So many paths—is hard to see what to do."

Sinibaldo looked up suddenly, as did Jack: both stared at the outer door. Then Hob, alerted by the warlike pair's instincts, heard it too—a faint scuffling noise.

Da Panzano, a man of plots and schemes and purloined information rather than a man of action, looked back and forth among the others. "What? What is it you are hearing?"

Sinibaldo pointed to the outer door, and da Panzano swung around in his chair. Even as they watched, the locked door gave a *clank* and silently swung inward.

A moment later the elongated form of the Marroch sorcerer stepped out of the night, and behind him a small band of *bouda* pressed into the room, fanning out against the wall to either side of the doorway. The Cousins wore their hooded cloaks and nothing else, but they carried bags of coarse cloth, presumably with the ash so necessary to their transformation, and around their necks, slung on fine but strong chains, were sheathed the ornate curved daggers of the Berber folk. There were ten or eleven of them, and every man put a hand to his hilt, but none drew steel. One reached behind him and swung the door shut.

At once Sinibaldo stepped in front of da Panzano; Jack

and Hob came to their feet. Hob put his hand on his own knife-hilt, and beside him he felt Jack tense and widen his stance for stability, the floorboards actually creaking beneath his bulk. There was a moment's stasis, and then the sorcerer threw up a long thin hand: *Wait*. Yattuy was so cadaverously gaunt that he seemed even taller than he was, and Hob, looking up into the dark face with its taut cheekbones, its prominent brow ridges, the high forehead from which the crisp hair marched back in tight waves, was shocked to see something close to amusement—an angry, a dark amusement, the pleased expression of a cat with a mouse between its paws—in the sorcerer's eyes.

And what eyes they were! In the shadow of those strong brow ridges, they glittered with intelligence. Here was a man who had mastered the arcana of sorcery, who spoke several languages, who inspired obedience in hundreds of malefic beings, who could gain and hold the confidence of the irascible and headstrong king of a foreign nation.

Now he held the room, with its two factions poised on the brink of violence, immobile with his commanding presence, his gaze, and his upflung hand. He spoke, a mellifluous bass, with the faintest of accents—plainly he had mastered English, and the Norman high speech at that. "Be at peace. I seek only two women, witches of great power—you know who I mean. These ones"—he indicated the *bouda* behind him—"have trailed them here by scent."

He lowered his voice, and said gravely, "I have come to avenge my children."

Yattuy smiled upon Jack. Hob wondered to see what a

sweet and beneficent smile it seemed; almost one could believe that this was a kindly man, an uncle perhaps, reacting to his favorite nephew. He said to Jack, "You are what the people who dwell south of the great sands call the *ebóbó,* the hairy man of the mountain forests; my children can smell it upon you, the change, the animal inside your skin. Come, child, be my friend."

Jack seemed fascinated; it was as though he were unable to look away. He moved restlessly; his feet shuffled; his head began to turn, but did not, and always he was gazing into the sorcerer's eyes.

Yattuy reached behind him, blindly; the nearest *bouda* opened his bag of ashes, and held it so the magus could feel it. Still smiling upon Jack, he reached into the bag behind him, seized a handful of ash, and tossed it over Jack with a motion as of one who bestows a blessing. The Amazigh's long arm and narrow hand flashed out and snapped the leather thong about Jack's neck, the thong that held Molly's amulet, a little deerskin bag with herbs, a lock of Molly's hair, an image of the Horned Man, Lord of the Beasts. He tossed the amulet behind him.

Jack coughed, and began to shake his head. He staggered a bit in place, and reached a hand out to the nearest chair back. Hob stared at him in a mix of astonishment and horror: Had the dark man's outline begun to blur a bit? Hob blinked. No, Jack could be seen clearly enough—but was he a little coarser in feature? Were his shoulders even wider than before? There was a little tearing sound, and a rip began to open up at the sleeve of his shirt. Suddenly Hob caught sight of Jack's hand where it rested on the back of the chair—it *was* different: broader, darker, covered with coarse dark hairs.

Jack had begun to change into the Beast.

The Amazigh sorcerer, still smiling, turned his head slightly, addressing the *bouda* behind him. He pointed to Hob and the two Italians. "Kill these men."

CHAPTER 34

ONE OF THE COUSINS SPRANG at Hob, whipping his curved dagger from its sheath; the young man caught the descending knife wrist, applied a technique that Molly had taught him, and rolled the Berber over his hip, throwing him headfirst against the wall, to fall lifeless to the floor, his neck at a disquieting angle. As soon as the first *bouda* left his hands, Hob snatched out the heavy war dagger given to him by Sir Balthasar and went to one knee with his right arm extended, as that ferocious knight had shown him. The vicious horizontal swing that the next man had aimed at him thus passed harmlessly over his head, and the attacker's forward momentum carried him onto the dagger's point.

Da Panzano had backed away, Sinibaldo standing like a wall in front of him. The bodyguard's right hand flicked into his coat, flicked out, and did it again, and two men were down, convulsing, foaming, sliding down to death, the graceful Venetian darts quivering in their necks. In Sinibaldo's left hand was the gray silk cord: now the pierced golden coin of Venice, stamped with St. Mark's winged lion, flew out and coiled about a third man's neck. The Italian gave a fierce and clever pull, a move like a riverbank fisherman heaving a fish from the current, and there was a *crack*, muted by the muscle of the *bouda*'s neck, that told of a snapped spine, and the Berber, dead on his feet, fell straight down and rolled to his side.

At this moment Molly, breathless from running, appeared in the archway that led to the cloister passage, and Yattuy threw out his arms to either side and snapped out a command in Tamazight. The *bouda,* just preparing a concerted rush, stopped immediately and retreated to the wall behind them.

"Why, welcome," said the sorcerer, smiling pleasantly at Molly. "I am so pleased to find you here."

And now Nemain appeared behind her grandmother, and the sorcerer's smile widened. "And here is the whelp as well. We have a saying: *Ayna ikka tisgnit, ikt ifilu*—wherever the needle goes, so too goes the thread."

The women gazed in dismay at the scene: Jack's transformation was nearly complete. Da Panzano stared, his face drained of blood, his dark eyes wide and glassy, his palms flat to the wall behind him, as his mind fought to accept what he was seeing.

Jack's clothes had burst apart and fallen from him; his back had broadened, covered with a coarse black pelt, the hairs tipped with silver; his arms had lengthened and thickened, as big around as a strong man's thighs, with elbows knobbed with sinew and muscle, and the wrists and hands of a giant. Jack's legs had shortened and bowed and greatly increased in girth.

And his face! His face was a bestial mask of ferocity, small red-tinged eyes peering out from under a shelf of bone, a jutting mouth with four enormous fangs. He dropped to all fours, his leathery knuckles functioning as forefeet, and ambled forward a step, to peer uncertainly up into Yattuy's eyes.

The sorcerer looked down from his great height, placed an avuncular hand on the monster's shoulder, and pointed at Molly and Nemain. He bent down to the great head, where the skull rose to a casque-like ridge, and murmured in the Beast's small black ear. As he muttered to that which had been Jack, Yattuy's expression lost its veneer of urbane amusement, and became more and more savage. Hob had no doubt that he was ordering the women's destruction; that it would be accomplished by Molly's man added spice to the sorcerer's vengeance.

And now the Beast turned its muzzle; slowly its gaze left the wizard's face and sought out Molly and Nemain. It swung its stiff-backed torso about, and took a pace forward, still on all fours. Hob looked on in utter horror: the Beast was enormous, and immune to iron, and under Yattuy's control, and Molly unprepared and without the potions she used to induce a return to Jack's human state. It seemed that doom was inevitable.

But after a moment of frozen distress, Molly recovered herself, and extending a smooth white hand, she spoke to Jack in Irish, her beautiful deep voice calm and calming, her expression one of utmost kindness. The Beast's lips drew back: two great fangs above, two below, a terrifying sight, and then it roared, a tremendous leonine sound in the confined space, a thunderclap that seemed to shake the walls. From the corner of his eye Hob had a glimpse of da Panzano slumping back against the side table, his face ghost-white, and even Sinibaldo was in a deep defensive crouch.

And still Molly spoke to the Beast, and crooned to it, she and Nemain standing there empty-handed, and Hob could make out the name "Jack" amid the stream of Irish, and some Irish endearments he had come to learn—*mo mhuirnín,* and *a chuisle,* and *stór mo chroí,* and the like. He remembered what she had said about the wild white cattle, how they did not really understand Irish, but that the Irish helped Molly and Nemain focus their communication with the bulls, communication at a level below words. And the Beast was not a true animal; there was some Jack far down in that creature, and Jack had heard Molly murmuring those words, those Irish endearments, to him—on the pillows, in the dimness of the wagons, in the intimacy that they two shared with no one else.

Now Molly began to approach the Beast, still speaking in

that soothing voice that was almost singing, almost a lullaby. The Beast raised a fist the size of Hob's head, and hammered it down upon the floor, the planks giving off a muffled *boom*, and still Molly came on and she came up to the Beast and put a hand to its cheek, and bent forward—it flinched back a bit, but then stayed still—and she kissed it, full on the wide thin lips.

The Beast sat back on its haunches, looked off to the side, and gave a few desultory slaps at its black leathery breast, producing a popping sound. It almost looked embarrassed, thought Hob, if such were possible for so demonic a figure.

Now Molly put an arm about its neck, and she kissed it again, this time on the long flat cheek, and yet again, on the heavy supraorbital bone, and she looked up and past it, and into Yattuy's face, and her expression slowly changed from the utmost tenderness that she had shown to the Beast, to a grim minatory glare; gone was the fond lover, and in her place was this stern and vengeful queen. She raised her arm; her sleeve fell away and revealed her graceful forearm, her white wrist and hand and pointing finger, all extended toward the tall Berber: a lovely sight in itself, but signifying only *Death*. Slowly the Beast shifted to face Yattuy; it came forward onto its knuckles and took a pace toward him.

However evil Yattuy might be, he was not slow of wit. Those keen eyes had at once seen and weighed the shift in power: he was faced with two women of the Art, two dangerous warriors—da Panzano could be ignored for the moment—and this uncanny monster; he had his remaining *bouda,* still in human form, his own deep knowledge of the Art, and his force of will.

He stepped back rapidly five, six paces, almost running backward, and rapped out a command to the remaining *bouda.* At once they unslung their bags of ash and dumped the contents to the floor. A gray cloud rolled out from their side of the room. The Imazighen dropped in place and began to roll about in the ashes. Almost immediately their forms began to blur and distort.

Jack-the-Beast began to advance on the Berber magus, but the wizard fixed it with a glance and began to mutter in Tamazight, and the Beast stopped a moment, holding its head to one side and shaking it, as one does to clear water from the ear, but it was only for a moment: Molly's control over the Beast was complete, and it had the unholy strength of the shapeshifter, and the sorcerer's ability to control it was negligible.

Yattuy ceased his mumbled spell, and cried out a command, and transferred his attention to the two women. Behind him the band of *bouda,* now fully transformed, rose up from their bed of ash, burst into a cacophony of growls and yelps and titters, and surged around the tall form of their chieftain, who stood with both arms outstretched, one lean brown forefinger pointing at Molly and the other at Nemain.

Sinibaldo was immediately submerged beneath three

of the monstrous creatures, bitten and torn to death in the space of a heartbeat. Another hyena came around Yattuy's left side and made for Hob. The young man went into a defensive stance, his dagger out before him, although he knew it was hopeless, but Jack-the-Beast swerved from his slow advance on Yattuy and snagged the hapless Cousin with an outflung arm as thick and hard as a balk of timber. The hyena crashed to the ground, and before it could arise, the Beast's vast weight landed on its back; two enormous hands seized its head and wrenched the muzzle sideways. There was a dull crackling noise and the creature slumped to the floor, its dead eyes staring, its dead jaws dribbling saliva onto the polished oak boards.

The Beast turned away from the corpse and toward Yattuy, but a wave of the eerie hyenas, all that were left, leaped at it, and on the instant the room turned to a chaos of bestial snarling and roaring, the great bodies swirling and tumbling, hyenas thrown against the wall, scrabbling to their feet, and launching themselves back into the fray.

Hob backed to the wall near Molly and Nemain; da Panzano was already pressed tight against the wainscoting on his side, and even Yattuy stood aside somewhat. Hob could hardly make out what was happening; the combatants moved and dodged and swirled with the speed of fighting dogs, huge though they all were. He saw what had been Jack sink two-inch fangs into a hyena's sloping neck, shake it as Sweetlove did with a rat, and drop it, dead, at Yattuy's feet.

Then two more of the unnatural hyenas sprang at him;

he smashed one with a fist like a small boulder, and it fell on its side and slid perhaps a foot and did not arise. Jack-the-Beast began to throttle the second *bouda*, and then a third and fourth leaped on him, the collision driving the whole group through the arch and into the hallway, where they rolled and bit and smote and tore at one another, a sight to make Hob think of a war between tribes of devils.

But inside the room, Yattuy and the women had turned their attention back to their struggle. Hob tore his eyes from the tumult in the hall. In response to whatever unseen attack the magus was projecting toward Molly and Nemain, the women each had both arms extended toward him, the left palm out, and the right with first and last fingers extended, making Hob think of the Horned Man. He pushed himself off the wall and started toward Yattuy, dagger extended.

As he stepped in between the women and the Berber, Hob went blind. A humming ran along his bones, his limbs grew weak, and bile rose in his throat. He took a step but could not feel the floor, and a heavy blow to his shoulder told him that he had fallen. His ears heard only silence. He began to sweep a hand over where the floor should be, and then realized that he could not feel his hand. A fierce shining panic ran up through him, and he rolled aimlessly back and forth.

Mercifully his sight began to clear: at first it was around the perimeter of his vision, then the dark center faded to clarity. The three adepts still stood waging their silent battle, and the roaring of the Beast and the snarls and hysteric laughter of the *bouda* began to be heard, muffled at first and then, as whatever dire element Hob had stepped into began to wear off, louder and then yet louder. His limbs shook as though with fever, and he was weak, very weak, but sensation and strength were seeping back, however slowly, and he was giddy with relief.

From the floor he cast a glance at the women—what must it be like for them, standing full in the gale of the wizard's malice? Sweat stood out on Nemain's brow, she took tottering steps backward and forward again, and even as he watched, her eyes rolled up in her head and she collapsed.

A red rage ignited in Hob's chest, and seemed to seep into his limbs, thawing their chill, dampening their tremor; he forgot everything and began to creep. At first he was dragging his body along by his arms and one leg, then he progressed to a hands-and-knees crawl. He went past Yattuy and crossed behind the mage, grimly making for da Panzano's side of the room.

He came to Sinibaldo's corpse. With a great effort he seized hold of the bodyguard's arm, and, with a heave that took all of his diminished strength, turned the body on its back. He was dimly aware that da Panzano was watching him and the others, in ashen horror. Sinibaldo had been terribly torn, and Hob's hands were red to the wrist with his blood. He could hear the bodyguard on the day they had met: "The *dardo*—he is envenomed." The shock of stepping into range of the sorcerer's spell-casting had loosened the solid planks of the real world on which Hob stood, and for a moment the memory and the present became one, and he thought that Sinibaldo's corpse had spoken.

Hob shook his head; he wiped his gory hands on a dry section of Sinibaldo's surcoat, and folded back the lapel to reveal the leather baldric with its loops and their deadly cargo. Hob pulled out three of the Venetian darts, all that were left. He shuffled around, still on his knees, and painfully got to his feet.

With two darts held together in his right hand and one in his left, he advanced on the Amazigh sorcerer. He raised the darts high, and Yattuy became aware of him. The magus half turned, and aimed a forefinger at him, keeping the other hand trained on Molly. A terrible hot tingling began in Hob's face and swept down his neck to his body, and he felt his vision darkening again, and with a wrenching effort born of desperation he took a step forward and fell toward the wizard, all three darts sinking into the angular hard body, two in Yattuy's chest and one into his back, high up near the shoulder.

Again Hob collapsed, but his vision cleared almost at once, and so he was able to see the success of his attack: there was a moment when nothing happened, and then the sorcerer's long body curved backward into a bow, his mouth gave forth a shriek that was muffled at once by a gush of yellow foam, and he crumpled to the floor in a writhing tangle of narrow limbs. He flailed about for endless terrible moments, his shoulders whipping back and forth, his hands striking the floor, the knuckles making a sharp *crack* over and over; finally Hob could hear the *snap snap* of the long bones of forearm and shin as Yattuy's own convulsing muscles broke them like dry branch wood. At last the Marroch conjurer lay motionless.

As soon as Yattuy ceased to move, Molly sprang to Nemain's side and cradled her; Hob crawled over to them and Molly had him hold her while she rooted in her gown's pockets. She brought forth a small linen bag with a pungent odor of mint and yarrow, and held it beneath Nemain's nostrils. Hob settled his wife so that she lay back against his chest, and took to chafing her wrists, repeating her name in a desperate voice.

She was so very still! Was she dead? He had an instant of terrible despair so potent that his vision actually darkened again, and he thought that he might be dying himself, and he thought that perhaps it was of no great moment whether he did or did not.

Just then she gave a barely audible moan, and rolled her head from side to side; her legs moved in random restless movements. He buried his face in her hair, his soul upwelling from the lightless seawater cavern into which it had plunged, and he wept.

But only for a heartbeat or two; he felt Molly's hand grip his shoulder, and he came back to himself, and looked around the field of battle, that he might see what was still to do. He realized that there was near silence from the hall, save for a rapid rhythmic scraping sound. He glanced behind him. The Beast held the last *bouda* in the air, the two-hundredweight animal suspended as though from a gallows by the enormous black hands about its neck just behind the jaws, while the life was slowly crushed from it. The scraping sound was made by one hind foot, that just reached the floor, the claws scrabbling at the oak.

The kicking slowed, then stopped, and Jack-the-Beast dropped the *bouda* like a sack of grain; it landed with a blunt heavy thud and the *clack clack* of clawed feet limply striking the floor.

Molly was holding a bottle to Nemain's lips; she coughed and sat up, put a hand to steady the bottle neck, and drank again. She took Hob's arm where it was draped across her shoulders and drew it tight about her. To Molly she said, looking at Yattuy's contorted body, a knot of twisted limbs in the center of the room, "Is he dead, then?"

"He is."

She leaned back against Hob and sighed wearily. "He had horse-strength; wasn't I feeling his will battering at me, battering at me; 'twas like Jack's hammer, and then 'twas all red, and then 'twas all black—" She sat up suddenly and took deep rapid breaths, and Molly took her hand, and she calmed down again and fell back against her husband.

A shape loomed in the archway into the hall: Jack-the-Beast. It stood on all fours, blood from its wounds and the blood of the *bouda* dripping onto the floorboards, surveying the room, then gave an enormous, heart-stunning roar. For a moment everyone froze, white faces turned toward the Beast. Then the monster sat down in the doorway, looked up and off to the side, and slapped at its breast. Its lips writhed back from the appalling menace of its teeth, but closed again. Then it sat back, its short bowed legs out before it, and propped itself to one side on its powerful left arm, for all the world like a workman resting for a moment from his labors. It did not seem hostile; it did not seem in a mood to do anything but sit awhile.

In the center of the room, just behind Yattuy's corpse, lay the little amulet bag Molly had prepared for Jack; now she got up from Nemain's side, went and picked up the amulet, and retied it about the Beast's short thick neck. She murmured prayers in Irish and gave the Beast a sip from a small flask produced from the recesses of her gown.

The Beast moved its legs a bit; were they somewhat longer? Hob could not tell. He had seen Jack-the-Beast transform once before, both to and from the Beast state, and the onset had been sudden and the recovery gradual, and so it proved now. Silence held in the room, da Panzano watching in horrified fascination, standing pressed back against the wall, his right hand holding the crude cross that he wore about his neck on an iron chain, his lips moving silently.

Hob, cradling his wife, felt curiously calm after the paroxysms of the last hour. He was content to watch Molly, with her murmured spells and endearments, administer who-knew-what potion to the Beast, which all the while grew slimmer, and longer, and less hirsute, until it was no longer the Beast, or Jack-the-Beast, but Jack: weak, naked, wounded, and a bit dazed, but recognizably Jack.

From where he stood, frozen, watching Molly with Jack, da Panzano said in a small dusty voice, "You are far more enmeshed in Satan's snares than even I had thought, madam." Molly ignored him.

In one corner of the room was a handsome cabinet of dark wood, a cross carved into the doors. Da Panzano pushed himself away from the wall and walked stiffly over to the cabinet; he withdrew a small vial of oil and went back to where Sinibaldo's ruined body lay. The papal legate knelt and began to administer the last rites.

Hob stroked Nemain's hair; she seemed almost asleep. He watched the priest attending to Sinibaldo with the same bemused detachment with which he had observed Molly attending to Jack. There was a certain similarity in the two activities.

Da Panzano finished. He looked up and his eyes met Hob's. "He was a *ragazzo,* a street urchin, and he grows up, he is leading a gang of young thieves and brawlers, and one day I catch him breaking in to steal from the rectory. He was a *duro,* a street tough, but I see something in him, I see something in him. I say come with me, I make you something more than this street garbage."

Molly had run out to the wagons and returned with bandages, ointments, and a little jar of pain's-ease. Now she was administering to Jack, cleaning and wrapping his wounds, and Nemain was nearly asleep. It was as though da Panzano and Hob were the only ones in the room: he held Hob's eyes and he spoke quietly, though his voice was shaking a little, and his English was slipping.

"I take him in, I show him how to dress, to behave. He is already a brawler; I get him men who are deadly, who train him to kill with weapons and without weapons. He is flourish in my service: he is happy—he *tell* me he is happy, though he is not a man to smile; and he is save me many times."

To his surprise Hob realized that the dark eyes, normally keen as a hawk's and just as pitiless, were shining with tears. Da Panzano patted Sinibaldo's chest. His hand came away reddened, but the legate did not seem to notice.

"Sinibaldo, my son: there was no dog on earth so faithful as he."

CHAPTER 35

AFTER A WHILE NEMAIN SAT UP and put her clothing and hair in order, and Molly took one of the hooded cloaks that the *bouda* had worn and got it around Jack. The dark man, drained from the rapid and unanticipated change into Beast form, the forced return to himself, and the bites and bruises inflicted by the *bouda,* sat quietly on the floor, propped against the wall. His wounds did not seem serious, although he was plainly very weary. Hob stood and stretched. He was very tired himself, but happy to see Nemain feeling well enough to go to Molly and to help with Jack.

Da Panzano roused himself—he had been sitting and staring at Sinibaldo—and began walking about the room, which, like any battlefield, was drenched in blood and strewn with corpses. And now Hob, really looking around for the first time, realized that the hyenas had reverted in death to their human form, with all the wounds and broken bones that Jack-the-Beast had inflicted. The papal agent walked about among them, his lips moving; occasionally, with a richly made shoe, he would shift a tangle of limbs to show each individual more clearly.

Hob wondered at the legate's odd behavior: Was he praying for these demons? But da Panzano seemed to say only a word or so at each corpse. The twisted, foam-smeared body of the sorcerer, frozen in a silent eyes-wide gape-mouthed scream, a sight to engender nightmares, he avoided completely. Now the legate went through them all again, going out into the hall where there were more bodies, and back in again. He poured wine into a goblet, and sat, and sipped at the wine, his gaze far away.

At last he seemed to remember something. He said to Molly, "Madam, I have made you the promise, no? You will have our support, and when I reach Durham I will send a good amount of silver to Castle Chantemerle; Sir Odinell can keep it safe for you. Then I must leave this country for a little, or this king, he may find me, and be unpleasant to me. But I have also prepared a letter for you; it is with the papal seal, and when you are need the help, you show this to a bishop, an abbot, a prior—not some country priest, he is not understanding what to do—and they will give you the help. It is for the unusual difficulty, *vero*? And when you are ready to go to your home in Ireland, we will speak together; we will decide what help of ours will be best for you."

He spoke to Hob. "Squire Robert, perhaps you can do

me a service—I am fatigue', and you are young, and strong.
. . . Go into that hallway, go all the way to the end—it runs
the length of this house and down to the monastery. There is
a door to the monastery to the left, but it is locked; go into the
room at the very end, to the right. The letter of assistance,
he is there, on the table, in a little packet with the papal seal;
like so." He showed Hob his ring, with the crossed-key seal
prominent.

Hob looked a question at Nemain; she just nodded, and
indeed she seemed quite herself, if a bit subdued.

He stepped out into the hallway. He found himself in a
long narrow corridor, flagged with close-fitted stones and
paneled in dark wood. It went on for quite a long way, leaving
the guest house; at one point, through windows in the side
wall, he could see that the corridor ran along one side of the
cloister; beyond the cloister columns he could see the garth,
the grassy open area in the center of the cloister. Then he was
past, into a windowless section of the hallway. He thought
that he must be alongside the monastery itself now, although
the one doorway opening into that building was closed and
locked.

At last he came to the archway on the right, just before
the corridor ended in a blank wall. He stepped through into
what must be a study: rolls of parchment were thrust into
pigeonholes; two writing desks stood along one wall; there
were pots of ink and quill pens in holders, and oil lamps,
unlit, in brackets on the walls. The only light in the study
came from the fireplace, the fire burning low and filling the
space with moving shadows. Someone had laid and lit the

fire against the night damps of England, but at the moment the room was deserted.

Much of the room was dominated by a long trestle table, the surface the usual planed-smooth oak, rubbed with bees-wax cloths. Hob could just detect the faint scent of the wax: an earthy musk, a suggestion of honey. He looked about for the packet. But the table was empty save for two large silver candlesticks, the candles unlit.

Hob stood a moment, idly running a palm over the table, resting. He was weary unto death, swaying as he stood. But clearly this was a cul-de-sac; he must retrace his steps down the corridor and ask da Panzano if the priest was sure of his directions, or perhaps determine that Hob himself had made some misstep, and taken a wrong corridor.

Even as he thought this, a sound came to his ears, stopped, began again. What was— It was an irregular *tick, tick,* a pause, then *tick tick tick.* Claws, claws on stone! Hob snatched his dagger from its sheath and shrank back against the table, his heart pounding. His fatigue dropped from him like a discarded cloak.

The archway that led back into the corridor showed an impenetrable black. The ticking footsteps resumed, then paused. With hideous slowness, the misshapen mask of a hyena peered around the jamb of the arch. Black lips drew back from a jumble of huge teeth, and round mad eyes glared in at him. From the creature's lips broke an eerie titter, fol-lowed by a bass snarl. A moment later it loped around the corner and sprang at him.

Hob dropped at the last instant beneath the table, and

the beast, missing its target, crashed into the table edge. It sprawled awkwardly for a moment, claws scrabbling on the stone floor, and Hob plunged the dagger into its neck.

The hyena wrestled itself up to a standing position and backed away a few paces, shaking its head. The dagger, which for a moment had seemed so strongly embedded in its neck, began to loosen. A few drops of blood came out around the steel, but not the throbbing gout that might be expected from a wound in the throat, with its great blood vessels.

The dagger slid from the wound, which was hardly bleeding at all—even as Hob stared in dismay it seemed to be closing—and fell with a dull clatter to the floor. Hob rolled to the other side of the table, and stood, unarmed, defenseless. The hulking beast began to move toward him again, shoulders high, demon-mask head slung low on a long neck. There was nothing between Hob and this monstrosity but the table, empty but for its two candlesticks—no weapons on the walls, no window behind him to escape through. Hob looked about the room and back to the slowly approaching shapeshifter, and again back to the room, trying to search for something to aid him but also anxious to keep an eye on the death advancing upon him.

He moved sideways a bit, down toward the end of the great table, and the beast paused, perhaps assessing the best way to come at him. Its gaze seemed to display— afterward Hob could never fully explain how, even to himself—a more than bestial, but less than human, intelligence. *Tick.* Certainly it seemed in no hurry to spring: it took a step or two, paused, then took another two steps, all the while staring into his face, its lips writhing back from its fangs. *Tick, tick. Tick.* A continuous low rumble issued from its chest. *It plays with me,* thought Hob, and the voice of Monsignor da Panzano came to him again: "With perhaps a bit of the cat as well, no?"

Hob looked about him in a frenzy: He must act, but what was there to do? He had no weapon, and bare hands against two hundredweight of dagger-toothed demon would never prevail. Then *tick,* the beast took another step, and Hob shuffled sideways, his mind blank.

DESPERATION, FEAR, perhaps even the faint scent of beeswax from the candles and the table's surface: through Hob's mind ran a bolt of memory, swift as summer lightning, of a lesson from Sir Balthasar. The grim castellan would set Hob problems to solve, at all hours and in all places. On this day, months ago, they were on their way to a practice session with wooden knives, to be held in the castle's herb garden, when Sir Balthasar stepped into the castle's small chapel, redolent of incense and beeswax, a little room set aside for private prayer, as opposed to the larger chapel where Father Baudoin said Mass.

They knelt, prayed a moment, and then Sir Balthasar stood, put one of the wooden knives aside and gave Hob the other.

"Were a knife to come at you, and you unarmed, what would you do?" he asked.

"I, uh . . ."

The knight spread his arms wide. "Here, come at me, come kill me."

Hob was used to this sort of thing from the knight, and he knew that it was almost impossible to get the better of Sir Balthasar, and at any rate the knives were blunt, and wooden, and so without hesitation or warning he lunged at his mentor.

Sir Balthasar sprang backward, close to the wall behind the little altar. With his back to the wall he leaped straight up and seized the crucifix fastened there and dropped lightly back. He held the cross by the bottom and swung it like a hammer; Hob threw up the wooden knife to block the blow, and Sir Balthasar, by some cunning twist, snagged the wooden knife blade in the angle between the upright and the crossbar, wrenched, and sent the knife flying into a corner. The huge knight swung the cross up and over, a tremendous overhand blow aimed at Hob's forehead and stopping a few fingers' breadth from its target.

Hob, caught on the wrong foot, off balance, astonished at the loss of his dagger, would have been stunned like a steer at the harvest slaughter, had the castellan not stopped with such perfect control.

"You must make shift with what is around you," said Sir Balthasar. He kissed the crucifix and set it on a nearby bench.

"But—but, my lord," began Hob, concerned about sacrilege, "to use a cross . . ."

"Nonsense," said Sir Balthasar. "Do you think the Sieur Jesus wants to see you gutted like a fish?"

The knight was as devout as the next man—Hob had often seen him at Mass—but he was not a fussily pious sort.

At this moment a castle servant came into the chapel, bearing a broom and a basketful of fresh rushes; seeing the two standing there, he bowed and prepared to withdraw.

"Stay you," said Sir Balthasar, and he pointed to the cross. "See that that's put back up."

"My lord."

THE UNNATURAL HYENA was stalking along the far side of the table; soon it would be round the end and at him. Even across the wide table, Hob could smell its blood-and-carrion breath, hear it rumbling deep in its throat, like the purring of an enormous cat.

Make shift with what is around you.

In a despairing rage, Hob seized the nearer candlestick and threw it with all his force at the *bouda,* striking it full on the shoulder.

To Hob's utter astonishment, the hyena screamed and coiled around on itself, snapping at its own shoulder, the mindless reaction of a fighting dog or wolf. A sudden pain in the wild often means a bite, and a swift savage snap at the pain often catches the biter in the act. Molly had said that shapeshifters in their Beast form could not think as men and women did, and the turnskin before Hob acted with animal illogic, snapping again and again at the air by its injured side.

Where the candlestick had struck, there was a furrow in the hyena's hide, the furred edges smoking, the interior beginning to run with blood, the wound widening a bit even as Hob watched. The candlestick, dropped to the floor, had rolled toward the wall, and it was coated with smoldering skin and fur. Hob looked at the remaining candlestick, gleaming softly in the firelight. He had a moment when he could hear Molly telling of the uses of iron against witchcraft. But shapeshifters were creatures that no iron would bite. He was thinking at a furious pace. This candlestick, it was not iron, but, but, it was silver: Could it be that—?

The hyena had begun to turn its attention to him again, and was limping back toward the end of the table. Hob came to himself with a rush; a storm of fear and rage swept through his mind; there was a redness at the edge of his vision. He snatched up the remaining candlestick, put a palm to the table, and vaulted over to the far side.

The hyena swung its heavy snout toward him and he bashed at the side of its head, the candlestick visibly denting the horrid countenance. The hyena emitted its shrieking laugh, signifying excitement or distress, and shook its head as if partially blind, backing away a few paces. The side of its face was smoking; it seemed about to burst into flame. Hob charged after it, raining blow upon blow at its head; he was cursing breathlessly but his arm rose and fell without cease. He felt as though he would never tire; paroxysms of fury shook him; he was filled with a frenzy, spasms of madness, a savage joy at seeing his enemy finally helpless before him.

At some point he found himself half squatting, leaning over, cursing in English interspersed with occasional Irish maledictions he'd acquired from Nemain, striking again and again at a misshapen, blood-soaked, scorched bundle—the shapeshifter, now quite clearly dead.

He ceased. He stood up, breathing heavily, and put his free hand to the table and just leaned there a moment, the candlestick dangling by his side, and then Molly and Nemain burst into the room and came to a halt, staring at the tableau of Hob and the hyena, already beginning to fade into its human form. Behind them came da Panzano. Upon seeing the half-human corpse, from which wisps of smoke still drifted upward, a curious expression of satisfaction, even triumph, came over his face. Hob, still catching his breath, was facing the legate, and thought that he looked like someone who has wagered on a footrace and won.

"Let us return," said Molly, "for I'm not wishing to leave Jack to himself."

"There was no packet," Hob croaked.

Da Panzano said, "Yes, yes, I am remembering now—I have it in the guest house." Nemain turned and looked closely at him, but he shrugged and set off back up the corridor. Nemain came to Hob and put an arm about his waist, and then Molly was on his other side, and he limped along between them till he felt a little stronger, and stood up more straightly, and then they were back in the guest house, in the dining room.

"Sit," said Nemain to Hob sternly, pointing to a chair by the wall. She herself seemed to have recovered completely from her swoon.

Hob, exhausted and numb from his encounter with the *bouda,* sat down heavily; his side ached—at some point he must have bruised his ribs. But generally he felt a great contentment.

Molly went to Jack and got him on his feet; the dark man shuffled over, and dropped into a chair, which creaked alarmingly but held. Hob grinned at him, but Jack, still with a wisp of the Beast-dream on him, had not yet recovered the capacity for self-distance that lets one smile at grim events, and he just nodded at Hob.

From a chest in the far corner da Panzano withdrew a packet with the papal seal, and tendered it to Molly, who put it into a fold of her garments without looking at it.

"You do not look?" asked da Panzano.

"I will look later; if 'tis not what you promised, sure I'll come to you again, my lad."

For something said so unemphatically, thought Hob, this managed to convey a sense of terrible menace: the creak of a longbow at full draw.

"Is well, is well," said da Panzano, still pale and shaken from the loss of Sinibaldo. He looked around the room. "I am counting these *lupi mannari,* and I say to myself, surely there was one more? I had hoped, when I sent this young man down that so-long corridor, that this beast-thing would show itself. They are *feroci,* ferocious, they have the, how do you say, the blood-love? The blood-lust. But I think to myself, it will be afraid to face these two women, with their unholy—forgive me, but yes, unholy—powers. This young man, so strong and tall, does not have such powers; it will attack, and then these women will come and destroy it. I did not think that you could do so yourself, my son."

Had Hob not been so weary, he might have noticed the stillness that had come over Nemain; how she slowly pulled herself up in her chair, weary though she herself must be; how she drew her legs under her; how she put her feet flat to the floor.

"You're after using my husband as bait? You're after using my husband *as bait*?"

Suddenly she was on her feet, almost without seeming to rise; suddenly she took a pace toward da Panzano, and another, whirling like a dancer to add force to the coming blow, the spin bringing her near to the monsignor, her hair, tangled, disheveled from the long night, whipping out behind her like a flag, her outstretched hand having acquired a dagger in some fashion, the arc of the blade inscribing a silver circle in the air that was destined to end in da Panzano's neck, Hob frozen with shock, and there was a *slap!* as Molly's strong hand caught her granddaughter's slender wrist, the point an inch or so from the pulsing vessel in the priest's neck.

The women stood like carved figures for a moment, but Molly was far stronger, and forced Nemain's arm down. She put her other arm around her granddaughter and guided her back to her chair.

"We're needing him in the future, and any road he's one of those whose nature is to play chess with other people's lives, and he's not to be changing his nature. Let him aid us," said Molly, looking back over her shoulder to make sure that da Panzano heard her, "and we will let him live his life."

The papal agent, drawing his hand-cloth from his sleeve,

dabbed carefully at his forehead. "I apologize, madam; I have no wish to act other than honorably toward you."

Molly straightened and faced him. "Monsignor," she said in a calm, almost kindly, voice, "it's friends that we'll be from this night forward, but think on this question. You have seen what we can do. Do you think that you can hide, even in the mighty Church, from us?"

"No, I . . ." he began, but she held up her right hand, palm out, the universal gesture for *stop*.

"Nay, 'tis not that I need to hear it; 'tis not that I'm asking it of you. 'Tis for you to ask yourself, on those nights when sleep will not come to you, and you lighting your bedside candle again and looking at the ceiling till the break of day. Ask it of yourself then, and study the answer, and live your life by that answer."

CHAPTER 36

THERE MUST BE A NEST SOME-where nearby, thought Hob. Some irregularity in the walls, a jutting stone that provided enough of a ledge to build upon. He could hear, above the rhythmic crash of the sea against the headland far below, the burbling of rock doves, a pleasant sound on this summer day.

They were in Sir Odinell's favored meeting room, high in a seaside tower of his castle, Chantemerle: Molly and her family; and Sir Odinell, the Sieur de Chantemerle; as well as, from Castle Blanchefontaine, Sir Jehan and Sir Balthasar. On the bright cloths that covered the broad main table, jugs of wine and platters of meat pastries were set at convenient intervals.

On a sideboard, its oak surface bare of covering but highly polished, was a single object: a square of parchment, and on it, in Latin, the terms of the agreement signed at Runnymede by King John and his rebellious barons. The sideboard stood beneath a window; the day was fine and with little wind, save for the inevitable breezes that blew in little starts and stops from the German Sea.

"And I fear 'twas all for naught," said Sir Odinell. "The king breaks this part of the treaty, and we that part, and in the end 'tis so many empty words."

"It will be war, and the French will be in it—some want Louis to come over—and there will be chaos. . . . Precious Christ! It will be the days of Stephen and Matilda all over again," said the grim Sir Balthasar.

"We'd do as well to light this evening's fire with it," said Sir Odinell. "It might be of some use, then."

But Molly had gone over to the sideboard and was feeling the parchment, running her fingers along the edge, then smoothing it flat against the wood and running her finger slowly along the lines—she could read Latin, but not well, not easily, and so she had to pause, and think, and slowly derive its meaning. Now she looked up, her fingers still rubbing gently at a corner of the Charter.

"Nay," she said, "there's a tinge, a taste, a faint . . . I feel it has some power and some use, but not now." She turned to Hob. "You remember when you found those caltrops, and they lying in the road?"

Hob nodded.

"And wasn't I saying that I had no idea what good they might do for us, but that it seemed that they *would* do some good for us, and we carrying them along from that day, and they saving you and Jack from those *arrachtaí,* they bounding up the path, and so eager to get at you?"

Again Hob nodded, and Jack gave a growl that, to those who knew him well, merely signified assent, although the three knights gave a slight start: it was the sound of a bear, grumbling in its den, deep in the earth.

"Doesn't she have the second sight, now," said Nemain, "and that more strongly than any I've seen, and what she foretells coming to pass, time and again."

"*Al-Kahina,*" said Hob, who could recall virtually anything that he had once heard. When everyone looked at him, he said, " 'Tis what the Arabs called that Amazigh woman, Dihya, their hero, that Father Ugwistan said you were like— *al-Kahina*; it means 'the soothsayer,' because she could foretell the future."

"You can foretell what is to be, madam?" asked Odinell. He had seen too much of Molly's powers to be openly skeptical, and yet, and yet . . . "How can you do such?"

" 'Tis like explaining the *clairseach* to a deaf man," said Molly, "but . . . that pigeon we're hearing, we hear it because it's right there outside the window, and the wind calm. Think of a wind that blows strongly toward you—it carries sounds of things you're traveling toward, things you cannot yet see. Is the sound of children laughing just over the hill you're going round, children you'll meet in a little while, is that not a sign from your time to come? You're saying to yourself, 'Sure I'll be meeting children soon,' and so 'tis—you come around the hill, and there are the children, and you meeting them, but you knew that you *would* meet them, soon, when you were coming round that hill. 'Tis like that with me—only 'tis not hearing, 'tis some other way, and how can I tell you of it, you as it were deaf to the sound of time to come. I feel this parchment, as I felt the steel of those caltrops, and something within me is saying, 'This will be of use'; I know not how, nor when, but 'This will be of use.'"

"But the treaty is broken on both sides; of what further use can it be?" asked Sir Jehan.

"'Tis not that I can see myself what use it might have," said Molly slowly. "'Tis not clear even to me; but what I feel is, is . . . a sense that an arrow has left the bow, and 'tis not to be taken back."

She turned again to the parchment, and bent to peer at the bottom. "This is one of those in the meadow with you that day by the Thames," she said. "'Tis never a monk's copy, for here is the king's signature."

"Yes," said Sir Odinell, "'tis one of several copies signed that day."

"Be said by me," said Molly, tapping the parchment where John Lackland had signed, "this king wi—" and then her face went slack and she slapped a hand to the sideboard and held to it a moment, swaying, very pale.

"*Seanmháthair!*" cried Nemain, and came up and around the table to her; Jack arrived a heartbeat later and caught Molly around the shoulders, and eased her into a chair. Hob and the knights had come to their feet, but there seemed to be nothing to do. Jack hunkered beside Molly's chair and took her hand in his, looking keenly into her face. She was a big woman, but her hand disappeared into Jack's huge paw.

Molly made waving-off motions with her free hand. "Nay, 'tis nothing, 'tis nothing. I'm just after seeing . . ."

"What is it, *seanmháthair*, what?" Nemain sat down beside her.

"I'm just after saying that I'd a sense about the parchment, but that it's vague, and more a feeling than a clear thought, and then I'm tapping that signature, where the king's hand itself rested; I was about to say of him—well, 'tis gone, but it was concerning King John. And then . . ."

"What, *mo chroí*?"

Jack took a goblet of wine from the table with his free hand and held it to Molly's lips as though she were a tot, and she drank, and shook herself, and patted the hand that held hers. The color was coming back into her cheeks.

" 'Twas as though I were blind for a moment; this room, wasn't it gone entirely, and myself on a bleak shore, a rocky shore, and the waves crashing on the rocks, and with every crash saying '*Faoi cheann bliana. Faoi cheann bliana.*' And this went on for a long time."

" 'Twas but a moment till you spoke to us."

"Sure it seemed a very long time, and after a while I'm noticing a crown caught in the rocks below, very near the water, and washing to and fro with the waves, and they saying '*Faoi cheann bliana.*'"

"This is Irish, then?" asked Sir Jehan.

" 'Tis," said Molly. "These dreams, or visions, from Herself are always in Irish, or it seems like Irish to me in the dream."

"But what does it mean?" asked the knight.

"It's meaning 'one year,' or 'in a year's time,'" said Nemain.

Molly said, "And the waves were chanting it, as it seemed, and then a wave caught the crown and pulled it out into the water, and it sank from sight. And wasn't it that very moment that the waves stopped their chant, and were just waves, beating on the rocks, and then I was here, and glad to return to you, so I am. 'Twas like an ill dream. 'Tis a vision: some sign from the Mórrígan. I have had such before, but not for a while. And strong as it was, clear as it was, I know not what to think of it."

"Do you not?" said Nemain.

Something in her granddaughter's voice made Molly turn to look into Nemain's face. The young woman's green eyes glittered with intensity. Hob and the knights had resumed their seats, but were reduced to onlookers, Hob a family member and the others powerful magnates of the North Country, but all excluded from these matters of Art. Jack was concerned only for Molly's health and well-being; he did not care about the meaning of portents, so be it that she was safe.

"What is it, child?" she asked Nemain.

"A crown caught in the rocks on a desolate shore, and the waves chanting 'One year,' and trying to pull the crown from the land into the deep, and then succeeding, and the crown sinking into darkness, and the chant ceasing at that moment. Think, *seanmháthair,* what can it mean? I have a thought, but I'm not wanting to say it, lest I taint the purity of your message—'twas to you it came, and not myself."

Molly thought, and then said, "Ah!" and turning to Jack,

said, "Give us another sip of that wine, *a rún*." When she had drunk again, she drew a deep breath. "Sure the crown is King John, and the bleak shore the perils that compass him about, and one year is the time, and at the end of that year it's down into the dark he'll go, so he will."

" 'Tis my thought exactly," said Nemain.

Sir Jehan looked from one to the other. "You mean that in one year John Lackland—"

"Will be dead," said Nemain with just the least trace of impatience.

"Precious Christ!" said Sir Balthasar.

There was a general silence, as everyone reflected on this, and what it might mean, and what, if anything, should be done in preparation. Then: "Things seemed simpler when I was young," said Sir Odinell.

Sir Jehan roused himself, and said, "The world is wide, and many things therein."

THERE ENSUED a pragmatic political discussion among the three knights: What would be the effect were King John to die? Who would be regent for the boy Henry were he to take the throne? Was Anjou, then, lost completely? Hob, sitting quietly, his mouth full of a pork tart and a goblet of good red wine at his elbow, listening to his elders debate, thought that a few years ago these men would have thought Molly a witch or a charlatan; now they accepted her prediction as iron-hard fact, and discussed the possible consequences without hesitation. *Al-Kahina!*

CHAPTER 37

AFTER A WHILE SIR JEHAN, coming round to some of the business for which the meeting had originally been called, stood, raised his goblet, and said in formal tones: "Let us drink to Queen Maeve, who has saved us yet again from foes too terrible for simple knights to face."

The other knights also stood and raised their wine to Molly, who stood by the window with the light finding silver wavelets in the gray flood of her hair, and acknowledged their praise with the slightest inclination of her head.

Hob and Jack and Nemain also stood, and drank to she on whom they all depended.

And then there were salutes to Queen Nemain, and to Squire Robert, and to Master Jack Brown, for their parts in saving the Northern nobles from a ghastly end.

Nemain alone was not drinking wine, but saluted with her cup of tea brewed from herbs that Molly collected as they traveled. Hob noticed it; suddenly he could not remember when she had last drunk anything stronger than mint tea, or well water. It was odd, and—

Jehan broke into his thoughts. "There's war coming, soon or late though it be, and Balthasar and I must return to Blanchefontaine—I wish to see how the crops are coming along, and I have not held court in far too long, and we will be delighted to see Lady Isabeau and Dame Aline again. I trust you will come with us, madam?" This last was to Molly.

"We will that," said Molly.

"But before that," said Sir Jehan, "there is this that we must do."

Sir Balthasar stood, and went into the next room, returning with a large burlap sack, such as might be used on campaign in a supply wagon, so capacious that its folds concealed any hint of what it contained. In his brusque way, he dropped the bundle without ceremony on the end of the table. He drew out a scabbarded sword, a gold-buckled belt, golden spurs.

"Squire Robert," said Sir Jehan formally, "no one here can doubt your courage, your good faith; you have killed men, one of them fairly described as a giant; you have killed a sorcerer; and you have killed a monster from some pit of Hell. Sir Balthasar says he has never had a more apt pupil. Kneel before him."

Hob, taken all unawares—he knew he was to be knighted someday, but this had been kept a surprise from him—went down on one knee before the grim castellan. Sir Balthasar, without ceremony, pulled the sword from its sheath, banged the flat down on Hob's left shoulder and then on his right; nor were they love taps. Hob felt them, and was sore for a few days afterward.

"Rise, Sir Robert," growled Sir Balthasar, sheathing the sword again.

Hob, the blood singing in his ears, rose. The huge castellan knelt before him, causing Hob no end of embarrassment, and fastened the spurs about his ankles. Then he threaded the gold-buckled belt through the scabbard loops, and strapped the sword to Hob's side. He embraced Hob, saying "Welcome, brother," and stepped back, and here came Sir Jehan and Sir Odinell to do the same.

"Both Sir Odinell and myself offer you service, if you wish to swear fealty to either of us," said Sir Jehan.

Hob—Sir Robert, now—looked at the lord of Blanche-fontaine. "I thank you both, sirs. But I cannot swear to either; there is one to whom I must swear, and that is Queen Maeve."

"We thought as much, but wished to make the offer," said Sir Jehan. Sir Balthasar drew from his belt pouch a small crucifix, and handed it to Hob.

Hob had studied the forms of knighthood and the

swearing of allegiance. Although it felt strange, it did not feel ludicrous, for him to pledge formally to the woman who had raised him from child to knight. She was Molly, but she was also Queen Maeve, and a more powerful woman had rarely walked the earth.

He went to Molly and knelt before her, the cross between his two palms, and said the old words. "I am at thy service, madam. I swear, upon Our Savior and this cross, that I will always be a faithful vassal to thee and to thy successors in all things in which a vassal is required to be faithful to his lord, and I will defend thee, my lady, and all thy successors, and all thy castles and manors and all thy men and their possessions against all malefactors and invaders, at my own cost and of my own free will, so help me God and His saints."

"Rise, Sir Robert," said Molly, not a bit troubled by Hob's oath being sworn on a cross. He stood and she embraced him, and kissed him on both cheeks. Then, the mother overwhelming the queen for a moment, she straightened the scabbard on his sword-belt, muttering to herself "There, that's better" almost inaudibly.

"To Sir Robert," said Sir Jehan, raising his goblet, and this was echoed by all, and Hob stood there, extremely happy but for his fear that he would blush in front of the company.

He looked around him: everyone was smiling, even Sir Balthasar, although that grim knight's smile rather resembled the expression one sees on a wolf, just before it springs.

Sir Odinell turned to Sir Jehan, and said, "As anxious as you are to return to Blanchefontaine, brother, 'twill have to be the day after tomorrow, for tonight we will have a great feast to honor our new knight, and on the morrow I trust you will have neither desire nor capacity to travel."

WHEN THE MEETING had concluded some time later, Sir Odinell drew Hob aside, and said, "Sir Robert, there is something I would have you see. Come with me, if you please."

Hob had been a knight as long as it might take Milo to walk a league, and here was the Sieur de Chantemerle addressing him as "Sir Robert" and, more significantly, asking his cooperation—"if you please"—where before he might just have told the young man to come with him. Hob was not his vassal, but one did not easily refuse a lord in his own castle. To be treated as an equal by a man approaching middle age, and a knight, and a lord of extensive lands, was dizzying.

He followed Sir Odinell down the winding stone stairs to the hall, and thence to the outside stairway to the bailey. The men-at-arms at the little gatehouse at the bottom of the stairs threw bolts and hauled open the door to the outside; they saluted Sir Odinell and then they saluted Hob, with his knight's belt and his spurs. The day was fair, and Sir Odinell's bald head with its fringe of graying hair gleamed in the sunlight. He put an arm about Hob's shoulder and steered him toward the stables.

Hob was acutely conscious of the longsword in its scabbard swinging against his left leg, and he put his hand on the hilt to still it. They crossed the beaten earth of the bailey.

Against a far wall the dog grooms were working with Sir Odinell's pack of Irish wolfhounds, descendants of the pair Sir Jehan had given him. In the other direction housecarls had strung a line between two poles set in the dirt, and were beating some of the castle's tapestries with wooden paddles in which holes had been cut; small clouds of dust arose and were whirled away by eddies of the endless breezes whistling in from the German Sea.

And here they were at the stables, outbuildings stretching along half the length of the northern curtain wall. They stepped into sudden gloom, cool after the sun-warmed bailey. Here was a long corridor divided into stalls, some of them large enough for more than one animal. They went along the corridor, the air rich with the warm salt smell of horse, the sweet nose-tickling scent of hay, the ammoniac bite of urine. Away down toward the far end a groom called something unintelligible to one of his mates; the answer, even farther away, was as faint as an echo.

Sir Odinell stopped before a large enclosure, perhaps three stalls' worth, with a chest-high board wall in front of it. Within were a groom as well as a large mare and her colt; the big-boned mare was black, but the colt—Hob leaned forward eagerly, a hope growing in his heart. The colt had a soft halter on it, and the groom led it over to the front wall. Hob reached over, felt the warm neck, the soft nose; the colt whickered a little and pushed against his hand, perhaps moved by some nursing instinct. It was a beautiful gray, the color of dull steel on a cloudy afternoon.

"My lord, that colt—it resembles your . . ."

"You have the right of it, Sir Robert: this mare is Larmes; her colt here is the get of my destrier, Ferraunt. I know you have admired him, and especially his color, so like steel it is, and fortunately the colt takes his color from his sire. We will train him up for you, and he is yours."

Hob was leaning into the stall, stroking the small velvet nose. "My lord, this is too—"

Sir Odinell broke in, putting a hand to Hob's shoulder: "Sir Robert, consider. Everyone in this castle owes life itself to you and your family, and our gratitude will never fade. This is but a little gift; your gift to us was the greater. Let us have no more protests; 'tis your destrier, and I wish you joy of him."

"I thank you, my lord."

The colt pushed at him, breathing warm air into his palm, tickling him. Hob smiled at the earnest little face. A destrier of his own! The colt sneezed against his palm, reminding him of Milo, and he had to laugh.

CHAPTER 38

IRELIGHT AND TORCHLIGHT and candlelight: it seemed to Hob that the great hall of Castle Chantemerle was more brightly lit than ever he had seen it. If Molly's wagons were what he considered his home, and Castle Blanchefontaine his second home, surely Chantemerle was his third, another place where Molly's troupe was assured of a lifelong welcome, and a refuge, strong not only in its walls but in the knights and men-at-arms in residence there, each of whom was cognizant of the little family's role as their saviors: saviors from a particularly horrid evil.

This goodwill, this gratitude for their deliverance, which was accomplished primarily by Molly and Nemain but in which Jack and Hob were essential partners, perhaps contributed to the exuberance with which folk were celebrating Hob's elevation to knighthood.

He had reluctantly laid his sword and golden spurs aside for the feast, but of course one wore the belt of knighthood. He was in the seat of honor at Sir Odinell's right hand. To Hob's right was Sir Odinell's daughter, Mistress Eloise, now a young lady of fourteen years. Around the table on the dais were the rest of Hob's family; Dame Maysaunt, Sir Odinell's wife; and Chantemerle's household knights. The long trestle tables and benches of the lower hall were filled with the castle folk: men-at-arms, housecarls, servants of all kinds— everyone not on duty. So tight-knit a community, working and eating and sleeping within the same walls, is itself like a large clan, and although they might not be privy to each last detail, they knew in general that the horror that had come to prey upon this stretch of the German Sea coast in past years had been destroyed by Molly's folk, and they were happy to see Hob's advancement.

The chefs had outdone themselves. Dish followed dish— chicken and rice cooked in almond milk and sugar; the poached dumplings known as quenelles, some made with veal, some with herring; and later, sculptures of ships, of castles, of miniature jousting knights, all made of sugar. Pitchers of good red wine were constantly replenished, and there were various punches, apple cider, perry. Hob—he found it hard to think of himself just yet as Sir Robert—was enjoying himself, eating and drinking with great gusto, listening to Sir Odinell's tales of campaigns that he and Sir Jehan had been on together and to Mistress Eloise's anecdotes about her adored wolfhounds.

Mistress Eloise had been a girl of perhaps eleven when Sir Jehan, having acquired two litters of wolfhound pups from Ireland, had given Sir Odinell a male and a female, one from each litter. Mistress Eloise had promptly named them Erec and Enide, after the characters in her favorite romance. Sir Odinell had let her have them as pets till they grew to adulthood, and one or the other was still her constant companion. They were the parents of the wolfhounds Hob had seen being trained in the bailey.

Between Hob and Eloise lolled an enormous brindle-furred shape: Enide, the matriarch of Sir Odinell's pack. Sir Odinell would jest that Eloise needed no guard—there was always one of the fiercely devoted dogs within arm's reach of her. Now Eloise took a morsel of beef from her trencher and held it below the table. Enide, lying on her side, lazily lifted up head and shoulder, daintily took it in her wolf-killer jaws, and lay back down, chewing dreamily.

Now came the moment Hob had been dreading: Sir Odinell rose, called for attention, and embarked on a speech, not overlong, detailing Hob's virtues, while Hob, acutely embarrassed, found the whole hall looking at him as he was showered with praise. Then Sir Jehan rose and did the same, and even Sir Balthasar growled his way through a discourse on how much Hob had exceeded his other pupils in the arts of murder.

And worst of all: the cry went up for a speech from

Hob himself. Afterward he was never sure what exactly he had said—gratitude to Sir Jehan and Sir Odinell, for their instruction in the conduct of knights, and to Sir Balthasar, his especial teacher for the Norman martial arts, and then he spoke of techniques shown him by Molly and Nemain, and Jack, who had taught him both how to become strong and various useful, if somewhat low, sleights to use in combat. Somehow he managed to acquit himself reasonably well—Molly herself told him afterward that he seemed both calm and polished, which he found ludicrous but was nonetheless relieved to hear.

Sir Odinell had two jugglers, and musicians—none so good as Molly's troupe, thought Hob—and a troubadour from the Continent who performed a long section from *Aucassin et Nicolette.*

Finally, when at last the speeches and pledges and healths had been exhausted; when Mistress Eloise had gathered up Enide's leash, kissed her parents good-night and Hob as well, and wandered off to bed; when most of the lower hall had cleared; when Sir Balthasar and Sir Odinell were deep in a technical discussion concerning the cross-breeding of horses; and the only ones still drinking hard were the younger castle knights, Hob said his farewells and went down the table to join Nemain.

She took his hand and rose and, in turning, staggered a bit; she put a hand to the table to steady herself, knocking over her goblet, spilling the little left in the vessel across the layers of cloth draped over the table. Hob steadied her, and they began to make their way along the table. Hob was thinking idly that Nemain must have drunk deeply: usually she was as agile as a cat.

This drew his gaze back over his shoulder to the goblet lying flat on the table, and the cloth there, unstained, wet but colorless—Nemain had been drinking well water, and not wine.

He had barely time to be puzzled when here came Daniel, Sir Odinell's seneschal and a friend, with his young wife, Hawis, and another round of congratulations began, and for the moment the incident of the goblet of water was forgotten.

CHAPTER 39

ON THE SECOND DAY AFTER THE feast, in the predawn darkness, Hob was breaking his fast in the troupe's solar. This was one of Hob's favorite places when they were guests in Sir Odinell's castle: high rooms in one of the seaward towers of Castle Chantemerle's keep, with a clear view out across the German Sea. The table held honey beer, hard rolls, and the sheep's-milk blue cheese brought up from Yorkshire, the work of the monks at Jervaulx Abbey. Molly's little family were all ready to take the road; it remained only to hitch up the animals and form up in the bailey with Sir Jehan's party, and they were off to Castle Blanchefontaine.

Nemain had picked at her roll, and had drunk only mint tea brewed from leaves Molly had gathered, and looked out the window at the slowly lightening sky. Suddenly she got up and, excusing herself, hurriedly left the solar. Hob looked after her, surprised. The sea wind rattled the shutters a bit; gulls mewed; and suddenly a dark cold shadow swept across his life.

He had seen Nemain, with Molly, engage in a battle of will and magecraft with a sorcerer at least as powerful as Yattuy, if not more powerful, a battle that lasted from the middle part of the night until dawn. Yet the Berber had overwhelmed her. And her appetite had been waxing and waning for some time now. And today, if he read her sudden departure correctly, she could not even keep her breakfast down.

Hob considered Nemain's cup of mint tea, and her digestion, so sensitive of late that she could not face the thought of wine. He was worried. She seemed a bit weak, and weary, she who had always been so active, a slim and formidable warrior. Yet she looked healthy, even robust: she had gained a bit of weight this summer, and her bosom had swelled, so that she seemed to be flourishing, and yet was tired and irritable.

It was one of those moments when a host of small observations, having plucked at one's sleeve again and again, and having been ignored in the face of more pressing demands, suddenly rise up to block the path ahead. He turned to Molly.

"Mistress!"

"Aye, Sir Robert?"

He ignored Molly's attempt at a pleasantry; he was imagining all sorts of terrible explanations for what afflicted Nemain, and who better to turn to than Molly, that wise woman?

"Mistress, what, what is it that ails Nemain? She—is she— She is ill, is she not?"

Molly put her hand to her face and turned away for a moment, and Hob's heart began to pound at the back of his throat. Jack's face was, if anything, more expressionless than usual, and he seemed very involved in scratching behind Sweetlove's ears.

Sweetlove began to growl, looking at the door to the solar, and just then Nemain, very pale, opened the door, and the little dog, recognizing her, subsided. Nemain went to the table. She had washed her face at one of the castle's fountains, where the cold water ran down to each floor from tanks on the roof, and her pale face was not quite dry: it had a slight sheen of moisture to it.

She took her cup and went to the seaward window seat. She sat, sipped, swirled the mint tea around her mouth; she leaned out the tower window and delicately spat the tea into the German Sea, crashing so far below into the headland on which the castle sat.

Out there, past the saltwater vastness, the sun began to breach the rim of the world; a river of fire burned along the surface of the German Sea from the horizon to the castle; the dawn breeze began to blow, rippling the edges of Nemain's veil. She took it off and, here in the privacy of her family, pulled pins from her hair and let the incoming salt air blow it back from her face.

The sunrise cleared the windowsill; the new rays struck red flame from her hair; her still-damp face glowed white.

She was gazing out over the water, and Hob looked from her to Molly. Fear for her gnawed like a badger at his heart.

But Molly was still turned away from Hob, her face partially hid in her hand. Now she said, "Nemain, *mo chroí.*" Hob's concern grew as he heard the quaver in the older woman's voice. "Your husband here is fearful for your health, and he's after asking me what ails you, and I about to tell him, but 'tis your place and not mine to tell him what troubles you."

Nemain, with a mixture of exasperation and amusement, turned back toward the room and said, "I'm after thinking you told me everything about men, and sure you gave me a mort of advice about them, but not that they were as thick as the door to a keep." She turned to Hob. "If I'm off my meat, 'tis your fault."

"My fault—" said Hob, and now he noticed that Molly was laughing behind her hand, and Jack was suppressing a grin, and his heart began to lift, ever so little.

"Your fault, and your bairn's," said Nemain, and then Molly and Jack burst into laughter at the sight of him, sitting there staring and his mouth actually open. He shut it with a snap and was up from the table and at the window in a moment, lifting her to her feet, to his hug, to his kiss.

He reached back to the table and retrieved his goblet of honey beer and set it on the broad windowsill, and sat down in the window seat, and pulled his young wife to his lap, the better to kiss her and tell her how happy she had made him, and just to grin and beam at her. And there he sat, content, smiling on the world.

She said to Molly, "Sure he's slow of understanding, but you'll grant me he has a lovely smile."

"He has that," said Molly. She said to Hob, " 'Twill be a daughter, you know."

"How can you know that, Mistress?" he asked.

"Our firstborns are always daughters," said Nemain. "Our wise women—in this case, Herself—arrange it so, by studying the wind riffling the water, the movement of the stars around the hinge of the sky, birdcalls at dusk. *Seanmháthair* gave me the signs to watch for—a shaft of the late sun, and yourself speaking of the sun falling into the Western Ocean out beyond Erin." She looked down, suddenly a little shy. "Do you not recall that day in York?"

It came back to him: "That day in the stables? With Milo?"

"The very one, and 'tis on that day that you're founding your tribe there in the straw."

Hob sat there, his mind whirling, his heart full; in memory's eye he could see again the boards of the loft above him, and the wisps of hay, and that sentinel spider.

"Your firstborn," said Molly, "and a queen also."

"She will be a queen?" asked Hob.

"In our tribe it passes down the female line," said Molly. "You will be the vassal of a queen; you will be the husband of a queen; you will be the father of a queen; but yourself will never be a king." She took a deep drink. "On the other hand, you will be the founder of a dynasty, and you will be Robert the Englishman, and those are no small things."

At this point Jack took his goblet, peered into it, and

realized that it was empty. He filled Molly's goblet from an earthenware jug that Sir Odinell's servants had provided, and then refilled his own. He stood by the tableside, a man who might have been a model for some pagan war god, and he looked deeply embarrassed. He squared his shoulders, faced Hob and Nemain, raised his goblet, and said, "Gorh ble' zhou bo'!" and drank.

Nemain—who, even as a little girl in the first days that Jack came to live with Molly, was the one who could understand Jack best—translated: "God bless you both."

Everyone applauded, and Jack sat down—Hob suspected that, had Jack not been so swarthy, he would have been seen to blush—and then Molly rose, and lifted her goblet, and said, "Health and safety to you both; increase to your family; death to your enemies."

Hob, drinking to the pledge, thought this a little grim for so early in the day, but Molly's thoughts were on the future, and in the future was Erin, and in Erin were people who would happily see Nemain and her child dead, and so, Christian or not, he echoed Molly: "Death to our enemies!"

Nemain stood, indicated her mint tea a bit ruefully, drawing a smattering of laughter from the others, and, turning to Hob, said, with all seriousness, "To our bairn."

More applause, and they all drank.

Hob pulled Nemain down again on his lap. His arm was around her waist; his hand rested on her still-flat abdomen, with its precious passenger. The wind blew into the room, and he could smell salt mingled with the scent of Nemain's hair, and he thought of Father Athelstan, who would often say that all life was a miracle.

He considered Nemain: when they were children they would play long games of hide-and-seek, and pelt each other with balls of snow, and here sat this woman—dangerous, beautiful, powerful: an adept of the Art. And now, from Nemain and himself, and this new game that they played, came this third person, who would be a little girl at play one day, and then some other day would herself be a beautiful and dangerous woman. In what way was this not some form of miracle?

He realized that they were waiting for him to pledge another drink. Suddenly he thought of Molly's explanation of the Mórrígan. "It reminds me of what you told the monsignor of your . . . Patron," Hob said, unwilling as a Christian to say the word *goddess*.

He kissed Nemain again and grinned at the company; he raised his goblet of honey beer.

"To three queens in Erin!"

Glossary of Irish Terms

a chuisle	pulse, heartbeat [uh KOOSH-la] (direct address; literally: "O pulse"—that is, the one so addressed is as important as life itself to the speaker)
arracht	monster [are-OCHT] (plural: *arrachtaí*) [are-OCH-thee]
a rún	love, dear [uh ROON]
claírseach	Irish harp [KLAUR-shock]
conriocht	werewolf [kun-ricth] (even emphasis) (plural: *conriochtaí*) [kun-ricth-thee]
draíodóir	wizard [DREE-a-duhor]

Faoi cheann bliana	one year; in a year's time [fwee kheawn BLEE-uh-nah]
geasadóir	enchanter, spellbinder [GAYSH-a-duhor]
Mavourneen	my sweetheart (Irish: *mo mhuirnín*) [muh VOOR-nyeen]
mo chroí	my heart [muh KREE]
mo mhuirnín	My sweetheart [muh VOOR-nyeen]
ochone	an exclamation of sorrow; woe (Irish *ochón*) [och-OWN]
seanmháthair	grandmother (literally: "old mother") [shan-VAUGH-er]
spalpeen	rascal, layabout (Irish *spailpín*, itinerant laborer) [SPAL-peen]
stór mo chroí	treasure of my heart [STORE muh KREE]
Tapaidh	speedy (Irish: *tapaidh*) [TOP-ee]
uisce beatha	whiskey (literally: "water of life") [eesch-uh BAH-ha]

Glossary of Archaisms and Dialect Terms

boohter	butter; Derbyshire dialect
coney	a rabbit
coom	come
culver	a dove (term of endearment)
Gammer	Grandma
gie	give
John Lackland	King John I of England; so called because of losses of his territory in France
Mahomet	Mohammed
Mahometan, Mussulman	Muslim
Marroch	Morocco

mort	a great deal, a great many (lit. "death"; a mortal amount)
nowt	nothing
oot	out
owt	anything
rissom	a small amount; Derbyshire dialect
scran	food
sennight	a week (seven-night)
sithee	see thee:

As a question:

   "Do you see?"

   "Do you understand?"

As a command:

   "Look" or "Look here," as in "Look, I'm willing to [etc.]."

staunchgrain	thin white paste of lime, flour, egg whites, milk; used to smooth and whiten parchment
theer	there
unco	strange [*adj.*]; very [*adv.*]
weel	well
yon	over there, yonder; *but also as pronoun:* that [one]

Acknowledgments

One of the pleasures of introducing a new book is the acknowledgment of those who've been such a help and support during its writing. Let me pause this hour to thank them:

Emily Bestler, my astute and very supportive editor, and her assistant editor, the always helpful Megan Reid; my excellent copy editor, Jaime Costas; George Hiltzik, agent extraordinaire; and many dear friends, especially Patricia and Michael Sovern. Thanks go to Hilary Mhic Suibhne (Glucksman Ireland House, New York University) for help with the guide to the pronunciation of Irish words, and my thanks as well to reader Marie Botkin for suggesting the inclusion of such a pronunciation guide.

And I must thank, for their help and support, the Fairy Bride, Theresa Adinolfi Nicholas, and the delightful Tristan, who, despite his distant Yorkshire origins, actually came from a kennel in faraway Hungary, and from thence straight into our hearts.

About the Author

Douglas Nicholas is an award-winning poet whose work has appeared in numerous publications, among them *Atlanta Review, Southern Poetry Review, Sonora Review, Circumference, A Different Drummer,* and *Cumberland Review,* as well as the *South Coast Poetry Journal,* where he won a prize in that publication's Fifth Annual Poetry Contest. Other awards include Honorable Mention in the Robinson Jeffers Tor House Foundation 2003 Prize for Poetry Awards, second place in the 2002 Allen Ginsberg Poetry Awards from PCCC, International Merit Award in *Atlanta Review*'s Poetry 2002 competition, finalist in the 1996 Emily Dickinson Award in Poetry competition, honorable mention in the 1992 Scottish International Open Poetry Competition, first prize in the journal *Lake Effect*'s Sixth Annual Poetry Contest, first prize in poetry in the 1990 Roberts Writing Awards, and finalist in the Roberts short fiction division. He was also recipient of an award in the 1990 International Poetry Contest sponsored by the Arvon

Foundation in Lancashire, England, and a Cecil B. Hackney Literary Award for poetry from Birmingham-Southern College. He is the author of *Something Red* and its sequel, *The Wicked,* fantasy novels set in the thirteenth century, as well as *Iron Rose,* a collection of poems inspired by and set in New York City; *The Old Language,* reflections on the company of animals; *The Rescue Artist,* poems about his wife and their long marriage; and *In the Long-Cold Forges of the Earth,* a wide-ranging collection of poems. He lives in New York's Hudson Valley with his wife, Theresa, and Yorkshire terrier, Tristan.